SPELLSTONE

ROSS
MONTGOMERY

**WALKER
BOOKS**

First published 2023 by Walker Books Ltd
87 Vauxhall Walk, London SE11 5HJ

2 4 6 8 10 9 7 5 3 1

Text © 2023 Ross Montgomery
Cover illustration © 2023 David Dean

This book has been typeset in Garamond

Printed and bound by CPI Group (UK) Ltd, Croydon CR0 4YY

British Library Cataloguing in Publication Data:
a catalogue record for this book is available from the British Library

ISBN 978-1-5295-0193-3

www.walker.co.uk

For Honey

PRA

"Riveting, punchy, with surprises around every bend.
Ross Montgomery is a flawless storyteller."
Carlie Sorosiak

"Another absolute triumph from one of
my favourite children's authors. Heartfelt and humorous,
while fizzing with magic and fun."
Catherine Doyle

"A cinematic roller-coaster ride of a book."
Katharine Orton

"Utterly infused with magic, adventure and imagination.
This is Ross Montgomery on top form,
and the result is spectacular."
Katya Balen

"A magical book that is both clever and gripping. A joy!"
Lisa Thompson

"Montgomery's playful imagination floods every page,
creating a magical adventure full of high stakes,
charming characters and unexpected twists."
Joseph Elliott

"Spellbinding … brimming with original magic
and the most charming cast of characters."
Jenny Pearson

"Sparkling with magic, danger and that
wonderful Montgomery wit. A fabulous,
crackling adventure. Utterly gripping."
Amy Wilson

"Ross Montgomery just gets better and better!
Crackling with magic and swirling with mystery."
Jennifer Bell

INTRODUCTION

I T WAS RAINING INSIDE THE THEATRE.

It came down in sheets, streaming from the chandeliers and turning the aisles into carpeted rivers. There was so much rain that it had nowhere to go: gathering in the balconies; flooding the orchestra pit. Sodden paper programmes floated on the surface like leaves as they were swept past the rows of spectators.

The audience didn't move. They sat in stock-silence as the rain came down in torrents around them. The champagne in their glasses slowly filled, and then overflowed, soaking into their suits and ballgowns ... but no one seemed to mind. No one even seemed to notice.

They were all fast asleep.

It was true: every single member of the audience was slumped in their chair, sleeping like a baby. One man had leaned so far forward that his monocle floated in his champagne glass; the woman beside him had leaned so far back that her open mouth had filled with rainwater. Beneath the downpour, you could just make out the steady rise and fall of a thousand sleeping breathers.

Wainwright stood at the back of the theatre, gazing around himself in amazement. He had been inside many dreams before, but never one *quite* like this. He was so entranced that he almost forgot why he was there in the first place.

He found the others quickly. They were squabbling in the front row.

"Soaked! Absolutely soaked!"

"He said he'd be quick."

"I don't understand why we had to do this *here*…"

"Next time, *I* choose where we're meeting."

Wainwright strode down the aisle to join them, his footsteps squelching into the sodden carpet. He didn't bother with an umbrella. He'd been in enough rainstorms in his life to know when it was pointless to try and stay dry. Besides, his boots had so many holes in them that they were already absorbing every puddle he stepped in. His overcoat was covered in patches, too. He looked like a man who'd lived on the streets his whole life, which was precisely the point. When you dress like a pauper, no one ever suspects you of being a magician.

He found the others huddled under their umbrellas. There were four in total. The first was a man of no more than twenty, gangly, pale and clean-shaven, shivering beneath a cheap three-piece suit. Next to him sat an old woman, dark-skinned and elegantly dressed, brushing raindrops from the hem of her skirts with a tut. Beside her sat a young boy, wide-eyed and baby-faced beneath a neat side-parting, his hands patiently folded in his lap. Last of all was a very wet, and very angry, black cat. One of her eyes was yellow; the other eye was blue. Both were fixed on Wainwright with absolute fury.

"You're late," snapped the cat.

"Sorry – I got distracted," said Wainwright. He nodded to the rainswept theatre around them. "Quite something, isn't it? And all thanks to Rish!" He nodded to the young boy. "Can you believe it? Only ten years old, and he *already* has enough magic inside him to bring all five of us into a dream. Why, when I was his age—"

"Get to the point!" hissed the cat.

The old lady smiled diplomatically. "Lady Alinora is right. I don't see why you insisted on us meeting inside a *dream*, Wainwright. I am a busy woman! I have things to do!"

The pale man sniffed. "I think I'm getting a cold."

"We should probably hurry up, sir," said Rish politely. "The dreamer could wake up any time – we might not be able to stay in here for much longer."

That was the problem with magicians – they always took amazing things for granted. Wainwright sighed. "Very well, then. I'll be frank."

He cracked the knuckles beneath his fingerless gloves, ran a hand through his big orange beard, and leaned against the stage. The others listened obediently. Wainwright might be late, but he was still their leader.

"We have to face facts," he said. "We're running out of time. Vale's catching up with us. His eyes are everywhere – all over the city. It's only a matter of time before he gets his hands on the Spellstone. And when he does…"

Wainwright trailed off. He didn't need to say any more. The magicians knew *exactly* how bad that would be. Wainwright paused. He had to choose his next words very carefully.

"I know I've asked a lot from you over the years," he said. "As leader of the Order, I'm entrusted with secrets that I can't share with you. That's the way it's always been – the way it has to be." He looked at each of them in turn. "You may not always understand the choices I make – you may not even *like* them – but every single one is for our cause. To protect the world from what's inside the Spellstone. And we can't hide it from Vale for much longer." He cleared his throat. "So I've made some decisions. Some big ones, in fact."

There was another pause. The magicians leaned forward in their chairs, craning their necks to hear him better over the downpour.

"I moved the Spellstone," said Wainwright.

The effect on the others was electric. All four leaped to their feet at the same time.

"You *moved* it?!"

"Wainwright!"

"To *touch* the Spellstone, let alone *move* it…"

Wainwright waved his hands to stop them. "I had no choice. Last night I was checking on it, in the usual hiding place … and Vale's men followed me. He must have made them more powerful somehow. They were able to chase me for longer than before. I couldn't risk him finding the Spellstone, after all these years. I *had* to move it." He sighed. "Don't worry; no one saw where I took it. It's still hidden – it's still safe."

"For how long?" said the cat.

She gazed calmly at Wainwright, her tail flicking. She spoke – as she always did – with the unmistakable tone of a duchess. "You said so yourself – Vale's catching up with us. He's getting more and more powerful every single day, and we don't know why. Sooner or later, he's going to find the Spellstone again. So how are we supposed to—"

"Hush!" The old lady waved her quiet. "Wainwright has his clever look on him. See! He has some plan to beat Vale. A new magician for the Order, perhaps?"

The magicians stirred. Finding a new magician was always a cause for celebration, and they had never needed one more than right now. It meant, for the first time in a long time, that there was some hope.

But Wainwright shook his head. "No, Campbell. I'm afraid you're wrong. I haven't found a magician." He smiled. "I've found a *sorcerer*."

If Wainwright's first revelation had been a surprise, this was twice that. The others didn't jump or shout: they stayed fixed to the spot, staring at him in shock. Then they dropped their umbrellas, one by one. Their clothes soaked through in seconds, but they didn't even notice.

"I mean it," Wainwright continued. "A sorcerer. The most powerful magician there is, with the strongest magic that I've ever seen, right here in our own city. Strong enough to defeat Vale, I think. Maybe even strong enough to... Well, let's not get ahead of ourselves." His eyes were gleaming. "But I think she's our answer. Our hope. We're not going to hide the Spellstone from Vale any more. We're going to fight back. We're going to stop him, once and for all. It's why I asked Rish to bring us here tonight."

The others looked confused.

Wainwright laughed. "Don't you understand? It's so you can see her for yourselves." He held out his arms to the theatre. "This is all *hers*. This is *her* dream." He nodded. "Rish?"

On cue, Rish closed his eyes, muttered some silent words ... and the red velvet curtains onstage lifted, trailing long necklaces of rain. The magicians gazed over Wainwright's shoulder, to the person who was finally revealed on the stage behind him.

It was a girl. She was barely twelve years old, wearing a top hat and holding a wand. She was standing ankle-deep in rainwater on the flooded stage. She didn't seem to notice the magicians: she was too focused on her act. She gave a grand bow to the sleeping audience, and her top hat fell off. It landed with a splash in the water and began steadily pumping out rabbits. She squawked and tried to stuff them back into the hat, but it didn't work. Then a shower of playing cards burst from both her sleeves.

"*Her?!*" said the cat incredulously. "*She's* a sorcerer?"

Wainwright nodded. "The magic hidden inside her... I've never seen anything like it. I've been watching her for a while, waiting for the right moment to recruit her." He sighed. "We'll have to train her, of course ... and we won't have much time to do it. Not when Vale's already so close. But she came just when we needed her the most."

Onstage, the girl's head suddenly snapped up. She looked directly at the magicians, blinking with surprise, as if she was only just able to see them.

"She's ... looking at us!" Rish gasped in amazement. "She can *see* us!"

"Of course she can," said Wainwright. "She's magic. She just doesn't know it yet."

The magicians were speechless. Wainwright held out a hand to the girl onstage.

"Ladies and gentlemen – meet Evie," he said. "She's going to help us save the world."

PART 1

EVIE

1
EVIE

E VIE WOKE UP.

She'd been having the strangest dream. She was doing some kind of magic act inside a raining theatre, but it had all gone wrong. The stage had been flooded; her tricks had fallen apart in her hands. None of the audience had noticed, because they'd been fast asleep.

Except for the five people in the front row.

Evie blinked, trying to remember them. She hadn't spotted them at first. But once she'd noticed them, she couldn't look away. They were the strangest collection of people she'd ever seen. There was a man with a big orange beard, and an old lady, and a boy about her own age, and a man in a suit, and a talking cat...

"Evie! School!"

Dad's voice cut off her train of thought. The dream faded from her memory like breath on a windowpane, as dreams so often do, and within seconds it was gone.

She dragged on her school uniform and found her parents in the kitchen. Mum had already started work:

her stuff was spread across the table, and she was dividing her attention between a phone and two laptops and five newspapers. There was never quite enough room for Mum. Dad was frantically making three breakfasts.

"Quick! Get that down you," said Dad, handing Evie a plate without looking up. "I've got a meeting in five minutes. You overslept."

"I had a weird dream," said Evie.

Dad didn't reply – he was too busy trying to knot his tie while stacking the dishwasher. Evie sat dejectedly down at the kitchen table, making a space for herself among Mum's notepads. The house had been like this ever since her parents had both started working from home. Mum answered emails while having a bath; Dad did conference calls in the living room while wearing a suit jacket and pyjama bottoms. She went to take a bite of her toast and stopped. "This is peanut butter."

"Very observant of you, Evie," said Dad, closing the dishwasher with his foot.

"But I *hate* peanut butter."

"Since when?" said Mum, still looking at her laptop.

Evie bristled. *This* had been happening for months, too. No matter what she told her parents – whether it was about food, or about school, or about *anything*, in fact – nothing seemed to stick any more. Some days, she felt like they couldn't even hear her.

Still – being ignored had its benefits.

Evie cleared her throat. She had recently discovered that if she slipped something casual into a conversation, Mum and Dad would agree to it without even realizing.

"School's cancelled today," she said breezily. "I don't have to go in."

"No," said Mum and Dad at the same time.

Evie groaned. Trust Mum and Dad to be paying attention the moment it mattered.

"But I *hate* it there!" she said. "I've been at that stupid school almost a year and no one even talks to me."

"Nonsense," said Mum, still looking at her laptop. "You've got loads of friends. Kiera. Jaya. That silent boy with the eyebrows."

Evie stared at Mum in amazement. "Are you serious? Jaya and Kiera are in different classes to me now. I haven't hung out with them in months." A ball of irritation swelled inside her. "I've *told* you about all this!"

Her parents must have heard the hurt in her voice. Dad put down the plates and swept her in for a hug. Mum finally looked up and pushed her work away.

"Oh, Evie – you are a special, wonderful girl," she said, squeezing her hand. "Everyone takes a while to settle in to secondary school."

"That's right, Squidge," said Dad. "Just be yourself and you'll find your people."

Evie glowed. Mum and Dad always noticed the big things, when they happened. She just wished they noticed the little things as much. She knew her parents cared: in fact, they thought she was great. She wondered if one day, they would realize that they had an extremely dull daughter who wasn't particularly good at anything. Surely, if she really was special and wonderful, someone else would have noticed it by now. "Love you, Mum. Love you, Dad."

"Now off you go!" said Dad, shoving her towards the door. "Don't forget your toast."

Evie stared at him. "Dad?"

"Yes?"

"Peanut butter."

Dad blinked for a few seconds, before the information finally registered. "Oh! Right. Er … have a banana."

Evie made her way to the front door with her banana, grumbling. She had no idea why Mum and Dad were forgetting everything she said at the moment. It had started months ago – some time around her twelfth birthday – and it was slowly getting worse. Was it because they were busy? Or maybe she was just really, *really* boring? Or maybe it was…

She stepped outside, and the thought was instantly blown away in a thick wave of heat.

She gasped. It was even hotter than yesterday; she didn't know how that was possible. It had already become the hottest summer on record, and the city felt like it was about to crack. Weather reports kept saying that the heatwave would break soon – that it *had* to break soon –

but, day after day, the temperature kept on rising. No one had any explanation for it; it was as if something momentous was about to happen. As if something was stirring beneath the earth, rising after centuries of sleep.

She slammed the gate behind her and strode down the street, wincing at the heat that was seething off the tarmac. Maybe *that* was why Mum and Dad were so scatterbrained at the moment: thinking in weather like this was impossible. She tried to get her own thoughts in order. *School.* She really was late. If she wanted to make registration in time, she was going to have to go by the main road, and *that* meant…

Evie stopped. There was something sitting on the wall beside her that she hadn't expected.

"You!" she said, taken aback.

It was the cat from her dream – the *exact* same black cat, with one blue eye and one yellow eye. The memory of the theatre came back in an instant – the rain, the sleeping audience, the people in the front row…

Evie shook her head. It couldn't be the same cat. Just because its eyes were the same colours, that didn't mean anything. There had to be millions of black cats in this city.

But she knew, just *knew*, that it was the same one. There was something about it that was special. It was staring right at her, for one thing. It was weird, being stared at by a cat.

"I have to go now," said Evie. "I'm late."

The cat didn't reply, which struck Evie as rude, until she remembered that cats didn't actually talk. She strode away quickly, without looking back.

The main road was even busier than usual this morning, jam-packed with stalled traffic. The pavements were clogged with sweaty commuters, dragging themselves to work with blank, exhausted expressions.

Evie gulped, and took a final moment to collect her thoughts. Here it was: the morning assault course. She lowered her head, gritted her teeth, and stepped into the flow of people.

It took five seconds for the first person to crash into her. They didn't stop to apologize: they just kept walking, as if Evie wasn't even there. Evie lost her balance and was barged directly into the path of a cyclist, who knocked her into a woman who was shouting into a phone, who sent Evie sprawling into a stack of cardboard boxes beside a fruit and veg shop.

"Hey!" she yelped.

No one stopped to help her up: no one even heard her. Everyone strolled right past, as if Evie were just another empty box on the pavement. She fumed. *This* had been happening for months, too. Why had everyone suddenly become so rude? Why did no one notice her any more?

She staggered to her feet, pulled a banana peel off her shirt ... and stopped. Someone *was* looking at her – someone sitting at the end of her street, staring at her.

It was the black cat from the wall outside her house. It had followed her.

Evie shook herself awake. No, not *the* black cat – *a* black cat. Besides, cats didn't follow people.

She raced to school, keeping all her attention focused on not being knocked over. Even so, she made sure not to look over her shoulder, just in case the cat was still behind her.

Class had already started by the time Evie arrived. It didn't matter: her teacher didn't even glance at her as she walked in. They never did. Evie sat down, took out a book from her desk, and started reading.

Being overlooked certainly had its bonuses. Evie could read in every single lesson and no one ever stopped her. In fact, she could put her head down on the desk and fall asleep, and no one even noticed. Teachers never told her off; they didn't even ask her for homework any more. If Evie *wanted* to draw attention to herself, she could – usually by waving both her hands and yelling – but the effort of doing that whenever she needed something was, frankly, becoming exhausting.

It was the same at breaktime. Evie could join in with any conversations or games she wanted to, but there was always a nagging feeling that if she stopped talking and walked away, no one would even care. Her old friends, Kiera and Jaya, were happy to chat when Evie found them … but she always had to find them. They never came looking for her. And whenever Evie *did* wave to them across the playground, there was always a brief moment when they would stare at her, baffled, before remembering who she was.

It was a horrible feeling, and it was getting worse and worse every day. Whether she was at home with Mum and Dad, or out in the streets, or at school … no one noticed her any more. She felt like she was in the middle of the ocean, watching everyone else swim away in different directions while she stayed exactly where she was. No one came back for her: no one even knew that she'd been left behind. It was like she had become a ghost.

The school day ended. Evie watched her classmates run off in gangs and pairs. Dad's words echoed through her head: *Just be yourself and you'll find your people.* The problem was that she was *already* being herself, and it wasn't working. Otherwise, she'd have found her people months ago.

Evie sighed. She didn't know if she could face another endurance-assault course back home along the main road. After days like this, there was only one place left to go.

The canal.

The canal had been important once. There was a time when it would have been filled with narrow boats taking goods in and out of the city, but then cars and tarmacked roads had made them obsolete. The old waterways had been left to rot for over a hundred years. The cobbles on the towpath were cracked and broken. The iron railings that ran beside it were strung with cobwebs and littered with burger boxes. There was graffiti everywhere.

But Evie loved it. The canal was lined with houseboats, stretching for miles in either direction, their sides strung with tyres and old rope. The newer ones had names like *Fisher King* and *Galahad* painted in big gold letters along their sides; the older ones were barely boats at all, their paintwork cracked along the waterline and their windows smoked with dust. One or two had even been abandoned, left to rot along the water's edge, with ducks nesting on the deck between old tins of paint.

It was peaceful here. The city noise fell away the moment you stepped onto the towpath, leaving nothing but the distant pecking of moorhens and a hush of water at the locks. It was blissfully cool too, hidden down beneath the shade of the buildings. Finally, for the first time that day, Evie felt herself relax. She slowed her pace and walked along the towpath's edge, peering down at the water. There, beneath the rippling skin of duckweed, she could make out bike frames and old abandoned trolleys, gently swaying in the backwash of passing boats. They felt close enough to touch and yet strangely out of reach: an underwater graveyard of forgotten things.

That was what Evie liked most about the canal. It was a place for things that didn't belong anywhere else:

for things that only showed themselves when you took the time to notice them. She wondered what else could be hidden down there, in the murk at the bottom of the water, if you only took the effort to—

A bicycle shot past, so close it almost sent Evie flying headfirst into the water. She swung around to catch her balance, tripped on a mooring rope, and cried out with pain as her knee struck the cobbles. The cyclist didn't stop to apologize, or check if she was OK. He zoomed away without so much as a backward glance. Evie watched him go, outrage boiling up inside her.

"Don't mind me!" she bellowed. "I'm just a twelve-year-old girl, walking home! Don't make room for me or anything! I'll just lie here and bleed to death and—"

"Terrible, isn't it? Some people never notice anything."

Evie snapped around. The voice came from much closer than she expected: from the man sitting on a bench behind her. She had no idea how she hadn't noticed him before – he was barely two metres away from her. And what's more, he looked absolutely extraordinary. Despite the heat, he was wearing a large black overcoat, a big black hat and thick black boots. All of them were tattered and threadbare and held together with patches.

But that wasn't the most extraordinary thing about him. The most extraordinary thing of all was that Evie recognized him.

It was the man from her dream.

2
THE STRANGER ON THE TOWPATH

Evie stared at the man on the bench in disbelief. It really was him – the man she had seen in her dream. He was wearing the exact same clothes; he had the exact same bright orange beard. Here he was, in real life, reading a newspaper and eating a ham sandwich.

"That's a nasty scrape you've got there," said the man.

Evie looked at her knee. It was slowly, confidently bleeding. The man offered her the paper napkin from his sandwich and nodded at the bench.

"Sit down, if you like," he said. "Until it stops."

Evie paused. She wasn't supposed to talk to strangers. But she had always been good at reading people. She could pick out a friendly person from a hundred paces; she knew the difference between a dog you could pat and a dog that would bite you if you tried. And somehow she knew, just knew, from the moment she had first seen the man, that he was nice. She'd known it the way you know a good peach when you pick one up.

Besides, he had somehow stepped from her dream and into real life – she had to find out what was going on.

"Thank you." She took the napkin and sat down on the other end of the bench, as far away from him as she could. The man nodded and went back to his newspaper. Evie waited to see if he would start talking to her again, but he didn't. They sat in silence for a while. The words that demanded to be said swelled inside Evie's chest, bigger and bigger, like a balloon ready to pop. "I saw you in my dream."

The man turned to her. "Is that right?"

"Yes," said Evie. "It was one hundred per cent, definitely you."

It sounded like an accusation – perhaps it was. Thankfully, the man didn't seem to mind. He folded up his newspaper and crossed his legs. "Do you always walk home this way after school?"

Evie's blood froze. How did the man know that? Had he been following her? "H-how did you know I'm walking back from school?"

"It's home-time," said the man. "And you're wearing school uniform."

Evie looked down at her shirt. "Oh yeah."

The man nodded at the bench. "Well – I'm always here. You probably saw me while you were walking home yesterday, and the memory of me turned up in your dream.

That's what dreams are: bits and pieces of memories, rearranging themselves into a story in your head. *Dream-work,* they call it."

This man knew a surprising amount about dreams. Evie hated to admit it, but his explanation made a lot more sense than a person stepping out of her dream and into real life. It even explained the black cat from earlier – she could have seen *that* yesterday, too. "But you were wearing the same clothes."

The man laughed at his shabby overcoat and broken boots. "I don't have much of a wardrobe, to be honest."

Evie blushed. She was being rude: the man was clearly homeless. "Sorry. I've just never noticed you here before, that's all."

"Not many people do," said the man. "See?" He gestured at the people walking past them, looking at their phones. "All this stuff going on around them, and they never notice it. It's a miracle they don't walk straight into the canal, frankly. How's the knee?"

Evie lifted the napkin and checked. "Still bleeding."

"It'll stop by itself soon enough," said the man, with confidence. "So – what was I doing, then? In this dream of yours?"

Evie thought back. The dream was fainter than ever now, like the imprints left by sunlight when you shut your eyes. "We were in a theatre. It was raining. I was doing a magic act."

"Magic!" said the man. "Cards, rabbits out of a hat, that sort of thing?"

Evie nodded.

The man stole a glance over his shoulder and then leaned forward conspiratorially. "Of course – that's not *real* magic. A *real* magician would never perform on a stage like that. *Real* magic never draws attention to itself. It hides in plain sight. And I should know!" He adjusted his coat with an air of self-importance. "You just so happen to be talking to one of the last *true* magicians left in the world. Consider yourself lucky!"

Evie frowned. "You don't look like a magician."

"What did you expect – wizard's robes?!" said the man. "I'll have you know that *these* clothes are just what a magician needs – they help me slip perfectly into the background, where magic belongs, so no one ever notices me." He waved his hands above his head. "Oi! Everyone! Look over here!"

Not a single person turned to look at him as they walked past – they kept their eyes fixed on the ground, clearly trying to avoid eye contact with the strange man shouting at them.

"See?" he said, folding his arms smugly. "My magic's working perfectly."

Evie giggled. She understood what was going on: the man was pulling her leg, teasing her to pass the time until her knee healed. He held out his hand.

"The name's Wainwright. Pleased to meet you."

Evie paused, deciding whether or not to keep playing along. It was nice to have a silly conversation like this: it was the first time in months that she hadn't had to fight to keep someone's attention. She decided it was safe to stay, so long as she didn't tell the man her real name. "I'm Sophie. Tell me, Wainwright, what do magicians do with their spare time?"

Wainwright crossed his legs. He was clearly enjoying this. "Spare time! What I wouldn't *give* for spare time, Sophie. I'm far too busy protecting the world."

"From…?"

"Evil magic! Dragons, ogres, monsters, that kind of thing."

"I haven't seen many dragons around here lately."

"That's because I'm doing such a good job."

"I see."

Wainwright smiled. "I'm joking, of course. It wasn't *me* who defeated the creatures of darkness. That was Emrys."

"Who's Emrys?"

Wainwright was scandalized. "*Who's Emrys?* The greatest magician who's ever lived, that's who!" His eyes were sparkling – he was on a roll now. "There'll never be another like him, mark my words. He was no mere magician, you see – he was a sorcerer. A magician born with *incredible* magic inside him. If it wasn't for him, the creatures of darkness would still cover this land from end to end. Emrys was the only one strong enough to imprison their magic inside the Spellstone!"

Evie blinked. "Spellstone?"

Wainwright turned to face her, his expression darkening. "That's right. The most powerful magical weapon ever created. When Emrys defeated the creatures of darkness, he took all their evil magic and stored it inside a stone – then he hid it from the world, so no one could ever find it. It's the sacred duty of magicians like me to make sure that the Spellstone is never found. And for one and a half thousand years, we've succeeded…" His voice dropped an octave. *"Until now."*

Evie giggled. Wainwright was good at this. "Oh dear."

"Oh dear, indeed," said Wainwright gravely. "You see, Sophie, there's a man who's been trying to get his hands on the Spellstone for forty years. A man who wants to unleash the evil trapped inside it and use it for his diabolical ends!"

Evie gasped theatrically. She was enjoying this. It was just like all her favourite fantasy stories rolled into one. "An evil wizard?"

"The most evil one there is," said Wainwright. "His name is Vale, and his powers are only growing stronger. He's been hunting me down for years … after all, I'm the only one who knows where the Spellstone is really hidden."

Evie mulled this over. "Don't you have anything you can use to fight him? A wand? An invisibility cloak, maybe?"

"You've been watching too many films," muttered

Wainwright. "But I *do* have this." He reached around his neck and pulled something out from inside his coat. It was a piece of old metal on a worn length of string.

Evie frowned. "What is it?"

"You tell me," said Wainwright.

Curiosity got the better of her. Evie took the necklace and turned it over in her hands. There was nothing special about it. It was just an old, ugly piece of metal, covered in rust. She wondered if she was going to have to wash her hands after holding it. "It doesn't look like anything."

"The most powerful magic," said Wainwright, "is always the most well-hidden."

The change in his voice was remarkable: it was almost trembling with emotion. Evie looked up and saw that Wainwright's eyes were shining. He wasn't joking any more.

"I did everything I could," he said. "But it wasn't enough. And now, I'm handing it on to you." He closed her hand around the metal. "It's precious. Take care of it. Never let it out of your sight. Keep it safe and keep it hidden until you're with the others. Alinora will find you and explain everything."

Evie was lost. She had been flung from out of the story they were making, and now she had no idea where she was. "Who's Alinora? What others?"

But Wainwright just smiled. "You're going to be very important, Evie. I wish I had the chance to see it."

Evie was so confused that it took her a moment to

realize what had just happened. It hit her in a sudden rush of fear.

"H-how do you know my real name?" she asked.

Wainwright didn't reply. He wasn't even looking at her. He was gazing at something in the distance over her shoulder ... and his face had drained of all colour.

Evie turned to follow his gaze. There were two men standing on the towpath behind them, about ten metres away. They were road workers in high-vis jackets – the kind you saw digging up pavements all over the city. But they weren't ignoring Wainwright, like the other passers-by. They were staring right at him, as if locking him in place with their eyes.

The moment Evie saw them, she felt their badness the way ice burns cold in your hand. There was nothing good in these men: not a single shred of warmth, or life, or humanity. A movement suddenly caught the corner of her eye: in the distance, a line of people had appeared along the bridge. There were more road workers, and a police officer, and a businessman in a suit. They all filled Evie with the same feeling of cold dread ... and every single one of them was staring at Wainwright.

"There were so many things I needed to tell you, Evie," said Wainwright, "but I fear we've run out of time."

The sorrow in his voice was heartbreaking. He still wasn't looking at her. He was speaking quietly to her out of the corner of his mouth, as if trying to hide what he was saying. Evie could barely hear him over the pounding in her ribcage. Wainwright leaned forward to stand, gave her hand a final tight squeeze ... and at the last moment, when he was close enough to whisper, he spoke once more.

"Tell them: it's safe. The last place he'll look."

Evie's head was spinning, but Wainwright was already on his feet and casually dusting down his coat. The two men in hi-vis jackets immediately started walking towards him; the people on the bridge began to move, too, quickly making their way down the steps to the towpath. Wainwright didn't seem bothered. He folded his hands behind his back and strolled towards them, whistling. He was trapped: the two groups of men were closing in from either direction, like the jaws of a beartrap...

With a sudden burst of unbelievable speed, Wainwright spun on his heels and leaped over the metal railing beside the towpath. He was already tearing down the street on the other side before the men even had a chance to react. At once, they shot after him – and suddenly, they weren't the only ones.

Dozens more men were appearing from every street and every corner and racing towards Wainwright, but he was far too quick. He dodged and darted between them like someone half his age, until he had spun down a side street and disappeared from view. The men poured after him like a flood, and in an instant, they were gone.

Evie stayed on the bench where Wainwright had left her, trembling with shock. No one on the towpath seemed to have noticed what had just happened. The men were gone; the strange encounter with Wainwright had ended as quickly as it had started. Cars honked as they crossed the bridge, ducks drew lines in the water, and the world continued on its course. The simple everyday fell back into place, like a blanket settled on a bed. It was as if Evie had dreamed the whole thing.

And yet…

She opened up her hand. There, resting in the centre of her palm, was the twisted piece of metal that Wainwright had given her just before he ran away. The edges had left an imprint on her skin in the shape of a crooked question mark.

3
ALINORA

EVIE WALKED HOME ALONE. THERE WERE NO FURTHER signs of Wainwright; no signs of the men who had chased him away, either. Everything was back to normal: the bridge, her street, the gravel path to her green front door. Dad was making dinner, as usual; Mum was exactly where Evie had left her that morning, only now she was surrounded by several dozen mugs of stone-cold tea.

"Sorry, darling." Mum sighed. "I'll be finished soon. Honestly, I feel like I've spent the whole day chasing shadows."

"No one's getting anything done in this heat," said Dad. "How was school, Squidge?"

For a moment, Evie considered telling her parents about everything that had happened – about the men, and Wainwright – and showing them the piece of metal he had given her, almost to prove to herself that it had really happened...

But all of a sudden, she knew – just *knew* – that it was very important she did exactly what Wainwright had asked. She had to keep it all a secret. "I had double maths."

"Great," said Dad, not really listening. "Want to help me with dinner?"

Normally Evie would have complained, but today she was grateful for something to do. She dragged a stool over to the kitchen counter and started chopping vegetables, focusing all her attention on moving the knife backwards and forwards and passing things to Dad. She could feel the weight of the metal in her pocket, growing heavier and heavier. She couldn't risk looking at it again until she went to bed.

Keep it safe and keep it hidden until you're with the others.

The words kept circling in her head. What others?

Evie ate dinner and watched TV with her parents, waiting for the earliest moment she could go to bed without drawing suspicion. Luckily for her, night fell faster than usual: a heavy, premature darkness seemed to be settling over the city, pressing in at the windows. The weather was acting stranger and stranger. She stood up, yawning theatrically.

"Phew! I'm beat," she said. "All that double maths. I'm off to bed."

Evie didn't need to bother pretending. Mum was too busy shouting at the TV to notice.

"Look at it!" she said. "It's an absolute disgrace!"

She was watching a news report about the latest skyscraper that had been built in the city. It was the biggest one yet: a gleaming stack of glass and girders, twice the height of everything around it. It got thinner as it got taller, twisting to a jagged point in the clouds. Evie thought it looked like the remains of a broken sword, rising up through the crust of the earth. The scrolling message along the bottom said it was called Tower 99.

"Ninety-nine floors!" Dad read, impressed. "You'll be able to see the whole city from up there."

"Exactly," said Mum bitterly. "Everything but *that* monstrosity. You won't be able to go anywhere without seeing the damn thing! That's what big money gets you nowadays."

Mum and Dad started bickering about architecture and civil planning, and Evie used the opportunity to sneak upstairs. She closed her bedroom door behind her, shut the curtains, and, for some unknown reason, checked whether her wardrobe was empty. Only then did she dare take the piece of metal from out of her pocket.

It didn't look any more impressive the second time around. In fact, it was even smaller than she remembered. She turned it over in her hands, looking for anything she might not have noticed, but there was nothing: no writing, no markings, no clues about what it was for. She scratched it with a fingernail to see if there was anything hidden underneath the rust, but there was nothing. Its edges had presumably once been sharp, but now they were dulled and worn. It just looked like a piece of junk.

So why did it *feel* so important?

The metal felt more solid than anything she had ever felt in her life. There *was* something special about it: a weight that lay beyond its mere shape and size. Wainwright had told her it was important. He had said that *she* was important, too – but how?

There was a sudden slam against the windowpane. Evie nearly leaped out of her skin. She shoved the metal back into her pocket, without knowing why she was doing it.

"W-who's there?" she said out loud.

No one answered. Evie stood still for a moment, her breath held. The very last thing she wanted to do was open the curtains and see if there was something outside the window ... but what if it was Wainwright, searching for somewhere to hide?

There was another sound at the window – sharper this time, more urgent. Something was scratching at the glass.

Alinora will find you.

Evie swallowed. She couldn't just stand here, pretending it wasn't happening. She made herself walk towards the window. Then she took hold of a curtain in each hand, paused to take a breath, and threw them apart.

There, standing on the other side of the glass, was a cat.

"It's you!" said Evie.

It was the same black cat from that morning, scratching frantically to be let inside. Without thinking, Evie opened the window and the cat shot in at once, followed by a breath of scented night air. It jumped on the bed and glared at her with its blue and yellow eyes. Evie couldn't help but smile.

"You know," she joked, "I could swear you were following me."

"Don't be thick," said the cat. "Of *course* I'm following you. I've been following you all day. I've been sitting in your garden for over an hour, waiting for you to come to bed!"

Evie stared at the cat in shock. In a day where many strange things had happened, this was perhaps one too many. People didn't appear from dreams; strangers didn't know your name; cats didn't talk in a cut-glass English accent. Cats didn't talk *at all*.

And yet…

Alinora will find you.

"Wainwright," Evie whispered. "Did he send you here?"

The cat gave her a look that was indescribable.

"Wainwright's missing," she said. "No one knows where he is. And if he doesn't show up soon, then the smoke-men are going to come here next."

4
THE SMOKE-MEN

A T THAT EXACT MOMENT, WAINWRIGHT WAS RACING through the streets on the other side of the city.

He had been running for hours. His legs throbbed, his whole body was shaking, and his lungs felt like they were on fire. But he couldn't stop now: the men were still following him. There was a time when Wainwright could have outrun them, but *now…*

He shot from a darkened alley and pressed himself against a wall, heaving for breath. Wainwright knew the city inside out: that was what had kept him one step ahead all these years. He had run inside a housing estate that he knew well, filled with dark corners and hidden stairwells. The kind of place where you could lose someone easily, if you needed to.

He peered around the corner. Up ahead lay a dim flickering tunnel leading out of the estate. If he could sneak through it without the men seeing him, he had half a chance of getting back to the hideout safely. Wainwright was exhausted – *terrified* – he didn't know how much longer he could keep running. But he couldn't stay here. He had to keep moving, or it was all over.

He flew from the shadows and tore down the tunnel as fast as he could … and a man leaped from a doorway in front of him. He was wearing a suit and tie, and holding a briefcase and a newspaper. When he spoke, his voice seethed out of his throat like gas escaping a vent.

"He is heeeeere…"

It was a trap; the men must have blocked every exit in the estate. Wainwright acted fast. He took the crowbar he kept hidden inside his coat and swung it as hard as he could. The man erupted in a belt of black smoke. Wainwright ran straight through him. He couldn't stop now: in moments there would be more smoke-men coming here, who knew how many…

But he was already too late. The metal drains lining the tunnel were pouring smoke. It was no ordinary smoke. The black plumes twisted through the air and wrapped around him in a cloud. Wainwright swung the crowbar desperately, still trying to run. "No! Get back!"

But it was no use. Within seconds the smoke had filled the tunnel in both directions, blinding and choking him. Wainwright staggered to the walls and tried to feel his way out, but he couldn't breathe; he couldn't see. He fell to his knees, gasping for breath, his vision exploding with stars…

"That's enough," said a voice at the end of the tunnel.

The smoke disappeared instantly. Wainwright gasped

in a lungful of clean night air, spluttering with relief. He leaped to his feet in a final, desperate bid to escape ...

... and stopped. His muscles had petrified to solid rock inside him. His whole body had frozen in place. He couldn't even move his eyes.

"I *told* you not to hurt him," said the voice, getting closer. "He's no use to me dead."

Wainwright felt his whole body lift from the floor, as if raised by invisible hands. His head was twisted up against his will: now he could see that the black smoke that had attacked him had gathered into the shapes of men. There were dozens of them – traffic wardens and police officers and binmen and businessmen, lining the walls of the tunnel on either side. They formed an aisle for the man who was walking towards him, away from a sleek grey car at the entrance to the tunnel. The man was cast alternately in glare and shadow as he passed beneath the overhead lights.

In many respects, the man looked a lot like the car he had just stepped from. He wore a grey suit; his hair was grey; his skin was so pale it had become almost colourless. Both could pass through the streets unnoticed, without once inviting thought or comment. The man was almost boring: someone you wouldn't think to look at twice.

But there was nothing you could do about those eyes.

They were the eyes of a man with no goodness in him: no warmth, no love, no humanity. They were the eyes of a man who has hidden from sunlight for years on end and allowed the darkness to poison him. They were the eyes of a man who sees nothing but evil, and who has chosen to make himself worse. He came to a stop in front of Wainwright's floating, powerless body, and gave a sigh of genuine happiness.

"You have no idea," said the man, "how long I've been waiting for this."

"I know exactly how long you've been waiting, Vale," said Wainwright. His voice came out weak and wheezing, as if a great weight lay on his chest. "Forty years. And you've only just managed to catch me! Maybe you're not as powerful as you think."

Vale didn't even blink. "*Please.* My army of smoke-men fill the streets. I'm making more of them every day. Soon there won't be a single inch of the city that I do not see."

If Wainwright was afraid, he didn't show it. "You never learned, did you? You can surround yourself with as many false people as you like, but you're still alone. You were always alone."

Vale's smile fell. "Look at me, Wainwright. Look at my power."

He raised his arms. The surface of his palms began to prickle with threads of electricity; the threads grew and grew, until his arms, right up to the shoulders, were surrounded by tornadoes of blue-white lightning. They lit up the tunnel walls and flickered in the cold grey eyes of the smoke-men gathered around him.

"I am the greatest magician alive," he said. "The greatest since Emrys. My powers are only growing stronger. The Order of the Stone is finished. And when I finally have the Spellstone, my powers will be beyond reckoning."

Vale lowered his hands, and the lightning stopped. He stepped towards Wainwright, closing the space between them. Vale made sure not to touch him – he *always* made sure of that.

"Let's get to the point, shall we?" said Vale. "I know you moved the Spellstone. So, one way or another, you're going to tell me where it is. We can do it quickly, and I'll kill you quickly… Or you can take your time, and so will I."

Wainwright looked directly into his eyes – and smiled, for the first time. "You know, for someone so powerful … you don't really notice much, do you?"

Vale was confused. "What do you mean?"

"Look down."

Vale looked down at the space beneath Wainwright's floating body … and his eyes filled with panic. He spun around to the smoke-men.

"Stop it!" he cried. "Stop it, before it gets away!"

The smoke-men stared at him blankly. There was nothing to stop – the tunnel was empty. Vale pointed to the dark shape that was flying across the concrete floor. "His shadow!"

Wainwright's shadow had torn itself away from his body and was racing out of the tunnel as fast as it could, trying to escape. The smoke-men flew after it, dozens more materializing from nowhere to block it, but the shadow couldn't be stopped. It simply passed straight beneath their feet, or flung itself to the walls and raced along the ceiling to avoid them. It was already out of the tunnel and tearing out the estate.

"Follow it!" Vale screamed. "It's going to move the Spellstone again! It's going to—"

It happened fast. Vale's attention had been distracted for long enough to break the spell that froze Wainwright in place. With all his strength, Wainwright wrenched free ... and grabbed Vale's hand. Vale shot round, his eyes filled with horror. *"NO!"*

It was already too late. The moment their hands touched, a white glow began to pour down Wainwright's arm and pass into Vale. A kind of light dimmed in Wainwright's eyes. It was as if his life was draining out of him, drop by drop.

Vale tore his hand away, but the damage had already been done. Wainwright's body hung limply in mid-air, like a scarecrow strung from its supports. Then it slumped to the ground, and, at the end of the tunnel, the shadow stumbled to its knees. It stretched one arm out ahead, as if reaching for something only it could see ... then it vanished from view, dissolving on the concrete like a fading photograph.

Wainwright lay on the ground, dead. Vale gazed down

at his nemesis. He had been chasing Wainwright for forty years. He was the one and only person in the world who knew where the Spellstone was hidden … and his secret had just died with him. With his final act, he had used Vale's own powers to sacrifice himself. Vale could swear that Wainwright still had the faintest of smiles on his lips.

He took a deep breath. It didn't matter. The other magicians were useless without Wainwright. One of them would know something. Once Vale found them, the rest would quickly fall into place. He would have his hands on the Spellstone in a matter of days.

"Search his body," he ordered the smoke-men. "There might be some clues on him. Something that shows us where their hideout is. Find that, and we'll find the Spellstone."

The smoke-men tried to search Wainwright's body, but their hands passed straight through him. They looked at Vale helplessly.

"Oh, if I have to do everything myself…" Vale muttered.

He began going through Wainwright's pockets, but they were all empty. Wainwright wasn't carrying a single thing. Vale frowned. Something wasn't right. Something was missing. He turned around to his smoke-men. They stood, waiting for orders.

"Search the tunnel," said Vale. "Look for an old piece of metal. He must have dropped it."

The smoke-men obeyed immediately. They burst into a great cloud of smoke, covering every inch of the walkway in a single unbroken layer. But within a few seconds, they were standing back in their human forms.

"There is nothing," they said.

A look of alarm flashed across Vale's face. He fell to his knees and started searching Wainwright's pockets again. "Don't be ridiculous. It has to be here. He wouldn't go anywhere without it."

Vale kept searching. He checked around Wainwright's neck; he searched in his shoes; he tore apart the fabric of Wainwright's coat; he checked inside his mouth. There was nothing.

"It's a piece of metal. It has to be here. An old piece of metal. He wouldn't lose it. He wouldn't drop it. If he doesn't have the token, that means…"

But it was no use. Whatever Vale was looking for, Wainwright didn't have it any more. He had left this world with nothing but the smile on his face and the clothes on his back. It was the last, and greatest, trick that he had ever pulled – and it was the most important one of his life.

Vale turned to his smoke-men, his eyes burning with rage.

"Search the estate!" he screamed. "Search every inch of every street he came down! Do not rest until you find the token!"

5
THE HIDEOUT

B ACK ACROSS TOWN, EVIE WAS STILL IN HER BEDROOM, staring at the talking cat.

She could feel a rush of panic building inside her. The men on the canal – the ones she had seen chase Wainwright away – were coming *here*? Was that *really* true? She glanced at the bedroom door – she could still hear Mum and Dad bickering downstairs. "But my parents…"

"If we leave now, they'll be safe," said the cat. "It's you they're after. We'll go out the window."

Evie opened and closed her mouth, trying to form her thoughts into words. She had so many questions that it was hard to focus on a single one. Wainwright – the metal in her pocket – the talking cat – they all demanded her attention at the same time. "Wh-who are you? What are you doing here?"

The cat leaped onto the windowsill. "We don't have time for this. Our only hope of keeping you safe is to get you to the hideout and stay there until we know where Wainwright is. Grab what you need and come on!"

Evie blinked. "H-hideout?"

The cat glared at her in exasperation. "For heaven's sake, stop asking so many stupid questions and *hurry up*!"

Evie finally snapped. She sat down on the bed and folded her arms. "No. I'm sorry, but I have no idea who you are, or what you're doing here, or where you're taking me. I'm not going *anywhere* without some kind of explanation!" She paused, and then added, "Please."

For a moment, Evie thought the cat was going to shout at her again. Instead, she sat down on the windowsill, and spoke calmly for the first time that evening.

"Have you ever felt like there was something different about you?" she asked. "Something that feels important, but you have no idea what it is? Like there's a kind of hidden secret answer to your life that would explain everything, if you only knew what it was?"

Evie nodded, dumbstruck. That was how she'd felt for a long time now.

"Then come with me," said the cat, "and find out what it is."

And with that, she shot from the window ledge and disappeared into the warm summer night.

Evie stood, staring at the open window. A dark path lay before her: a new, dangerous and frightening world. She had two options. She could close the window and hide under the duvet and pretend that none of the last few minutes had happened … or she could follow the cat, and find out some answers.

You're going to be very important, Evie.

She clutched the piece of metal in her pocket. She had to know – she had to find out the truth.

She glanced at the bedroom door. Until she came back, Mum and Dad had to think she was asleep. She turned out the bedroom lights, tucked some pillows under the duvet to look like a body, grabbed what she needed, and clambered out of the window, quickly shutting it behind her.

The cat sat waiting for her on the garage roof. The last of the day's heat thrummed off the tiles beneath them.

"Good," the cat whispered. "You have everything you need?"

Evie gripped the metal in her pocket. *Keep it safe and keep it hidden until you're with the others* – that was what Wainwright had told her. She couldn't show it to the cat, not yet. "Yes."

The cat nodded. "Now stay close. I'm taking us to the hideout. Don't do *anything* unless I tell you to. Understand?"

Evie nodded. "Y-yes." She leaned down to pick up the cat.

The cat leaped back in horror. "What on earth are you doing?!" she hissed.

"I'm … picking you up," said Evie, confused. "So that we can get off the roof."

The cat was outraged. "Don't pick me up. Don't *ever* pick me up."

With that, she slipped over the edge of the roof. Evie lowered herself onto the wheelie bins, somewhat chastened, and silently followed the cat out of the garden. The cat was leading her through the back gate and down an overgrown pathway that joined the gardens on the rest of the street together, taking shortcuts. Evie kept up as best as she could, but following a black cat under hedges and over fences in the dark wasn't easy, especially when she had no idea where she was going. She was being taken to some kind of hideout — but where it was, or who would be waiting for her when she got there, was still a mystery.

The cat came to a sudden stop in an alleyway and peered around the edge of some bins, checking to see if the coast was clear. Evie crouched behind her, heaving for breath. At the end of the alleyway she could see a strip of water, its surface prickled with starlight.

"We're going to the canal?" asked Evie.

The cat nodded. "The hideout's down there. Stay close, and whatever you do, don't…" She turned around and trailed off. "Did you bring a *book*?"

Evie looked down at the book in her hand. "You said to bring what I needed."

"You're not going to need a book!"

"But I haven't finished it ye—"

The cat slammed herself up against the wall so fast that it took Evie by surprise. Then her brain caught up, and she flung herself to the wall as quickly as she could. She stood frozen in place, feeling her heartbeat pound against the bricks.

"Don't – *move*," hissed the cat,

Evie waited, not even daring to breathe. She had no idea what the cat had seen. There was nothing outside the alleyway except for a few pools of light cast by the streetlamps…

And then, on the other side of the road, a man appeared from the shadows. He was an ordinary businessman, wearing a suit, carrying a briefcase and a newspaper. The sort of person who faded quietly into the background.

But the moment Evie saw him, she knew that he was bad.

It was one of the men she had seen chasing Wainwright earlier. It was the *feeling* that the man left inside her: looking at him was like gazing down a hole in the bottom of the ocean. Every part of her wanted to turn away, sickened with fear, but she knew she couldn't afford to take her eyes off him for even a second. The man was walking with his head bowed, as if searching for something on the ground…

Then he suddenly stopped. With dreadful slowness, he began to turn and face the alleyway. Evie pressed herself tighter to the wall, fear sluicing through her. She was trapped: she had no place to run, no place to hide. She was certain that he was staring right at her. *Surely* the man could see her? Surely at any moment he was going to walk towards her, his grey eyes gleaming in the last of the streetlamps...

The man stood in place for another heart-stopping moment, and then turned on his heels and walked away. Within seconds, he was out of sight. The cat released a shuddering breath.

"Smoke-men," she whispered. "They're still looking for Wainwright. He must have given them the slip. Come on, quick!"

She shot over the road, slipping down onto the towpath and out of sight. Evie followed as fast as she could. The canal was pitch-black, lit only by the squares of light spilling from narrow boat windows. Here and there, a thread of woodsmoke rose from a chimney, or a fox darted from the darkness. Apart from that, Evie and the cat were completely alone.

"The hideout's there," the cat hissed. "Quick!"

Evie looked around, searching for a hideout, but there was nothing. Then she worked out what the cat was talking about.

"*That's* the hideout?" she asked, aghast.

It was one of the old, abandoned narrow boats that had been left to rot along the towpath. The paint was cracked and blistered; the windows were held in place with old gaffer tape. It looked like it had been here for decades, and it probably had. It even had a tree growing out of the roof. Evie must have walked past it every single day and never once noticed it.

"Come on!" said the cat impatiently. "Hop aboard."

Evie wasn't even sure that she *could* hop aboard. It looked like one hop would send her crashing through the floorboards and into the canal. Woodworm had chewed the deck to powder. "Are you sure it's safe…?"

The cat ignored her, leaping onboard and disappearing through a hole in a doorway without replying. Evie groaned. She had to follow – anywhere was better than out here, with those men walking around. She gave a whimper of fear and gingerly stepped aboard. The boat creaked with her weight, but it held. Evie turned to face the doorway in front of her, and her heart sank. Through a sheet of cracked and grimy glass, she could make out a dismal space riddled with rot and cobwebs inside. Was she *really* about to go in there?

Evie closed her eyes, threw open the door like ripping off a plaster, and stepped inside.

She had prepared herself for the stench of cold, damp decay. Instead, she was surprised to find herself breathing in air that was warm and scented with woodsmoke. The walls of the room felt wide and generous around her. She could hear voices coming from somewhere far ahead –

impossibly far ahead, she thought – echoing towards her like the inside of a cathedral.

"She's here! I've got her! We're safe!"

Evie opened her eyes ... and found that she wasn't standing inside a narrow boat after all.

She was standing inside a vast and gleaming mansion. A golden ceiling stretched high above her, every inch of it decorated with sparkling constellations. Before her was a hallway, flanked by four double doors, each one leading to a succession of rooms that seemed to go on and on, unfolding almost for ever, each one more beautiful than the last.

It was the most incredible place Evie had ever seen. In one room, there stood a great marble fountain, its jets pluming into the teardrops of a chandelier that hung above it. Through another door, she could see a giant spiral staircase, its steps carpeted in thick red velvet. At the end of another corridor she could make out a library filled with books: millions of books, a whole empire of books, shelf after shelf of dusty spine-cracked volumes stretching up to a roof beyond where she could see.

She stood, stupefied. She knew it didn't make any sense. She knew that a moment ago, she had been standing on a rotten narrow boat, and that all of this could not possibly fit inside it. But here it was, right in front of her. She could see it and feel it and smell it and touch it.

And she could hear voices, too: lots of voices.

"Alinora!"

"Oh, thank the Lord!"

"What took you so long?!"

"Where's Wainwright?"

Evie turned to the nearest doorway. The room inside it was smaller than the others, but no less decadent. It was lined with dark wood panels and rich, rippling wallpaper. On one wall stood a roaring fireplace, surrounded by high-backed leather armchairs. There were three people in the room, all of whom were talking to the cat at the same time. One was a young boy; one was an old woman; one was a thin, pale man.

Evie recognized the people, of course. She recognized them instantly.

They were the people from her dream.

6
THE ORDER

Evie's mind was spinning like a weathervane. She could find a way to explain the encounter with Wainwright. At a push, she might *even* have been able to find a way to explain a talking cat. But not this. Not a mansion that had materialized from nowhere, filled with people she had seen in her dreams only the night before.

They were the same people, all right. The boy was stocky and baby-faced with a neat side-parting. The old lady had a sensible cardigan buttoned over a brightly coloured dress, and glasses perched on the end of her nose. The pale man was wearing a three-piece suit in an effort to look older, but nothing could hide how pale and scrawny he was. His eyes darted between Evie and the cat.

"Where's Wainwright?" he repeated. "He *is* with you, isn't he?"

The cat stared at him. "He still hasn't come back?"

The others shook their heads. The cat swallowed, and turned to the fireplace.

"Then he's still out there," she said. "Running from Vale's smoke-men. If they haven't caught him already."

Evie felt the temperature of the room drop several degrees. The old woman shifted in her chair; the pale man wrung his hands; the boy bit his nails.

"I was keeping lookout on the bridge" said the cat. "They appeared from nowhere – dozens of them, more than I've ever seen before. Wainwright was right about Vale's powers. He's got stronger."

"Why didn't he come here, Alinora?" the boy asked quietly. "He'd have been hidden here. He'd have been *safe*."

"Because he'd have led Vale's men right to us," said the cat. "Right now, this hideout's the only thing that's keeping us safe."

Evie's mind was still spinning. *Alinora, the hideout, Vale...* All the things that Wainwright had mentioned to her were coming true.

The old lady reached over and patted the boy's hand. "Come, Rishi, dear. Do not fear. Wainwright has outrun Vale's men many times before. No one knows the streets like him!"

"That's right," said the cat. "And he gave me strict instructions when we left the hideout this morning. He told me that if anything went wrong, I was to bring Evie here the moment it was safe." She spun to face them, her blue and yellow eyes flashing in the firelight. "Don't you see? This must all be part of his plan. He led Vale's smoke-men away, so that I could bring Evie here safely. He'll be back any moment!"

The relief in the room was palpable. Everyone suddenly turned to Evie, as if only just realizing she was there.

"You're sure this is her?" said the pale man. "The one he showed us? The secret weapon?"

"Of course it's her," snapped the cat. "We all saw her in the dream, didn't we?"

Evie felt a jolt. *Secret weapon?* What did that mean? Before she could process it, the old lady leaned forward in her chair, giving Evie a big beaming smile.

"Well! I suppose we should introduce ourselves!" She placed a hand on her chest. "My name is Clara Campbell ... but everyone here just calls me Campbell." She gestured to the boy beside her. "The young man here is called Rishi."

"It's *Rish*," the boy muttered. "I told you, I want people to call me Rish now."

"Of course!" Campbell nodded indulgently. "The gentleman who does not look very well is Mr Onslow..."

"Pleasure," said Onslow, who still had his head in his hands.

Campbell gestured to the cat. "And I believe you have already met Lady Alinora."

Evie blinked. *Lady* Alinora? No wonder the cat sounded so posh. Before Evie could ask a single question, Alinora had raised herself up to her full height.

"Right — that's enough introductions," she said.

"Now let's find out what she knows, before Wainwright gets back. The quicker we get her up to speed, the better. Frankly, I think we have our work cut out for us." She gave Evie a distasteful look. "Well? Come on, then – what did Wainwright tell you?"

"That's right!" said Rish. "What did he tell you about us?"

Onslow leaped to his feet. "Did he mention Emrys? Or the Order of the Stone?"

"*Cha!*" snapped Campbell, trying to heave herself out of the chair. "Stop it! Don't crowd the poor girl!"

Evie's mind was completely scrambled. Suddenly remembering anything Wainwright had said seemed almost impossible – but then one of the most important things he mentioned pushed itself to the front of her mind. She clutched the piece of metal in her pocket.

"He ... he gave me something, just before he ran away. He told me I had to take care of it, and then show it to you…"

She held out the piece of metal. Evie could never have guessed the impact it would have on the others. It was like a bomb had been let off in the room. Alinora stood frozen to the spot, as if she'd been slapped; Campbell's mouth fell open; Onslow almost toppled over backwards.

"N-no," Rish whispered.

Alinora shook her head. "It's a mistake. He must have dropped it when he was running away and she picked it up. There's no *way* he would have…"

"No, Alinora," said Campbell wearily, lowering herself into her chair. "He would not have dropped it. You know as well as I do what has happened."

"I think I'm going to be sick," said Onslow, leaning against the mantelpiece.

Evie gazed around the group – at their stunned, shocked faces – and finally felt a burst of courage. For the first time that night, she felt like she was on solid ground. The metal in her hand had given her some kind of power over these people.

"Will one of you tell me what's going on?" she demanded. "I don't know who you are, or why I'm here, or what any of you are talking about. So, someone is going to explain everything to me, right now! Please."

The strangers shared a look. The space between them filled with silence: the silence of something huge that demanded to be said, but couldn't be. It was clear that no one even knew how to begin. It was Campbell who eventually answered.

"We are the Order of the Stone, my dear," she said. "A secret magical society sworn to defend humanity from darkness." She nodded to the others. "Standing in front of you are four of the last magicians left on the face of this planet."

"Four," whispered Alinora. "Only four of us left."

Campbell pointed to the metal in Evie's hand.

"The item you are holding is called *the token*," she said.

"It was the single most precious thing that Wainwright owned. He never let it out of his sight – he never let it leave his side." She shifted in her chair. "It was given to Wainwright by the leader of the Order before him … who was given it by the leader before them, who was given it by the leader before *them,* who was given it by the leader before *them.* Because whoever leads the Order of the Stone must hold the token, and keep it safe until the day they die. And with his final act, Wainwright passed it to you."

Evie felt a lurch of realization. "Wh-what does that mean?"

The four magicians stared at each other, waiting to see who would say it first. No one expected it to be Lady Alinora.

"It means that Wainwright's dead," she said, her voice steady and blank. "It means that you're a magician. And it means, Evie, that you are now our leader."

7
THE TOKEN

THE WORDS LANDED ON THE GROUP LIKE A TEN-TON rock. Evie looked at the others, panic rising in her chest. She was the leader? Of a society of *magicians*? Was *that* what Wainwright had meant when he said she was going to be important?

"L-listen," she said. "I think there's been some terrible mistake. I *can't* be your leader…"

"The token can only be held by the rightful person," said Campbell patiently. "Wainwright would not have passed it on if he did not believe you were worthy of it."

Evie stared at the metal in her hand. It felt even heavier than before. "But … I'm not even a magician!"

Campbell leaned forward. "Do me a favour please, Evie. Hold up the token."

Evie had no idea why she was being asked, but she did as she was told.

"Now – ask it to show you magic," said Campbell.

Evie blinked. "Out loud?"

"However you want," said Campbell. "It's different for every leader."

Evie shifted nervously. Everyone was watching her, waiting to see what would happen. She felt like it was all going to turn out to be a cruel joke. She looked at the piece of crummy metal in her hand. "Er … show me magic." She paused, and then added, "Please."

Nothing happened. Evie blushed bright red. "You see? I told you it's—"

She never finished the sentence. The token started to glow right in front of her eyes: dim at first, and then brighter and brighter, until the piece of twisted metal was so bright she could barely see it. She shielded her eyes in surprise. Within seconds, the token was blazing bright white in her hands, fully alight and yet somehow still cool to the touch.

And it wasn't the only thing that was glowing.

Evie gasped. A white light had appeared in the centre of Campbell's chest, pulsing beneath her cardigan like a second heart. *All* the magicians had one: a shining white glow in their chests, beating in time with the token. Lady Alinora's light shone beneath her fur like a moon behind clouds. Evie was so dazzled that it took her a moment to realize that the others were staring at her.

"G-good God," said Onslow.

"My my," said Campbell.

"He was right," said Rish in disbelief. "She's a sorcerer!"

Evie looked down at her chest, and cried out. She had a glowing white light inside her, too. But this one wasn't like a second heart. Her whole ribcage was a beaming white beacon, bright enough to light the room. And it was getting brighter and brighter…

Evie dropped the token in shock. At once, the white lights vanished, and the room fell dark and shadowed once more.

"Wh–what was that?" Evie cried. "What just happened?"

Campbell smiled. "The token did what you asked it to do, Evie. It showed you magic. Magicians like us are born with it inside us. But *you* have more than anyone. That is why Wainwright brought you to us. Why he chose you to lead us."

Evie was stunned. "But … I don't know anything about magic! I've never done *anything* special!"

"In fact, everyone looks right past you," said Onslow wearily. "And it's only started happening recently." He looked Evie up and down. "You're twelve, I assume?"

Evie was caught off-guard. "Exactly."

The others sighed knowingly. Campbell heaved herself from her chair. "Right! We have much to explain. You lot get started. I'll make the tea."

"No milk," said Onslow automatically.

"Two sugars," said Rish.

"Just show it to the water," said Lady Alinora.

Campbell shuffled out of the room, humming under her breath. Onslow glanced at the others, waiting to see if they were going to begin. When they didn't, he turned to Evie with a sigh. "The reason that no one notices you," he explained, "is precisely *because* you have magic inside you. Magic is meant to be unnoticed. It hides in plain sight. It lives just beneath the surface of things. People like us, who are born with magical powers ... we have to work hard to be noticed by ordinary people. Their eyes just slide right off us." He folded his hands. "Once the magic inside you switches on, people begin to notice you less and less. For most people, it starts when they turn twelve."

Evie blinked. *That* explained everything that had been happening lately: why people kept bumping into her in the street. Why no one at school talked to her. Why her parents had to be reminded of basic things a hundred times over. Why she hadn't noticed Wainwright sitting on the bench at first. "But ... *I* can see all of you now."

"That's because you're magic, too," muttered Lady Alinora. "It's not rocket science."

Onslow cleared his throat, trying to cover up the cat's rudeness. "Once the magic inside you does wake up, it means you're also ready to discover your magical skill. Every magician has one skill. I can do ... this. *Alacazam!*"

He held out an empty hand. There was a sound like someone striking a tiny triangle, and suddenly Onslow was holding a glass of water. It had appeared from nowhere.

The liquid inside it was still swaying, as if he'd caught it in mid-air.

Evie's eyes boggled. "Wow! You can make things appear in your hand?"

Onslow's smile held for a moment, then dropped. "Er … no, not anything. Just this." He held up the glass of water.

Evie stared at him. "Your magical power is to make a glass of water appear in your hand at will."

"Yes."

"And that's it."

"Yes."

There was an awkward silence. Now that Evie thought about it, the room was covered in identical glasses of water. They were on the floor, and the mantelpiece, and the tables, and tucked into all the corners.

"I can't make them disappear again," said Onslow, blushing.

Campbell returned with a tray of tea and biscuits, immediately knocking over five of the glasses. "*Cha!* Onslow, how many more of these do we need?" She kissed her teeth and put down the tray. "I'll get a towel…"

She stormed out the way she had entered and Evie nearly leaped out of her skin. She had only just noticed that there was no doorway to the kitchen. Campbell had walked straight through the *wall* beside the fireplace. "How – how … did she just…?"

"Campbell's skill is walking through walls," Onslow explained.

"She's not much of a knocker," muttered Lady Alinora.

On cue, Campbell reappeared with a tea towel, passing straight through the wall again. It was as if she had stepped beneath a waterfall: the framed paintings and wood panelling simply flowed around her body, making space for her before returning to their original places. Campbell handed out the tea, and then handed Evie a plate of biscuits, and some cake, and a sandwich, and a banana, and then another slice of cake. Evie had never seen so much food on a single plate before.

"Every person's magical power is unique," said Campbell, sinking into a chair and picking up where Onslow left off. "Something only they can do. Young Rish here learned his skill when he was only five."

Rish leaned forward excitedly. "You saw us all in your dream last night, correct?"

So many shocking things had happened in the last few minutes that Evie had forgotten all about this. She nearly spilled her biscuits. "That's right! I *dreamed* all of you…"

"You didn't *dream* us," said Rish, unable to hide his pride. "We were really there, in your head. That's my skill. I step inside people's dreams."

Evie was horrified. The knowledge that five strangers had been inside her head was mortifying: it was like waking up to find burglars in her room, reading her diary. What if she had been dreaming about something private? She turned to Lady Alinora, desperate to change the subject. "A-and you? What's your skill?"

The cat gave her a withering look. "I can fly."

Evie gasped. "You *can*?"

There was an embarrassed silence.

"Alinora turns into animals, dear," said Campbell kindly, popping a biscuit in her mouth. "She was just being sarcastic."

Evie turned bright red: sarcasm was not her forte. She got the impression, not for the first time, that Lady Alinora wasn't happy that Evie was there. In fact, she got the feeling that she was angry with her, and she didn't know why.

"What about Wainwright?" Evie asked. "What was his skill?"

It silenced the room. There it was again: the horrible truth. Wainwright was dead, and there wasn't a single thing anyone could do about it. The moment of excitement brought by Evie's power was gone in an instant, swept away in a wave of grief.

"He could separate from his own shadow," said Lady Alinora, her voice quiet with reverence. "He could send it wherever he wanted. Beneath doors, over seas, under stones. He could hide objects inside it. He could hide *himself* inside it, if he had to. It was beautiful, beautiful magic."

"He was in the Order for longer than any of us," said Onslow. "Our last link to the magicians of old. And now he's gone."

"He never said goodbye," said Rish quietly.

He looked like he was about to burst into tears. Campbell reached over and pulled him into her chair. "Oh, Rishi, dear. It's OK. It's OK."

He let himself be hugged. Evie had no idea what to say. A part of her felt almost ashamed to be there, standing in the middle of their grief – to be such a poor replacement for all that they had lost. Another part of her felt frightened – how on earth was she supposed to take over from the last great magician of old?

"What about me?" she asked. "What's *my* skill?"

The magicians looked at each other.

"Well – that's the question," said Onslow. "We don't know. Wainwright had a plan for you, but he kept it all to himself. And now ... well, I guess we'll have to wait until your skill appears by itself."

Lady Alinora suddenly swiped at her cup, spilling tea. "That's why making her our leader is so *ridiculous*," she snapped. "I was in the Order for a whole *year* before I learned my skill. We can't wait that long! For all we know, Vale has his hands on the Spellstone right now!"

Something suddenly clicked in Evie's mind. "The Spellstone. Wainwright told me about that. Something about evil magic, and a magician called—"

"Emrys," said Campbell. "That's right. You're looking at him, dear."

She pointed to the wall above the fireplace. Evie glanced up, and only then realized that she was looking at an oil painting so enormous she had mistaken it for wallpaper.

The painting showed a vast boulder in the middle of a forest. It was blazing red, bursting from the earth like solid fire. Before it stood an old man swathed in red and white robes, with a long flowing beard that rippled down the length of his body like oil in water. His eyes were wide and watchful; his face was peaked with age; and, clasped in his hands, high above his head, was a gleaming silver sword.

Evie understood, instantly, who she was looking at. "That's…"

"Yes, dear," said Campbell. "Emrys. The greatest magician who ever lived. The man who created the Order of the Stone. The reason all five of us are standing here today."

Campbell settled into the chair, ate her final biscuit, and began to tell the story of Emrys and the Spellstone.

8
EMRYS AND THE SPELLSTONE

"Long ago," said Campbell, "when the world was young, this land was a dark and dreadful place. It was filled with the creatures of darkness: monsters that terrorized and tormented the people who lived here."

Campbell pointed to the edges of the painting, where twisted, evil figures clawed at Emrys on every side. There were great scaled dragons with slit eyes, and snarling ogres with broken teeth, and bloodthirsty giants, and a thousand unseen creatures that slithered and crept in the darkness.

"Then Emrys appeared," said Campbell. "He was a sorcerer: a magician born with incredible power. The magic inside him was like nothing seen before or since. He breathed magic as we breathe air. He could talk to it, move it, train it to do what he wished. Next to him, we are all just children."

Evie glanced at the others. They were all gazing at the

painting in rapture. She could tell, with a single look, how much the story of Emrys meant to them.

"Emrys *could* have used his powers to rule the world," said Campbell. "But, instead, he chose to protect it. He believed that if he could destroy the creatures of darkness, and remove every ounce of their evil magic from the land, then the people would be saved. And, so, he created the Order of the Stone: a society of faithful magicians devoted to fighting evil and flushing it from wherever it hid. Emrys and his followers travelled the land, defeating every creature of darkness they found. And once they were killed, Emrys would use his magical sword to draw out their evil powers—"

"And trap them inside a stone," Evie said. Wainwright had told her this.

Campbell nodded. "That is correct – the Spellstone. Emrys found an ordinary boulder in an ordinary forest, and hid all of the evil magic inside it. Then he sealed shut the stone with his most powerful magic, so it could only be opened with his sword, by him and him alone." She gazed up at the portrait. "It took many years. But slowly, one by one, the creatures of darkness were destroyed, and their evil magic locked away inside the Spellstone."

Campbell's voice suddenly softened. "But defeating the creatures of darkness was not enough for Emrys. He wanted to heal people's *minds* as well. Wherever he went, he would make people forget about the monsters that had tormented them. He would erase their memories, one by one, so they would not even remember their fears. Soon, people believed that dragons and ogres and monsters were nothing more than stories. In order to protect them, Emrys made them forget that magic existed."

"They call it the Dark Ages," said Onslow. "Hundreds of years, where barely any records exist of what happened. And now you know why."

Evie was speechless. So that was the truth: dragons and monsters weren't just stories. They really *had* existed, all along.

Campbell shifted in her chair. "When all the creatures of darkness had been removed from the land, there was only one thing left for Emrys to do: destroy the Spellstone, once and for all. Rid the world of its evil magic for good." Her voice became grave. "But Emrys had made a terrible mistake. Without realizing it, he had created a weapon of enormous magical power: one that was too strong to be defeated, even by him. When he struck the Spellstone with his sword, the Spellstone fought back. It shattered his sword into a thousand pieces, scattering his powers to dust and mortally wounding him. Emrys lay dying, defeated by his own creation.

"With his final breaths, Emrys told his faithful magicians what they must do: find a way to destroy the Spellstone. Over time, he said, the evil power inside it would only grow stronger: there would come a time when not even the Spellstone itself could contain it. The Order of the Stone must dedicate their lives to finding a way to destroy it before that happened: and until then, they must hide it from the world and keep it secret and safe, so that its evil powers could never be released."

She settled back into her chair. "And that is just what they did. The Order of the Stone took the pieces of Emrys's sword and destroyed them, so that it could never be used to reopen the Spellstone. Then the Spellstone was hidden in a secret place, where it would never be found. Only one person – the leader of the Order – would ever know the location."

Evie felt a tremble of nerves inside her. The leader of the Order – that was her now. "But why would *anyone* want to open the Spellstone? Why release all that evil magic?"

Campbell shrugged. "Greed? Power? An accident? Stupidity? Sadly, people do not always do the right thing. To think what all that evil magic could achieve in the wrong hands…"

She gestured to the magicians around her.

"And so, the Order has hidden the Spellstone for one and a half thousand years. Only the best magicians – the ones who are most honourable, kind and true – can be trusted with the knowledge of its existence. Over the centuries, hundreds of magicians have come and gone. Every single one of them has dedicated their life to protecting the world from what is hidden inside the Spellstone…"

"Until Vale," said Lady Alinora.

The cat sat facing the fireplace, her ears twitching as she gazed at the flames. Evie swallowed. "Wainwright told me about him, too – an evil magician."

Alinora nodded. "He was a normal magician, once. He was recruited into the Order not long after Wainwright. He had great magic inside him – more than anyone had ever seen, in fact. Everyone thought that when Vale finally discovered his skill, it would be something important. Maybe even powerful enough to destroy the Spellstone. Just as Emrys predicted, the evil magic inside it had grown and grown – time was running out. The Order needed a miracle. Perhaps *that's* what clouded their judgement."

Lady Alinora turned round, her outline shadowed against the flames.

"When Vale did discover his skill … it was worse than anyone predicted. He is able to *steal* powers. He can take a magician's magic, just by holding their hand. And when he takes their powers, it kills them."

Evie felt a chill fill the room. The other magicians listened in silence as Alinora continued.

"When Vale realized he could take whatever magic he wanted for himself … it turned his mind bad. He realized that he could *absorb* the powers of the Spellstone, if he wanted to. By doing so, he would become a sorcerer:

more powerful even than Emrys himself. Powerful enough to rule the world." She swallowed. "So, he did the unthinkable – he turned on the Order and tried to make them tell him where the Spellstone was hidden. And when they refused … he stole their powers and killed them. He hunted them down, one by one."

Evie felt a shiver up her spine. Lady Alinora stayed facing her, eyes gleaming bright in the firelight.

"The more powers Vale stole, the more powerful he became. The magicians of the Order were no match for him. The greatest of their age have all fallen to him – O'Brien, Banda, Clairmont, Wang, Davenport. Even…"

"My mother," said Rish, his eyes fixed to the ground.

Evie gasped. Campbell instinctively held him closer to her.

Onslow nodded to the mansion around them. "Patel – Rish's mother – built this hideout five years ago, to protect what was left of the Order from Vale. Frankly, it's the only thing that's kept us safe from him. Rish and I haven't even stepped outside in five years. Magicians like *us* … we're no match for someone like Vale."

The sight of him slumped beside his useless glasses of water told Evie all she needed to know. The great magicians of the past were all gone. Now, all that was left of the Order were these four magicians and their weird powers. They hardly seemed like magicians at all. They looked like … well, three people and a cat.

"Then ... why not keep the Spellstone here?" Evie asked. "Or take it to some other country, where Vale can't find it?"

"Because the Spellstone couldn't be moved," said Onslow. "It's far too dangerous. The powers inside it are vast. It would be like trying to move a nuclear bomb." He sighed. "But then, the other night, while Wainwright was checking on the Spellstone ... he was nearly caught by Vale's men. He had no choice but to move it. It was an *unthinkable* risk ... one that Wainwright would only make if he absolutely had to. He found a new hiding place for it – somewhere no one knew but him. And now he's gone, we have no idea where he hid it. We have no idea what his plan was to defeat Vale!"

Evie perked up – finally, here was some good news. "Wainwright had a plan to defeat Vale?"

"That's right," said Rish. "With you."

Evie's face drained of all colour. *"Me?"*

Lady Alinora glared at her. "You were his *secret weapon*. He believed that the magic inside you is powerful enough to defeat Vale. And now, you're all we have!"

Evie felt sick. The significance of all this was finally beginning to weigh on her. The only thing standing between an evil magician and the most dangerous weapon in the world was ... *her*. How on earth was she supposed to fight Vale? She didn't even know where Wainwright had moved the Spellstone...!

The realization slammed into her like a wall. "Wait – Wainwright told me where he hid it!"

Everyone gasped with relief and leaped to their feet at the same time.

"He did?!"

"Oh, thank the Lord!"

"He told me to tell you." Evie closed her eyes, pulling the words out of her memory. "He said … *It's safe. The last place he'll look.*"

The others waited for her to keep talking, but there was nothing more to say.

"That's … it?" asked Rish.

Evie looked around nervously. "He whispered it to me, just before he left. Like it was a secret."

"The last place he'll look," muttered Onslow. "Well … he must have been talking about Vale. But where would Vale look last?"

"Who knows," muttered Lady Alinora. "He can see the whole city from the top of his hidden fortress. And what *he* doesn't see, his smoke-men will. It hardly matters where Wainwright moved the Spellstone. The Order is clearly finished."

Campbell shot the cat a warning look and tutted. Evie got the feeling she did that a lot. "Hush, Alinora. You forget that we have two things Vale does not have." She picked up the token from the floor. "We have the token and we have Evie. Together they have the power to see magic – both good and bad. We can track down the Spellstone, wherever it is hidden." She smiled, and hung the token around Evie's neck. "And we all saw the power inside Evie just now. Mark my words, when she discovers her skill, she will be nothing less than a sorcerer herself! If Wainwright believed in her ... then so should we."

The others muttered in solemn agreement. Lady Alinora flicked her tail angrily and turned away. Campbell pushed herself up from her chair.

"Tomorrow, we will begin Evie's magical training," said Campbell. "And we can begin our search for the Spellstone, too. We must be fast, if we want to stay one step ahead of Vale. For now, I think it's time we all went to bed."

Evie nodded gratefully. At least back home, in the safety of her own bedroom, she could finally begin to make sense of everything she had learned. "Thanks. I'll come back first thing tomorrow morning. I doubt anyone at school will notice if I'm not there..."

She trailed off. The magicians were all staring at her, and Campbell was shaking her head.

"No, child," she said quietly. "You do not understand. You are the leader of the Order of the Stone. Until Vale is defeated, you must stay here in the hideout with us. Where it is safe."

Evie stared at her in shock. Campbell wasn't joking. "But ... my parents don't know I'm here."

"Good," said Lady Alinora. "If they did, Vale would find us."

Evie looked at the magicians, and the truth came like a punch in the stomach. She couldn't go home. No matter how bad things had been, Evie had always been able to go home at the end of the day. Even if her parents had been inattentive recently, she could ask them for help. Mum and Dad were probably watching TV now, thinking she was asleep. Tomorrow they would call her down to breakfast, and discover nothing in her bedroom except some pillows pushed under the duvet. They'd think she'd run away. The thought made Evie want to burst into tears and never stop crying.

Campbell held her shoulder. "I'm sorry, dear. Being in the Order is a great sacrifice sometimes." She started to lead her away. "I'll show you to your room. Say goodnight, everyone."

Onslow stood up and knocked over three glasses. "Oh! Er – goodnight."

"Night," Rish mumbled quietly, staring at his lap.

Lady Alinora didn't say anything – she just stayed glaring at the fireplace. Evie felt a fresh wave of misery. Despite what Campbell had said, it was clear that none of the magicians really wanted her here. Who could blame them? Their beloved leader was gone. And Evie, his clueless replacement, was going to doom them all.

She let herself be led through the sprawling mansion,

barely taking in any of it. She didn't even have the wherewithal to cry. Campbell took her up a grand sweeping staircase and along a twisting corridor until they came to a master bedroom.

"Here we are, dear," said Campbell. "The nicest room in the hideout!"

Just like the rest of the mansion, the bedroom was lavish and decadent. Its ceiling was decorated with moons and stars; the pile of the carpet looked deep enough to swim in. In the middle of the room was the biggest four-poster bed Evie had ever seen in her life, stacked with luxurious pillows. Through a doorway on the far wall, she could make out a bathroom with golden taps, gleaming marble, and a bathtub the size of her garden back home.

Then she noticed the mahogany wardrobe in the corner. The door was ajar. Inside it were ten identical shabby coats, ten identical pairs of tattered trousers, and ten identical pairs of broken boots.

"This is Wainwright's old room," she said in horror.

Campbell nodded. "He would want you to have it, dear. Do you need anything before I go?"

Evie needed more things than she'd ever needed in her life, but right now she just wanted to be left alone. Campbell gave her shoulder a final kind squeeze. "Try and get some sleep, dear. Tomorrow's going to be a long day." With that, she left.

Evie gazed around the empty bedroom. Under normal

circumstances, she would have been thrilled to stay somewhere so grand. Now, all she could think about was how small she felt inside it. She went into the bathroom and stood in front of the sink, then remembered she hadn't brought a toothbrush. She hadn't brought *anything* with her – no pyjamas, no change of clothes, just a stupid book. After all, she thought she'd be going back home after a few hours. Now she might never go home again.

She felt her eyes fill with fresh tears and slunk back to the enormous bed, clambering inside the pristine white sheets. It was like sliding into a glass of cool, clean milk.

She lay in her perfect bed and stared miserably at the ceiling. The day had come and gone, and her life had been transformed beyond all recognition. She had woken up a twelve-year-old girl; she was going to bed as the leader of a secret magical fellowship. She was in a race against time to find an ancient weapon, defeat an evil magician, and save the world. Oh – and she had to discover what her secret magical power was, too. How on *earth* was she supposed to do it all?

She lifted the token from her neck and gazed at it. The light from the bed lamp gleamed along its edges: a curved question mark in the darkness.

"The last place he'll look," she repeated.

The words rolled over and over in her head. How was she supposed to work out where Vale would think to look? Didn't Alinora say that he could see *everything*?

And that made her think of something else Alinora had said. Something that didn't make any sense. She stared at the ceiling in confusion.

"How do you hide a *fortress* in the city?" said Evie.

9
VALE

Vale stood at the top of his fortress.

He could see everything from up here: every street and every house and corner of the city, spread out like a landscape before him. He could see how the city was split in half by a giant river; how the buildings were built so close to its banks that it seemed like the river was twisting itself to snake between them. From up this high, everything looked different: people became so small and insignificant. The city became a puzzle.

It was why he had built Tower 99 in the first place.

It had taken an enormous amount of magic to do it. After all, it was the tallest skyscraper in the city. Half a kilometre of glass and girders piercing the sky like the tip of a broken sword. The powers he had stolen from the Order had helped, of course. With the power to control smoke, stolen from Banda, he had been able to create an army of smoke-men who slipped perfectly into the background of the city. Spies who saw everything, who could tell him whatever he needed to know at any time of the day.

With the power to paralyse, stolen from Davenport, stealing money had become simple. With a single flick of his fingers, he could freeze any bank security guard to the spot and take as much as he wanted. Vale had been steadily amassing his fortune for years: in fact, more money than even he knew what to do with.

With the power to create buildings from nothing – stolen from Patel – he had created Tower 99. He had done it steadily, night after night, filling the site during the day with his smoke-men to look like real construction workers. No one knew that a fortress was being built, right here in their city: as far as anyone else knew, it was just another ordinary office block.

All of his other powers had helped in their way. Fireballs stolen from O'Brien, telekinesis stolen from Clairmont, lightning stolen from Wang... But the fact was, Vale hardly needed to use them any more. He had defeated any magicians who might stop him, and the ones that were left were too weak to even try.

As for normal people – well, they didn't even notice him. He was too grey, too indistinct, too ... *unmemorable*. People's minds simply slipped over him. He could do whatever he wanted, in plain sight, and the world simply let him get away with it.

That had always been Wainwright's weakness. He thought that in order to survive, you had to hide *beneath* society. He'd spent forty years dressing like a homeless man, slipping into his shadow, keeping to the alleys and dark corners. Vale alone understood that in this world, if you never wanted to be noticed, questioned, or stopped, then you simply had to behave like no one *could* stop you.

He stood at the window to his office, gazing out across the dark city. The office lay at the very tip of Tower 99, on the secret 100th floor. The sun had slunk over the curve of the earth like a wounded animal hours ago, but the streets below still thrummed with heat. Window after window was beginning to flicker with electric light. You never noticed a single one when they appeared – they were far too small to matter – but they all added up. Soon the city would be a million points of light, twinkling like coral in the gloom. It was beautiful, if you took the time to notice it. But Vale's mind was on other things.

Why didn't Wainwright have the token?

Vale knew the rules of the Order. Wainwright had sworn to keep the token with him until the day he died. Vale's smoke-men had been searching the streets for hours, but he knew the truth: Wainwright would never have dropped it. There was no way he would have left it in the care of those other useless magicians, either.

So, if *they* didn't have the token, who did?

Unless…

Vale froze. It finally struck him. Wainwright had recruited another magician. He had given *them* the token. And that meant…

"The Order of the Stone has a new leader," he said.

Vale's eyes flickered across the streets. His mind worked fast – it always did. Wainwright had found a new magician, rare in itself. But Vale knew, as surely as he knew anything, that Wainwright would not have handed over leadership lightly. He had passed on the token for a reason. There was some kind of plan at work. This new magician would be special; they would be powerful.

Could they be more powerful than him?

Vale had no time to waste. If he was going to find this new magician, he had to do it fast. It would take an enormous amount of magic to do what he had planned, but then, he had an enormous amount of magic at his disposal. That was the beauty of Vale's magic, and it was what separated him from all the magicians who had come before him. He had discovered a new source of power that never once ran out, that never grew weaker ... and no one knew about it but him. It was making him stronger every single day.

And when he finally had his hands on the Spellstone...

He quickly composed himself and focused his powers. There was a moment's pause, then a cloud of black smoke appeared from a vent in the office wall. It gathered itself into the dim form of a man that stood waiting on the other side of Vale's desk. Vale didn't bother to give this smoke-man an appearance. After all, he was alone. He gave the orders without even bothering to turn around.

"Forget the token," said Vale. "Search for the other magicians: the cat, the old woman, the boy, the thin man. Search every building, search every road – search beneath the roads. Leave not one inch uncovered. One of them will lead us to this new magician, whoever it is."

Vale gazed down at the city, spread like a landscape before him.

"Find them," he said, almost to himself, "and we'll find the Spellstone."

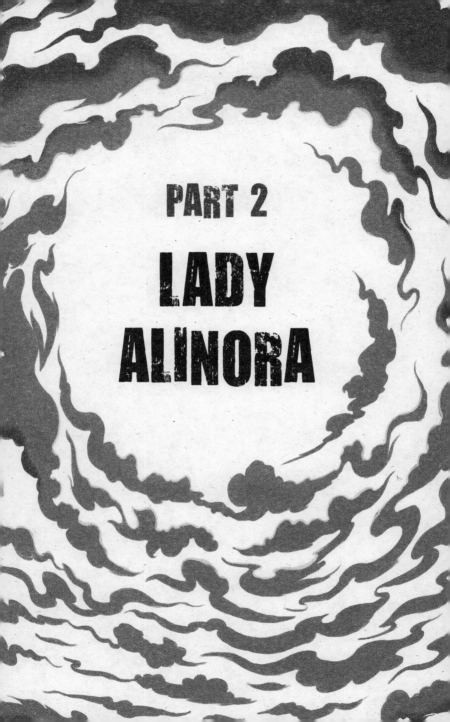

PART 2
LADY
ALINORA

10
ONSLOW

EVIE WOKE UP.

For a brief moment, she was shocked to find herself in a strange room, lying on a four-poster bed. Where was she?

Then it all came back, in one big, awful wave. The night before. Everything she had learned. Wainwright, the Order, Emrys, the Spellstone, Vale…

Her heart sank. It was no dream, then. She was still the leader of an ancient magical society, still caught in a battle between good and evil, and the fate of the world *still* rested on her shoulders.

She lay for a while, wondering if anyone was going to come and get her. It was eight o'clock: her parents would be awake by now. They'd have gone into her bedroom and discovered that she wasn't there. The thought was too awful to even consider, so she got out of bed and dressed forlornly. She felt ridiculous, wearing a school uniform in a place like this, but they were the only clothes she had. Taking something from Wainwright's wardrobe made her feel slightly sick.

She made her way down the grand carpeted staircase and traced her footsteps back to the drawing room. Evie noticed, for the first time, how dark the Order's hideout was. After all, there were no windows. It was morning, but there wasn't a shred of daylight to be found. It made the mansion feel like an old, abandoned museum.

She finally found the drawing room. Part of her expected to see the magicians waiting at the fireplace where she had left them the night before, but when she arrived the only person there was Onslow. He was still wearing a three-piece suit, but now he had an apron over the top of it. He was winding up a grandfather clock and humming to himself.

"Morning," said Evie.

Onslow jumped at the sound of her voice. "Oh! You're up."

Evie gazed around the empty room. "Where is everyone?"

Onslow seemed a little flustered. "Well – Campbell's still asleep. She went outside after you went to bed last night, to see if she could trace Wainwright's last movements, but she couldn't find anything. She gets tired much more easily nowadays."

"She went outside?" asked Evie. "I thought it wasn't safe."

"It's not," said Onslow grimly. "But we have to start taking more risks." He kept tidying, fussing at cushions and clearing away plates while he was talking. "Rish is sleeping, too. He was up all night as well, searching through people's dreams."

Evie frowned. "Why?"

"To see if he could find any clues about what happened to Wainwright," said Onslow. "People don't notice magicians, but images of them can still crop up in dreams. It's called—"

"Dream-work," said Evie.

Onslow seemed surprised that she knew. "Er ... yes, it is. We figured that if someone saw Wainwright over the last few days, they might dream about him. We could find out what happened to him. It might even help us find the Spellstone. It's a long shot, but then..."

Evie knew exactly what he meant. All they had were long shots. Onslow left the room and Evie followed him along one of the corridors.

"Lady Alinora went into town this morning," he continued. "She said she has a plan for finding out what happened to Wainwright, but she wouldn't tell us what it is. That's typical Alinora. She's been in an *awful* mood, ever since..."

He stopped himself, and blushed. Evie didn't need him to finish the sentence: she knew it was because of her. "And you? What are you doing?"

"Making a cake," said Onslow.

Before Evie could ask what he meant, they stepped

through a doorway, and her mouth fell open. He had led her into the library she had glimpsed the night before … but it was even more enormous than she had realized. It was like an ant colony of books, teetering in great stacks to the ceiling. She wasn't even sure if there *was* a ceiling, or if it was an optical illusion caused by the shelves stretching on to infinity.

"How … how many books are in here?" she asked.

"All of them," said Onslow.

Evie stared at him for a while, trying to process what he had just said. "*All* of them," she repeated. "All the books."

Onslow sought the right words. "Er … it's not *really* a library, truth be told. It's more of a portal, linking you to every library in the world. If it's been written – if it exists – then it's here somewhere."

Evie gazed at the endless shelves around her, stupefied. "How does it fit…?"

"Magic," said Onslow, stating the obvious. "The same magic that makes the mansion fit inside the narrow boat. It was Rish's mother who did it – Patel. If she hadn't made this hideout, I don't think any of us would still be alive." He sighed. "I wish I could have met her, but she died before I joined. She was an incredible magician. Poor, poor Rish – to lose his mother so young."

Evie thought about how she would feel to lose her own parents. It was too sad to even consider: even being apart from them was breaking her heart. She suddenly wanted to change the subject, very quickly. "But how do you find what you need in here? There isn't even a ladder."

Onslow looked pleased to be asked. He faced the nearest shelf and cleared his throat. "I need a cake recipe, please. Something dairy-free for Rish. No fruit, or Lady Alinora won't touch it. And nothing too sweet." He gave Evie a knowing look. "I'm trying to cut down Campbell's sugar intake. She basically lives on biscuits. What about you? Any requests?"

Evie smiled. "Chocolate would be nice."

On cue, a book shot out from a shelf fifty metres above them. Onslow caught it in mid-air. The book automatically fell open at a page for a low-calorie, dairy-free, chocolate cake. A suggestion for optional strawberries had been crossed out.

"See? Saves tons of time." He put the book on a side table and started untying his apron strings. "Right! I'll sort that out later. Time we got started."

Evie was confused. "Started with what?"

"Your training!" said Onslow, folding the apron neatly over a chair. "We need to discover your magical skill, remember?"

Evie's heart sank. The infinite library had allowed her to briefly forget how much trouble she was in. "How am I supposed to do that, exactly?"

"It's easy," said Onslow. "You think of what you want, and there it is. *Hey presto!*" He held out his hand – *ping* –

and a glass of water appeared inside it. He offered it to Evie, but she shook her head.

"That's it?" she asked, unconvinced. "You just think it, and it happens?"

Onslow shrugged. "It's different for everyone. We just have to find the right way of getting the magic that's inside of you, *outside* of you."

Evie swallowed. That sounded painful. "Do I have to say things like 'alacazam' and 'hey presto'?"

Onslow blushed. "Er … no, you don't. That's just something I do. But here – check this out!"

He held out his hand for Evie to take. She took it, slightly embarrassed. She hadn't held hands with this many people since nursery.

"Now – think about having a glass of water," Onslow instructed.

Evie closed her eyes, knowing it wasn't going to work. "*Alaca—*"

Ping!

Her hand sagged with the weight of something cool and heavy landing inside it. She opened her eyes, and, sure enough, she was holding a glass of water.

"Did I just do that?!" she gasped.

Onslow nodded. "It's because we're holding hands. If magicians hold hands, they can share their powers." He dropped her hand and took a step back. "Right, now try on your own. Think of something you want, and make

100

it happen!" *Ping!* Another glass of water appeared in his hand. "Like this! See?"

Evie closed her eyes and thought of what she wanted. She wanted so many things, she didn't even know where to begin. She thought of all the skills she'd like to have – flying, invisibility, shooting ice from her fingertips – but nothing happened. She waved her hands in the air, wishing with all of her might, but after twenty minutes the only thing she'd managed to conjure up was a strained muscle from waving her hands around. Onslow stood beside her the entire time, repeating the same unhelpful instructions and making glass after glass of water appear in his hands until the library was stacked with them.

Finally, Evie gave up. She flung herself into an armchair in despair. "Oh, this is hopeless! I'm no sorcerer. How am I supposed to defeat Vale if I can't even make a stupid glass of water appear by myself?!"

She hadn't had a tantrum in years – right now, it felt like the only sensible thing to do.

Onslow sat beside her. "You have great power, Evie. We all saw it last night. And Campbell was right: if Wainwright believed in you, then so do I."

Evie gulped. "What if Wainwright made a mistake? What if he was wrong?"

"Wainwright was never wrong!" said Onslow. "He recruited dozens of magicians in his time – back when he was able to, of course. The Order used to travel the world, using the token to seek out the best and brightest magicians for the cause. But when Vale began to hunt us down, Wainwright couldn't risk leaving the city."

Evie blinked. So Wainwright hadn't been able to recruit the best – he'd had to make do with what he could find near by instead. Maybe that explained why the magicians in the Order had such … *unusual* skills. "How did he recruit you?"

Onslow looked surprised to be asked. "Oh! It was five years ago. I was a door-to-door salesman, but I wasn't very good at it. It was the magic, you see – people would open their doors and have no idea I was there." He chuckled. "I got sacked pretty quickly. I was sitting on a park bench, feeling sorry for myself, and then Wainwright appeared. He told me all about the Order of the Stone, and showed me the magic inside me, and how he needed my help to save the world. I couldn't say no to that, could I? *Saving the world!* I didn't even have a savings account."

His eyes glossed over with the memory.

"We spent months trying to work out what my skill was. I used to lie awake at night, wondering what I could do: control the wind? Stop time, maybe?" He sighed. "Then one day, in the middle of training, I thought, *I could really do with a glass of water*, and…"

Ping. A glass appeared in his hand. Onslow gazed at it miserably.

"It's rubbish, having a superpower that no one else has in the world … and it's *this*. I must be the worst magician of all time." He nodded to the mansion. "Still – someone has to keep this place shipshape, don't they? You wouldn't believe how dusty it gets. Lady Alinora and Campbell might be able to go outside, but someone still needs to teach Rish maths and make everyone dinner."

Evie smiled weakly. Onslow was a little stiff and awkward, but she could tell he was nice. "How come Lady Alinora and Campbell can leave?"

"Because of their skills!" said Onslow. "They can hide easily if they need to. Lady Alinora could be any animal she wanted – a lion, an eagle, a sea-dragon … but living as a cat keeps her safe. No one notices a plain black cat, do they?"

Evie scuffed her feet. "I don't think Alinora likes me very much."

Onslow laughed. "I wouldn't worry too much about her. She's brilliant, but she can be a bit … unkind. She's been in the Order for longer than any of us, except Wainwright. Campbell's the oldest, but she was only recruited a decade ago. Rish is only ten. We all thought if anything ever happened to Wainwright, Alinora would take over." He shuffled uncomfortably. "That's why things are a little *weird* around here, with you being leader. The fact that Wainwright gave *you* the token instead of Lady Alinora … I think it's been hard for her to take."

Evie felt a sudden flush of anger. "It's not my fault! I didn't ask for *any* of this!"

Onslow nodded sympathetically. "I know. It can't be easy, finding out about all this in one go. I'm sure Lady Alinora will understand that, in time." He paused, as if deciding whether or not to keep talking. "That skill of hers... It's a great sacrifice, you know. She can only use an animal form once. Once she changes, she can never go back."

Evie didn't understand the point. "So?"

"So – that includes *every* form," said Onslow. "Including human. She lost her human form when she first discovered her skill. She hasn't been a human for forty years."

Evie's stomach fell. Alinora's skill had changed her entire life – would Evie's fate be the same? Would she discover her skill, only to find it meant she could never go home again? Or could she end up with a skill like Onslow's, and do nothing except produce freshly buttered toast at will?

There was a sudden sound at the doorway. Evie spun around – Lady Alinora was padding into the library, right on cue.

"You're back!" said Onslow, surprised. "And you've brought..."

"*Mmwppphph mmmwuuuppph mmmmrrr,*" said Lady Alinora.

There was something hanging out of her mouth — something mangy, and filthy, and very upset. Alinora spat it onto the floor in triumph.

"Took me ages to get one, but I managed it!" she said.

Evie grimaced. It was a pigeon, squawking and shedding feathers. Onslow tracked the mess it was making on his floor with thin lips.

"Delightful," he said. "And, er … *why* have you brought us a pigeon, exactly?"

The pigeon tried to escape out of the door, but Alinora pinned it down with a single paw.

"First rule of the city," she said. "If you want to know the truth, ask a pigeon. They go everywhere, they see everything, no one notices them … and they cannot keep their beaks shut. Mark my words – one of them will know what happened to Wainwright last night."

Evie looked at the pigeon. It didn't look like it was going to tell them anything useful. It looked scared, and swimming with disease. "How are you going to talk to it?"

Alinora gave her a withering look. "I was a pigeon for twelve years, girl. You don't forget a thing like that. It's not the easiest language in the world, but it's a far sight easier than French…"

She leaned in close to the terrified pigeon, her eyes thinning and her voice dripping with venom.

"Right, you," she said. "*Coo*."

11
THE CITY

THE MAGICIANS WERE GATHERED IN THE DRAWING room, watching Lady Alinora interrogate the pigeon. She'd been doing it for almost twenty minutes now.

"Hmph! It's *still* insisting it knows nothing about Wainwright!" she grumbled. "Time to get a little more persuasive, I think…"

She held up a paw, and a set of murderous claws swiftly appeared. The pigeon started flapping frantically beneath her, squawking with terror.

Evie gasped – this was a step too far. "Stop! You're frightening it!"

But Alinora ignored her, listening to the pigeon. "Now we're getting somewhere! It's saying it can take me to some pigeons who might have seen what happened last night." She turned to the others. "You wait here. I'll come back when I find out—"

"Not so fast," said Campbell. "You're taking Evie with you."

"She is?" said Evie.

"I *am?!*" said Alinora, aghast.

Campbell nodded. "No better training than to see a magician in action."

Evie felt a wave of dread. The thought of stepping outside the safety of the hideout after everything she had learned was terrifying. "But – Vale's smoke-men…"

"Vale doesn't know what you look like yet – that means his smoke-men won't, either," Campbell insisted. "You're safe … for now. If you want to discover your skills, Evie, you're going to have to take some risks." She shifted. "Besides, we need you out of the hideout. We have important Order business to attend to."

The others looked away, awkwardly avoiding her gaze. Evie blushed with embarrassment. She might be the leader of the Order, but the others were still trying to keep secrets from her. Clearly, she didn't belong in the world of magic any more than she belonged in the world outside.

"You're all forgetting one *very important thing*," snapped Lady Alinora. "Vale's smoke-men are going to be on the lookout for *anything* suspicious. *Anything* unusual. *Anything* that stands out." She glared around. "So, unless you can think of a good reason for a girl to be walking around in broad daylight with a cat and a pigeon…"

"Ahem."

Everyone turned around. Rish was rubbing his eyes sleepily … and he had his hand up. "I had an idea about that," he said.

Evie opened the mansion door and peeked outside.

Her skin instantly tingled in the summer heat. It was midday, and the towpath was filled with people on their lunch break. It all felt wrong, somehow. Evie's entire life had been turned upside down, but the rest of the world was carrying on exactly as she'd left it.

She stepped outside and quickly closed the door behind her. It was a sweltering day, even hotter than the day before. After the safety and darkness of the hideout, she felt blinded and exposed. It was like a thousand eyes were boring into her from every angle. Campbell had said that Vale's smoke-men wouldn't recognize her, but Evie felt certain, absolutely certain, that a smoke-man was going to leap out and grab her like a spider from a trap at any moment. Those road workers – that traffic warden – that couple on the grass – it could be any one of them.

Lady Alinora and the pigeon weren't helping matters.

"This is *outrageous*!"

"*Coo!*" added the pigeon.

"Never in all my life have I been so *humiliated...*"

"*Coo coo coo!*"

Evie glanced at the wicker cat basket in her hand. Lady Alinora was hunched inside it, with the pigeon peeking out from a moth-eaten blanket beneath her. Both of them were scowling at her.

"Stop gawping at me!" snapped Alinora. "Take us to the city centre. The pigeon's going to give us directions when we get there."

Evie swallowed nervously. "Won't it be crowded?"

"Exactly," said Alinora. "The best place to hide is in a crowd."

Evie frowned – that didn't sound like it made any sense at all. She glanced up and down the towpath. "Which way is the city centre? I've never walked there on my own before."

"Head for Vale's fortress," muttered Alinora. "You can't miss it."

Evie looked around, but there was nothing that looked like a fortress. All she could see were the towers dominating the skyline ahead…

And then it clicked. It was so obvious, she wondered why she hadn't seen it before. There, shimmering in the blistering heat, stood the tallest skyscraper in the city: Tower 99.

"*That's* his fortress?" Evie gasped. "But … it's right where everyone can *see* it!"

Lady Alinora gave her a cutting look – one that had an edge of triumph to it. "Goodness! You *really* don't know a single thing about magic, do you? The most powerful magic hides itself in plain sight. Now get a move on – you're supposed to be slipping into the background!"

Evie frowned. "It would help if you weren't talking so much."

"Stop arguing and do what you're told!"

Evie fumed. Here she was, risking her life, and she was being spoken to like an idiot. She marched towards the city centre, the cat carrier bashing into her leg every step of the way.

The walk to the city was long at the best of times; when it was the hottest day of the year, and people kept bumping into you, it was unbearable. Within minutes, Evie was pouring with sweat, but every time she stopped to catch her breath, Lady Alinora would berate her from the cat basket and make her walk even faster.

Step by step, mile by mile, the city began to appear around her. Terraced houses gave way to shops, and shops gave way to bigger shops, until finally, the buildings were so tall and tightly packed together that the sky was only visible in strips and patches. By the time Evie stepped into the busy main streets of the city centre, she was surrounded by people pressing in from all sides, constant and clamouring – tourists and shoppers and office workers and newspaper sellers. Any one of them could be a smoke-man. Surely, *surely*, one of them was going to notice her?

But Lady Alinora was right: the best place to hide was in a crowd. Evie walked past thousands of people, and no one so much as glanced at her. Everyone was far too busy eating lunch, checking directions, shouting at each other… No one had time to notice a young girl with a cat carrier. There were also, she realized, pigeons wherever she looked: they were lined up along the rooftops, perched on window ledges, gathered in groups along the gutters. The streets were filled with them. Evie had never really noticed them before. No wonder they saw everything.

"Over there!" hissed Alinora. "In that alley across the street. Cross at the traffic lights, *quick*!"

Evie did as she was told. She ran to the traffic lights, pushed the button, looked up – and felt her insides turn to ice water.

There was a man on the other side of the road. A businessman in a grey suit, holding a briefcase … and staring right at her. Evie felt a rush of panic – the man was striding towards her. It was too late to run. What could she do? How could she escape? Was he going to…?

The man stepped to one side at the last second and hugged another man standing beside her. They strolled down the road hand-in-hand, chatting excitedly. Evie felt the clutch of terror loosen inside her. It hadn't been a smoke-man after all – it was just a normal person. But the moment had rattled her. From now on, she couldn't let her guard slip for even a moment. Who knew how many smoke-men there were, woven through the tapestry of the city?

She scurried across the road and slipped into the alleyway. It was a gloomy, narrow passage hollowed out between an all-you-can-eat Chinese restaurant and an accountancy firm. There was nothing in it except some old overflowing bins and a handful of mangy-looking pigeons.

"This is the place," said Alinora. "Let me out, quick!"

Evie opened the front of the cat carrier and the pigeon scrambled out, cooing to the others desperately. Lady Alinora pinned it to the ground before it could escape. The other pigeons in the alleyway squawked with alarm, flapping their wings.

"Right – I'll do the talking," said Lady Alinora.

She faced the pigeons and started cooing in rapid bursts. Evie frowned. Whatever Alinora was saying, it didn't appear to be going down very well. In fact, the pigeons seemed to be getting more upset. "What are you saying?"

"I'm demanding they tell us about Wainwright," said Alinora. "If they saw him – what they saw – where he went. And I've said that if they don't start talking fast, I'm going to pluck out this one's feathers."

Evie gasped. "Why are you saying that?!"

"I'm not *actually* going to do it," muttered Alinora, rolling her eyes. "It's just a little threat, to get them talking. A little threat never hurt anyone!"

"I don't think that's true," said Evie nervously.

The pigeons were getting angrier and angrier, squawking in outrage. The noise was drawing even more birds to the alleyway. Within seconds, the rooftops and windowsills were lined with furious pigeons, all of them staring at Evie and Alinora.

"See?" said Alinora. "They're spreading the word! We'll find out what happened in no time!"

Evie's heart was beginning to beat a little faster. The pigeons didn't look like they wanted to help. "I – I don't think that's what's happening…"

A pigeon suddenly dived from the rooftop, straight for Alinora. The cat only just reared back in time: the pigeon's claws missed her by millimetres. Another bird swooped down, this time heading straight for Evie. She cried out as it flapped around her, batting her with its wings. The pigeons on the rooftops squawked with fury. "Quick – we need to run! Before…"

Evie turned around, and her stomach dropped. The exit was completely blocked by pigeons. Lady Alinora had been right about one thing: pigeons *did* talk to each other. Word had spread far and wide about what was happening in the alleyway, and now every pigeon in the city was here to stop them. She and Lady Alinora were completely surrounded, hopelessly outnumbered … and trapped. All hell was about to break loose.

It was a split-second decision. Evie leaped between Lady Alinora and the pigeons, waving her hands. "Stop! Everyone, just calm down!"

There was a tense stand-off. Lady Alinora glared at her with fury. "*What are you doing?!* I said to let *me*—"

"Tell them we're not going to hurt the pigeon," Evie whispered. "Tell them we know that they're worried about their friend – say that we're looking for *our* friend, too."

"How dare y—"

"Do it now, before they kill us!"

Lady Alinora made to argue again, but her eyes flicked to the gathering mass of pigeons. She knew she had no other choice: she passed on the message through gritted teeth. The pigeons stayed where they were, shifting from foot to foot and cooing suspiciously – but Evie could tell they were listening.

"Good," said Evie. "Now let the pigeon go."

Lady Alinora looked at her, horrified. "Are you out of your mind? It's our only bargaining chip! We let it go, and they'll peck us to shreds!"

"It's not a chip," said Evie. "It's a bird. Do it, now."

Alinora was so furious she could barely speak. She lifted her paw, and the pigeon scrambled away gratefully. The other birds greeted it like an old friend, swooping it into their crowd and pecking its neck affectionately. Evie felt a flush of endearment. It was touching, to see how much these birds cared for each other. She had known, just known, that the pigeons hadn't wanted to hurt them – they had just wanted to protect their friend.

Lady Alinora glared at her with loathing. "*Well?* Congratulations! You just gave away our one and only hope of finding out what happened to Wainwright. If you think a single pigeon in this city is going to talk to us *now*, you must be out of your…"

She trailed off. A one-winged pigeon had been bustled to the front of the crowd. It stepped shyly forward, picking its way towards Alinora. Then, encouraged by the others, it started cooing softly. Alinora listened in amazement.

"What's it saying?" asked Evie.

"It's … it's saying that it saw Wainwright," said Alinora. "Not last night – the night before he disappeared. It's saying it saw him go down a manhole, a few streets from here. It can give us directions, if we like."

Evie frowned. "A manhole? Wainwright went in the *sewers*?"

But Lady Alinora wasn't listening. Her eyes were gleaming with excitement. "Of course – that's what he meant! Vale's skyscraper can see everything in the city, but it can't see what's below the ground! *The last place he'll look!*"

"I don't get it," said Evie.

Lady Alinora sighed. "Don't you understand, you stupid girl? The pigeon saw where Wainwright went on the night he moved the Spellstone. He went into the sewers. *That's* where he hid it. And *we're* going to go down there and find it."

12

THE SEWERS

Ten minutes later, Evie stood in a quiet side street with Alinora back in the cat basket.

"There!" said Alinora, pointing a paw out of the front. "That's the manhole the pigeon saw him go down."

It was a square sheet of metal cut into the pavement, plain and unexceptional. Evie realized, with a feeling that was now becoming familiar, that she had seen hundreds of these before. She had walked over them every single day and never once noticed them. She wondered how many more things like that there were in the city.

"Well?" snapped Alinora. "What are you waiting for? Let me out!"

Evie glanced around to check the street was empty before she unlatched the door of the cat carrier and Lady Alinora shot out.

"Are we *really* about to go into the sewers?" Evie asked nervously.

"They're *drains*," said Lady Alinora primly. "It's just water. Now, stop dawdling and get on with it!"

Evie gritted her teeth with frustration – she was getting sick of being spoken to like this. She bent down and lifted the manhole lid. It was heavier than she'd expected, but after a few tries, she managed to haul it open. It dropped with a clang on the pavement. A square of darkness lay before them. Evie could make out a grey metal ladder inside, leading down to a brick tunnel. A breath of warm, fermented air wafted out from deep within, thick and muggy like a swimming pool.

Lady Alinora leaped down the manhole and disappeared, without thanking her. Evie hid the cat carrier behind some bins, climbed down the metal ladder, and carefully shut the manhole lid behind her.

The tunnel had been dark before; with the lid shut, it was pitch-black. The air felt old and dirty, filled with suspended damp that clung to you like wet clothes. At least it was cool down here, hidden away from the city heat. Evie couldn't help but let out a sigh of relief.

She climbed down the ladder until her feet met wet earth. She reached out her hands, trying to make sense of the space she was in, and felt cold, crumbling brick. She was in a narrow tunnel, just wide enough for a single person to walk down. The steady sound of rushing water echoed all around her.

"Well?" said Alinora in the darkness. "You still have the token, don't you?"

Evie reached around her neck. There was the piece of

metal, still on its tattered bit of string. "Why?"

She could almost *hear* Alinora's eyes rolling in the darkness. "The token shows magic, girl. Even evil magic. You can use it to find the Spellstone."

Evie held out the token nervously. She hoped she could make it work a second time. "Sh-show me magic, please."

The token glowed into life instantly, gleaming in her hand once more – so too did the light in her chest, illuminating the tunnel around them like a lamp. The relief at being able to see lasted about two seconds: then Evie saw the state of the tunnel and decided that sometimes darkness was preferable. It was revolting: every surface was covered in a thick, foul layer of ancient grey filth. She tried not to think too much about what it must be made of.

They walked down the tunnel and came to a shallow river. The tunnel it ran through was much bigger, and wider – and to Evie's surprise, it was beautifully made. The walls were covered with polished tiles, reflecting the glow of her chest as it pulsed in the darkness. The ceiling was pockmarked with holes and grates, leaking thin shafts of sunlight from the streets above. It was strange to think that something so exquisitely made was hidden down here, where no one ever saw it.

Evie glanced from left to right. The river ran into darkness in both directions. "So ... which way?"

"Use the token," instructed Alinora.

Evie didn't really understand – it felt like a test. She

held the token to the left – it stayed the same. Then she held it to the right, and the token changed. The white beam of light was suddenly tinged with the faintest pink, like a single drop of blood in water.

"You see?" said Alinora. "Evil magic. The token will glow redder as we get closer to the Spellstone. Upstream it is!"

She leaped onto Evie's shoulder. Evie stared upstream. There was no walkway: just river. "I ... I have to walk in that?"

"Stop complaining!" Alinora snapped. "It's just water."

Evie bit her tongue. It might be water, but it still looked absolutely filthy. She stepped into the flow, and instantly felt her shoes and socks soak through. She shuddered with revulsion.

"That's it!" said Alinora. "Keep moving! Chop, chop! We haven't got all day!"

Evie made her way up the tunnel with the cat perched regally on her shoulder. It was slow going. The tiles beneath her feet were slick with grey-green matter that slithered underfoot, and she had to steady herself on the walls to stop from falling. Step by step, the glow of the token changed: first to light pink, then to deep rose, making the shadows loom and pulse around them. She knew they were filled with rats. She could hear them shimmying along the pipes that lined the wall and scampering from the edge of the token's light.

I'm not really here, she told herself. *I'm back home, having biscuits in front of the TV with Mum and Dad.*

That was even worse. With a stab of sadness, Evie realized that she had left home almost twenty-four hours ago. She wondered what Mum and Dad were doing right now – if they were thinking of her, too. They would probably be out of their minds with worry. She pushed away the thought and kept walking.

The tunnel finally widened out into a large brick chamber. It was a junction for several tunnels, bringing drain water from different parts of the city.

"Well?" said Lady Alinora. "Come on! Which way do we go now?"

Evie stepped from tunnel to tunnel … but every time she moved from the centre of the chamber the glow of the token began to fade back to white. Evie gazed around, confused. There was nothing else here except a row of brick pillars, surrounded by dead leaves and gathered filth. There was no sign of any Spellstone.

"I – I don't understand," said Evie. "It should be here."

Alinora gave her a withering glare. "*Should, should, should.* 'Should' isn't going to help us now, is it? I suppose that's what happens when you give the token to a twelve-year-old girl…"

Evie finally snapped. "You know what? You're right. I'm *twelve*. I didn't know magic existed until yesterday. I know you're angry that you're not the leader, but I never wanted to be in charge!" She waved her hands for emphasis. "So, do me a favour and stop being so *rude*!"

The silence was heavy. Even the rats seemed to have quietly let themselves out. Alinora fumed, her tail flicking. Having an argument with someone sitting on your shoulder was incredibly awkward.

"I am trying to *help* you," said Alinora, hard as flint. "We have to find the Spellstone and discover your power, fast, or the world is doomed. I don't have time to be gentle with you."

"If you think *shouting* at me is going to help me discover my magical powers…" Evie began.

"As a matter of fact, I do!" cried Alinora. "Fear is important. When you're backed into a corner, and you think you have nothing left, *that's* when you discover what you're really made of!"

The silence was different this time – it was like a locked door had been opened, just a crack. Evie glanced at her. "Is that how you discovered your skill?"

Lady Alinora shuffled. "It was, actually."

"How old were you?"

"Eighteen. I was still living at Bambridge when Wainwright found me."

"Bambridge?"

"My family's estate. You may have heard of it."

Evie snorted. She knew Alinora was posh, but not *that* posh. "You grew up in a mansion?"

Alinora bristled. "Not really, no. My parents packed me off to boarding school whenever they could. And when I *was* home, they always made sure they weren't. Business meetings, holidays that I couldn't possibly join, that sort of thing."

Evie hadn't expected Lady Alinora to say anything like that. She was so used to her being cold and imperious, she'd forgotten that she must have been a child once. Evie knew all too well how it felt to be ignored – but her parents would never have treated her like *that*.

"The school holidays were the worst," Alinora continued. "I was always alone. I had my animals, but that was about it. Horses, dogs, rabbits ... my parents let me have as many of *those* as I liked. They were the only friends I had, really." She shuffled. "When my parents died, I inherited the whole estate, along with more money than I knew what to do with. So, I decided to turn Bambridge into a zoo – elephants in the hedge maze, flamingos in the fountain, that kind of thing."

Evie felt Alinora relax on her shoulder. Even her voice sounded different now: as if she could talk openly, here in the darkness.

"I had a few good years, running that place," said Alinora. "I'd still be there now, if Wainwright hadn't found me. That was back when he was still able to leave the city – before Vale got too powerful. He told me all about the Order of the Stone, and about the powers hidden inside me, and how I'd have to leave everything behind if I wanted to join. I didn't want to leave my animals – I really didn't – but I had to. It was my duty. How can you say no, once you've learned about something like that?" She shifted. "So I gave the zoo to a charity. It's still there, you know. I'd love to visit it one day."

Evie had a feeling that if she didn't keep asking questions, Alinora would stop talking. "So – how did you discover your skill? You said yesterday that it took a year to come out."

Lady Alinora was quiet for a while.

"We used to move around the city in groups, back then," she said. "We don't do that any more. One night, Vale and his smoke-men ambushed us – they were suddenly everywhere, on all sides, dozens of them. I don't think anyone realized how powerful Vale had become. We fought back as best we could, but it was no use. He took the others down and stole their powers. All of them. I just stood there, backed into a corner, watching the greatest magicians of their age fall in front of me, with no powers to fight back…"

Evie could feel her trembling on her shoulder.

"And it all came out in one go," she said quietly. "My skill. As if it had been waiting for the right moment, the whole time. I turned into a bear – a huge one, three times my own size. I took out every single one of Vale's men and sent him running." She shifted on her paws. "It was too late, of course. Vale had done all the damage he needed to. There were eight members of the Order when he attacked, and only Wainwright and I got out alive."

Evie was stunned. No wonder Alinora was so tough – she and Wainwright had built the Order back up from nothing. The cat hardened up again, all business. "So now you understand. Being mollycoddled by Onslow and Campbell isn't going to help you become a sorcerer. A little toughness would do you the world of good!"

Evie glowered. For a moment, she had glimpsed a softer side of Alinora. "Maybe you're *too* tough. You talk like you don't have any feelings, but I think you might secretly be much nicer than you make out."

Alinora scoffed bitterly. "Ha! You see too much good in people…" She stopped mid-sentence.

Evie glanced at her. "What? What's the…?"

She cried out in surprise. The water around them was rising, fast. Within just a few seconds, it had built up past Evie's knees and was soaking into her skirt. It was gushing from one of the tunnels that led into the chamber. Something was driving out the water, wave after wave of it. Evie turned to look closer … and felt a scream choke her throat.

It was rats – hundreds of them – pouring out of the tunnel like a flood. They were flinging themselves into the water around Evie's feet and boiling past her, swimming away from the tunnel as fast as they could. Alinora leaped from Evie's shoulder and flung herself behind one of the brick pillars lining the chamber.

"Move, you idiot!" she screamed.

Evie had no idea what was happening, or what Alinora was running from, but she wasn't going to argue. She waded frantically away from the tunnel and pressed herself tightly against the pillar beside her.

"The token," hissed Alinora. "Put it away!"

Evie gasped. She had forgotten she was still holding the glowing pink token. She stuffed it back into her skirt and the light snapped off at once – so too did the light in her chest. The chamber was instantly plunged into darkness.

She stood pressed against the pillar, panting with fear. The last of the rats flew out of the tunnel behind them. The water settled, lapping against the walls like a tide … then, the chamber was still and silent, resting beneath the beams of sunlight that bled through the grates in the ceiling. Whatever the rats had run from was nowhere to be seen.

And then Evie saw it. A cloud of twisting black smoke, creeping out of the mouth of the tunnel. It was no ordinary smoke: it moved silently, with thought and intent, passing through the darkness like a viper. Right in front of her eyes, it gathered into the shapes of two men. They stood in the chamber, dressed in overalls and hard hats like maintenance workers.

Evie knew exactly what they were. She knew it from

the moment she laid eyes on them. She knew it from the emptiness in her chest.

It was Vale's smoke-men. They had found her.

13
TRAPPED

Evie stood, pressed to the pillar in terror. The smoke-men were mere metres away from her — how could she possibly hide from them? She stayed frozen in place, trying to make herself invisible, praying that the men would continue down another tunnel without noticing them.

"There was a light," said one of the smoke-men in a steady monotone. "A light that disappeared."

"I saw it too," said the other.

The two men turned to each other, and together spoke as one, in a voice that was not their own.

"*The cat, the old woman, the boy, the thin man,*" they intoned. "*One of them will lead us to this new magician, whoever it is. Find them, and we'll find the Spellstone.*"

With that, the men began searching the chamber. Panic swarmed inside Evie like wasps. The men were going to find them in seconds. She turned to Alinora and whispered, "What do we do?"

"We have to run." Lady Alinora raised a paw. "Take

my hand — you can share my powers. I'll turn you into a cat and we can both slip past them."

Evie blinked. "Will I be stuck as a cat afterwards?"

"Probably, yes."

"Probably?!"

"Do you want to get out of here or not?"

The smoke-men were getting closer. Right now, the only thing protecting them was the sound of constant rushing water that covered their voices.

"I — I can't do it!" said Evie. "I'm frightened!"

Lady Alinora's gaze grew brighter. "Then *use* it, Evie. Use the fear! Dig deep and find your power!"

Evie swallowed. "R-right now?"

"It might be the only thing that can save us," said Lady Alinora. "Do it, before they find us!"

Evie whimpered. The men were mere footsteps away. Alinora was right — it was now or never. Could she really do this?

She clenched her fists, closed her eyes, and dug deep. Her whole body sang with terror. Blood drilled in her ears, and her mouth tasted like kerosene, but she focused everything she had. She blocked out the sounds of the men getting closer and fought her own fear, searching for the powers hidden inside her...

Come on, come on, come on!

But there was nothing. No discovery of magic; no sudden eruption of power. Evie was just a frightened girl, trapped in the cold and the dark. She turned to Alinora, her eyes filled with tears. "I – I can't do it," she whispered.

The look that Lady Alinora gave her was indescribable. "Have it your way," she growled.

The cat leaped from the pillar just as the smoke-men took their final steps. She darted past the men and flew down the tunnel that she and Evie had come from. The men swung around in unison, fixing the cat in their sights.

"There!" they cried.

In an instant, they burst into coils of smoke and shot down the tunnel after Alinora. Evie gasped: all around her, more smoke was pouring into the chamber through grates and pipes on every side. It seemed as though every smoke-man in the city was flooding into the sewers at the same time, chasing after Lady Alinora.

Evie stayed fixed to the pillar, reeling with shock. Alinora had abandoned her: now she was alone, trapped in the pitch-black sewers with Vale's army of smoke-men around every corner. She had no powers. How on earth could she ever get out of here, when she couldn't even use the token to light the way? The moment one of those smoke-men spotted it…

She swallowed. She couldn't be frightened now. She had to be brave. If she didn't think straight, she'd never escape. She knew what she had to do – she had to find another way out of the sewers, and make her own way back to the hideout. It was the only way she'd survive. If she stayed here, Vale would find her.

The sewers were silent; the smoke had passed. Slowly, with superhuman effort, she twisted her neck to gaze around the chamber. It was empty.

"Move," she said to herself.

She made herself step from the pillar and felt her way blindly to the nearest of the five tunnels. Evie had no idea where it led, but she couldn't stay here. She had to keep moving. The longer she stayed, the more likely it was that the smoke-men would come back and find her. She groped her way inside the tunnel and staggered upstream, her feet slipping and stumbling on the slick tiles with every step.

It was slow, tortuous going in the dark. It took everything Evie had not to panic, to keep herself focused on the task at hand. She made her way by touch alone, her hands feeling across the tiles and searching for a break in the wall. On she went, taking every turning she came to, all her senses trained for the sound of a voice in the darkness ahead or a footstep behind her.

Then, finally, her hand felt crumbling brick instead of smooth tile. She knew what it meant: she had found another side tunnel, like the one she and Alinora had come down. Evie scrambled inside, groping her way along the filthy walls, praying that she would find what she was looking for at the end.

Her hands met cold metal. A ladder, leading to

another manhole above her. Evie could have cried for joy. She could taste sweet summer air seeping through the gaps around the metal, fresh as nectar. The outside world was mere inches away. She scrambled up the footholds and pressed her hands against the lid...

Nothing. She pushed again, heaving against its shunting weight – but it didn't move. She forced all her strength against the lid, but every time she pushed, she could hear the *click* of a metal catch around its edge.

The manhole was locked. *Of course* it was locked. Wainwright knew the city inside out: he must have known which manholes could be opened and which ones couldn't. Evie hammered her hands against the metal lid, praying that someone above might hear her. "Help! Please!"

But it was no use. No one could hear. Evie could feel the rumble of cars passing near by: she must have been beside a main road. The waking world was separated from her by a sheet of metal, and there was no way she could reach it.

She tore back down the ladder, her breath coming in violent pants. There was only one way out now. She had to retrace her footsteps and find the original manhole she had come down. It might be the only way out of here. *That* meant heading back towards the smoke-men – but she had no other choice. She had to be brave, just for a little longer. She just had to get back to the chamber.

But where was the chamber?

Evie stood, horror rising in her chest. She had followed the tunnels wildly in the dark, taking every turn she came to. She had no idea how she got here. She had no idea how to get back. The sewers were like a labyrinth.

She was lost.

Evie slumped against the wall and slowly sank down to the floor. It was over. One way or another, Vale's men were going to find her. She would never see her parents again.

But for some reason, the thing that stung worst was the fact that Lady Alinora had abandoned her.

Evie stopped. She had just heard something move at the end of the tunnel.

She held her breath. Was it a smoke-man? Had they heard her shouting in the dark? Had they followed her?

Then the sound came again – a scuttling along the wall. Evie looked down and reeled with disgust. It was a great, filthy rat, slithering along the wall towards her. She clambered back, waving her hands. "Go away! Shoo!"

But the rat didn't stop. It kept getting closer and closer. Evie backed along the floor until she was pressed tight against the ladder. There was nowhere left to go. Finally, she snapped.

"Leave me alone!" she cried, kicking out at the rat. "Get away from me!"

The rat stopped – and gave a familiar, weary sigh. In the light seeping through the manhole, Evie could finally see that its eyes were two different colours.

"It's *me,* you stupid girl," said the rat, in an unmistakable cut-glass English accent. "Now, for heaven's sake, stop making such a fuss so we can both get out of here."

14
DAYLIGHT

Evie stared at the rat in disbelief. It had the same voice, the same eyes, the same regal composure. It was also very rude. There was no doubting it – the rat was Lady Alinora. "You came back for me!"

Alinora stared at her with indignation. "Of *course* I did! I wasn't going to leave you down here, was I? I figured our only hope was for me to lead Vale's men away, and change form once I caught up with the rats, so I could give them the slip. They'll be downstream for hours now, searching for a black cat."

Evie stared at her. "But … you've changed form. That means you can never be a cat again."

Alinora gazed at the walls for a while, as if there was something there to see. "Well! No point crying about it. Come on; let's get out of here, before we lose our chance."

She scurried past Evie and climbed the ladder.

"Tried this manhole already? Hmm – looks locked. I'll bet there's a catch hidden just under the lid. If you push the lid, I can squeeze around the edge and release the catch. We should be able to open it together. Ready?"

Evie didn't reply. She stayed right where she was, beaming at Lady Alinora.

"What's wrong with you?" Alinora muttered. "Why are you gawping at me like that?"

"You came back for me," said Evie.

Alinora groaned. "Oh, for the love of…"

"I knew it!" said Evie. "You *do* care! You don't save people you don't care about!"

Lady Alinora fixed her with a serious look. "For the record, Evie, being a member of the Order of the Stone is *precisely* about saving people you don't care about. I've devoted my entire life to protecting billions of people I've never met. If the magic inside the Spellstone is ever released, we *all* lose. The whole world – not just magicians. Emrys devoted his life to saving humanity, without reward. We have a duty to do the same."

Evie was caught off-guard. Lady Alinora had a point. No one in the world above knew that they were down here, fighting for their lives in the darkness. None of them knew about Emrys, or Wainwright, or the magicians who had given their lives to the cause. "Then let's stay down here. Let's keep looking for the Spellstone."

Lady Alinora sighed wearily. "No … I don't think the Spellstone is down here. It's the most powerful evil force in the world: if it was close, the token would have glowed bright red. I don't think Wainwright hid it here after all."

Evie was confused. "Then why did he come down here?"

"Who knows," said Alinora, with an edge of bitterness to her voice. "Wainwright kept a lot of secrets."

Evie stared at the darkness around her. That was certainly true. She knew so little about the man who had brought her into this world of magic. He had hidden everything from the people in his life: the Spellstone, his plan for Evie, the secret to defeating Vale. Trying to understand the choices he'd made was like feeling your way around these dark tunnels.

"He was the first person who ever cared about me, you know," said Alinora. "The first person who ever believed I could do something."

Her voice had changed again. It was softer: the voice she had used when she talked about her animals.

"I gave my whole life to the Order," she said. "I always thought that if anything ever happened to Wainwright, then he would want me to carry things on for him. We fought side by side for years. When he chose *you* as leader instead…"

Evie felt a flush of discomfort. "I never *asked* to be chosen."

"I know you didn't!" said Alinora, annoyed. "That's not what I'm saying!"

"Then what *are* you saying?"

There was a very long, very loud silence.

"I should think it's perfectly obvious!" said Alinora. "I clearly just apologized to you!"

Evie smiled. Lady Alinora hadn't actually used the word "sorry", or even come close, but she knew it was the best she could do.

The rat raised her head. "And for what it's worth ... I know you weren't able to find your skill back there, but I think you have the makings of an *excellent* leader. In the short time that we've spent together, you have displayed great bravery and courage. Finding your way out of here by yourself would not have been easy." She cleared her throat. "And, er ... you were right about the pigeons, too. The Order is lucky to have you, Evie. You're a leader, through and through."

Evie glowed. Being complimented by Lady Alinora was like stumbling upon the most precious jewel in the world. "I knew you were nice."

Lady Alinora scurried up the ladder. "Right! Quite enough of that! Time to get out of here!" She squeezed herself into the gap around the edge of the manhole. "Are you ready?"

Evie *was* ready. Everything felt a thousand times easier somehow now that Alinora was back. She climbed after the rat, pressed her hands against the manhole lid ... and suddenly had a thought.

"Wait – how are we going to get you back to the hideout? Vale's smoke-men could still be out there. I left the cat carrier by the other manhole, and I can't walk around in broad daylight with a rat on my shoulder!"

This time, the silence was so big you could build a house on it.

"I believe," said Lady Alinora, with great dignity, "that it would be prudent for you to carry me in your pocket."

Evie grinned. "Are you sure?"

"Yes, quite sure."

"I won't tell the others."

"Thank you, Evie."

Evie pushed the lid, Lady Alinora released the catch, and together they returned to daylight.

15
THE CEREMONY

THE WALK BACK TO THE CANAL WAS MUCH FASTER now that Alinora was tucked into Evie's pocket, rather than banging against her leg in a cat carrier. Even so, Evie couldn't help but feel like she was being watched the entire time. She glanced over her shoulder: sure enough, there was Tower 99, looming behind her. Sunlight was blazing against its tip like an eye, always searching, always watching.

This must be how the magicians feel all the time, she thought to herself. *Always being hunted.* Evie wondered if it was a feeling she would have to get used to: maybe she was never going to go home again. Maybe she was going to live in hiding for the rest of her life. Evie pushed the thought away. She couldn't bear to think about it.

The sight of the old narrow boat filled her with relief when it finally came into view. She ran the final few steps along the towpath and leaped on board, glancing over her shoulder one last time to make sure no one was looking. No one on the towpath was paying her the slightest bit of attention, of course: they were lazily walking home in the last of the day's heat, chatting to friends and sunning themselves. Evie paused with a hand on the narrow boat door and gazed at the people who were separated from her by only a few footsteps. None of them had the faintest clue what she had just been through. They suddenly felt very far away.

She pushed open the door and stepped into the hideout. It was just as she'd left it: dark, chill, gloomy. The other magicians were sitting where Evie had left them that morning, in the armchairs by the fireplace, whispering intently among themselves. They all stopped talking the moment Evie stepped into the drawing room.

"Oh!" said Onslow. "You're back!"

"We were just—" Rish began.

"Shh!" snapped Campbell, cuffing his shoulder.

Evie's heart sank. She had forgotten how cold the magicians had been that morning. Despite everything that she had just been through with Alinora, the Order were still hiding things from her. Clearly, they still didn't trust her. On cue, Alinora clambered out of Evie's pocket and scampered over to the fireplace, steaming her fur dry with a sigh of relief.

"Alinora!" said Campbell. "You're…"

"Filthy," said Onslow, glancing with distaste at Evie's uniform. "Where have you two *been*?"

"Long story," Alinora muttered.

She caught them up with everything that had happened – the pigeons' sighting of Wainwright, the sewers, the glowing token, the smoke-men – all while expertly avoiding the fact that everyone had just seen her climb out of Evie's pocket.

"So that's it," Alinora concluded. "We know that Wainwright went into the sewers with the Spellstone, but we don't know why."

A grim silence fell over the group. They were no closer to finding the Spellstone: it was still hidden somewhere in the city, where Vale might find it first. The fact was always there, like a ceiling slowly being lowered.

"Then we keep looking," said Campbell, determinedly. "We should lie low for the rest of the day – Vale's men will be on the hunt. Rish – tonight, you search dreams again for any memories of Wainwright. Alinora and I will go out again first thing tomorrow and see what we can find."

"Can I do anything?" asked Evie hopefully.

Campbell gave her a smile. "You go upstairs and get changed out of those filthy clothes, sweetie."

Evie's heart sank. The magicians were trying to get rid of her again. "I don't *have* any others."

"I put some on your bed," Onslow replied, nudging her out of the room. "Off you trot!"

Evie frowned. There was something strange about the way the magicians were behaving, but she couldn't put her finger on what it was. She could swear they were all watching her as she made her way up the staircase, but when she turned around at the top, they all pretended to be looking at their shoes.

Onslow had tidied her bedroom while she was out. The sheets were turned down; there was a chocolate mint on her pillow. There was also a neatly folded dress at the foot of the bed. It was made of red and white velvet, brocaded with golden thread. Evie picked it up: it felt creamy-smooth and deliciously warm to the touch. Then she saw that it wasn't a dress. It was a set of…

"Wizard's robes?" she muttered.

She glanced down – sure enough, a pointy red and white hat had been hidden beneath it. Beside the hat was a note, which read:

Put them on and meet us downstairs!!!!!! – O

And then scribbled beneath that:

(Onslow)

And then beneath that:

(from the Order of the Stone)

Evie pulled on the robes. She was surprised to find that they fitted perfectly. The sleeves ended exactly at her wrists; the hem brushed just above the carpet. The fabric was heavy, but the weight of it felt reassuring somehow, like being held in place with steady hands.

She made her way back downstairs and found the others waiting for her. They stood in a line at the foot of the stairs.

"They fit!" said Campbell, relieved. "Thank goodness. I was worried about those sleeves."

Evie was stunned. Each of them was wearing an identical set of red and white robes. Even Lady Alinora was wearing a tiny, rat-sized hat and cape. "You … have a set of rat-sized robes, just lying around?"

"No!" Campbell tutted bitterly. "I had to make them *just now*, using some off-cuts." She glared at Alinora. "Next time you feel like changing size before an initiation ceremony, some notice would be nice!"

Evie blinked. "Initiation ceremony?"

The magicians stepped to one side. There was a set of grand double doors open behind them. They had been shut the entire time that Evie had been in the hideout; now she could see that there was an enormous room hidden inside. The floor was covered in thousands of candles, arranged around the room like an audience. The floorboards had been polished to a shine; something rich and golden gleamed across their surface. It was *gold*, real gold, traced into the outline of the Spellstone. The room was arranged in the shape of a giant pentagon, stretching up to a high domed ceiling that was painted with the face of Emrys himself. A white glass lamp hung on a golden chain in the centre, carved into the shape of a crescent moon.

The others gestured for Evie to step inside. She was hesitant – she had no idea what she was supposed to do.

Rish quickly stepped forward and took her arm. "It's OK," he whispered. "I was nervous too, when it was my turn. Just repeat everything we say."

He led her inside the room. Evie saw first-hand just how huge it was – towering walls stretched around her, each one covered with...

She felt her breath catch in her throat. For a moment, she thought there were people gazing at her from the shadowed walls – then she realized that the walls were covered in long hanging tapestries, each one decorated with stitched faces. There were hundreds of them: men and women, young and old. Evie understood who she was looking at. They were all the members of the Order of the Stone, stretching back across the centuries. At the very bottom of the closest tapestry were two freshly stitched portraits of Rish and Onslow. Before them was a slightly faded portrait of Campbell, and then a woman with a thick plait and kind eyes – that had to be Rish's mother, Patel. The faces went on, and on, and on, magician after magician...

And there, gazing out with his bright blue eyes, was Wainwright.

The portrait was clearly made when he was much younger – before he had a beard, before years of hiding had weathered and worn him down – but there was no doubting it was him. Evie hardly knew how to feel, seeing his face again. She almost wanted to reach out and grab him, to *beg* him to explain where he had hidden the Spellstone and how she was supposed to defeat Vale. But it was impossible, of course. Wainwright wasn't here any more – he was gone, just like all these magicians before him.

"Stand here," Rish whispered, leading her to the spot in the room where the lines converged.

The other magicians took their places at different points on the pattern, until all four stood in a square around her. No one spoke. In the flicker of candlelight, it felt as if the faces in the tapestry were really with them too, waiting for the ceremony to begin. There was a moment of living silence, like the room gathering its breath, and then Lady Alinora spoke.

"The Order of the Stone have gathered once more in the Hall of Emrys to welcome a new magician," she said, her voice rising high to the painted dome. "Who holds the token?"

There was a long pause. Evie suddenly realized Alinora was talking about her.

"Oh – me!" she said quickly. "Yes, sorry, that's me."

She took the piece of metal from around her neck and held it out.

Lady Alinora scurried along the golden lines in the floor until she stood before her. "You kneel for this bit," she whispered.

Evie did as she was told. Lady Alinora sat on her hind

legs, trying to look as regal as she could while also being a rat.

"Evie, the token has been handed to you," she said. "Until the day you pass it on, the Order is under your charge. Do you promise to guard the token with your life, and be faithful in your duty to the Order? Will you devote your life to the work of Emrys until the Spellstone is destroyed, once and for all?"

Evie swallowed. It was a lot to ask of one person. But Wainwright believed she could do it: he had placed so much faith in her, and she still had no idea why. She gazed at the hundreds of stitched faces around her: all the magicians who had dedicated their lives to the Order. How could she possibly fail them?

"Y-yes," she said. "I will."

Lady Alinora nodded with approval. Evie swore that she could see her eyes redden for a moment, but the tears never came. "Very good," she said quietly. "Well done, Evie."

She returned to her appointed place. Campbell stepped /along the lines to stand in front of Evie, and addressed her directly.

"Evie," she said. "The Order of the Stone is only as strong as the links that bind us together. One magician will never be as powerful as two that work side by side. Will you be dutiful to the magicians in your care? Will you be the sword that defends us, and the shield that hides us, and the light that guides our way through darkness? Will you protect us as you would a brother and sister?"

Evie had never had a brother or sister. She had always wondered what her life would have been like if she'd had one. Now, beneath the gaze of the magicians around her, both past and present, she felt as if she had hundreds. "I will."

Campbell beamed. "Good job, sweetie."

She stepped back and Onslow took her place, looking extremely nervous.

"Right. Er … sorry, I've not done this bit before…" He brought a folded printout from his robes with slightly trembling hands, and cleared his throat. "Evie, a member of the Order does not just serve their fellow magicians. They protect all humanity, without borders or boundaries. Will you be dutiful to every person on this planet, and lay down your own life to protect them, even though it will be a secret to them?"

Evie thought of Wainwright, sacrificing himself for a single chance to protect the Spellstone. She thought of all the long-dead magicians, devoting their lives to a cause that no one even knew about. She understood now why she had to be brave – why she couldn't go home until her quest was done. She had to leave her parents in order to protect them. "I will."

Onslow nodded gratefully and leaned in to whisper. "Well done! You're doing really well. At my initiation, I was so nervous I was sick in my mouth."

He stepped back, and finally Rish came to stand in front of her. He closed his eyes and drew in a deep breath.

"Evie," he said, conjuring the words he had clearly taken the time to memorize. "The Order's duty is not simply to protect the world from the Spellstone. In order to defend humanity from evil, we must first be able to find evil in ourselves. We must know it and recognize it in order to banish it. Will you be ever vigilant against your own heart, so darkness can never find a place in it?"

Evie didn't understand what that meant. How could you be vigilant against your own heart? But she knew not to argue. "I will."

Rish beamed. "You're nailing it!"

He held out his arms, and all four magicians came together, linking hands around Evie – Campbell and Rish had to squat slightly to reach Lady Alinora's paws.

"Four magicians entered this room," said Lady Alinora. "Five now leave it. Arise, Evie: spell-binder, wonder-worker, Child of Emrys, new leader of our cause…"

"I wi—" Evie began.

"You don't speak for that bit," snapped Alinora.

Evie blushed. "Sorry."

A gap opened up in the ring of hands: Evie stood up and joined with them. There was a final moment of silence that reverberated off the walls like a set of bells. Then the room relaxed in a great exhalation of breath. The magicians laughed, and suddenly all four were congratulating Evie, hugging her and giggling.

"You did it!"

"You were brilliant, Evie!"

"We're sorry we had to keep it a secret; we didn't want to frighten you."

"At least Onslow didn't puke this time."

"Shut up."

Evie let them lead her back to the drawing room. There, on a little table, was the cake that Onslow had spent all day making. It was decorated with swirling stars and golden moonbeams, and iced across the top were the words: WELCOME EVIE.

"Dig in, everyone!" said Onslow. "It's chocolate – Evie's choice."

Alinora grumbled. "It'd better not have any…"

"No fruit," snapped Onslow. "And it's dairy-free, and it's low sugar too. I'm not having a repeat of my birthday."

"Low sugar?" Campbell sucked her teeth. "It's not going to taste any good if—"

"Eat the flipping cake," said Onslow, cutting her a slice.

They stood in a circle, bickering and laughing and dropping cake on the carpet. Evie let it all wash over her. There was a glow in her chest that she had never felt before: a feeling that was new and strange to her, and yet somehow recognizable. For the first time since she left her house, she didn't feel overwhelmed, or out of her depth, or suffocated by the duty that had been thrust upon her. She felt like she had found her people, and they had found her.

She took a mouthful of cake, and it was better than anything she had tasted in her life.

16
SMOKE AND SHADOWS

"Tell me again," said Vale, "how you let her get away."

A smoke-man stood on the other side of the desk in Vale's office. The smoke on the surface of its face was trembling ever so slightly, like oil on water.

"We searched the whole sewers," it said. "Every drain, every grate, every tunnel, every corner, but the cat is not…"

"Of course she's not there," said Vale, anger rising in his voice. "She's escaped. She's probably not even a cat any more." He turned to face the smoke-man. "What about the other magicians? Where are they?"

The smoke-man shifted. It wasn't able to think for itself much: after all, it was only smoke. It could only do what it was told to do. "We – we searched every road, every alley, every corner, but we could not find—"

It happened fast. Vale opened up his hands, and a bolt

of blue lightning shot across the room and passed straight through the smoke-man, erupting it into a cloud of vapour and boring a scorch-mark deep into the wall.

Vale stood, shaking with anger. He took a moment to allow the steady grey waters of calm to settle over him. Then he waved his hands, and the scorch-mark cleaned itself from the wall.

It was inexplicable. Vale was the most powerful magician alive. He had reached heights no one had reached before. His powers were growing every day. His smoke-men covered the streets below – binmen, traffic wardens, police officers. There was nothing he did not see.

So why was he no closer to the Spellstone?

He gritted his teeth. It was like a final, sick joke at Vale's expense. He had spent years chasing Wainwright, only for him to slip through his fingers at the last second. His replacement was still out there, laughing at him. And Vale knew *nothing* about them. That was the problem: the smoke-men were only his eyes, nothing more. They only knew what Vale told them. Until Vale himself knew who this new magician was, his smoke-men would never be able to find them.

He turned back to the window and gazed out across the darkening streets. It was evening now: night was spreading towards the city like a tide. *Someone* down there in the city must know who this new magician was – people always had someone who cared about them. *Someone* must be wondering where they had gone, or where they had disappeared, or…

The answer came to him in an instant. It was so simple, so clear and obvious, that he couldn't believe he hadn't thought of it before. It had been right in front of him the whole time.

His mind turned fast. He wouldn't be able to use his smoke-men – they couldn't carry anything. He'd have to rely on one of his other powers instead. But which one?

Vale smiled. Of course – his *newest* power.

He gazed at the floor. There was his shadow, stretched out in the lamplight. There was a moment of thoughtless adjustment … then, in front of Vale's eyes, his shadow peeled itself from his feet. It seeped over to the nearest wall and climbed it, standing to face him. Vale nodded approvingly. He had always secretly envied Wainwright's power … and now, it was his.

"You understand what I need you to do?" Vale asked.

The shadow tilted its head, as if amused. Then, with an air of casual arrogance, it stretched an arm to a vase of flowers on a shelf. In one swift movement, it pulled the vase inside itself. The vase disappeared, like being snatched through a hole in the universe. The shadow strolled across the office, reached inside itself again, pulled out the vase, and placed it on the desk.

All the flowers were dead.

"Very good," said Vale. "You know what to do. Bring

them here – all of them. Search every station in the city, if you have to."

The shadow nodded. Then it sank to the floor, slipped under the door like a pool of oil, and was gone.

Vale sighed. He could finally rest. He turned back to the window and sank into his chair with exhaustion. It had been a long day: the magic to cover a whole city with smoke-men had been far greater than he'd expected. But it didn't matter. By the time he woke up tomorrow morning, he would be even more powerful than today. Within hours, he would know who this new magician was. Once he found them, he would quickly find the Spellstone.

And when he finally had his hands on it…

Vale's eyes drifted shut, and he allowed himself to dream.

17
A RUDE AWAKENING

E VIE WAS DREAMING, TOO.

She was back on the bench where she had first met Wainwright. The towpath was empty, or at least, she assumed it was. It was almost impossible to see anything in the fog that surrounded her, billowing in grey sheets across the water. She could hear voices from every side, muttering secret incantations whose words she could never quite make out. Skyscrapers loomed like monsters in the haze around her.

Wainwright was sitting beside her. He was wearing the exact same clothes he'd been wearing on the day she met him. He was eating a sandwich and reading a newspaper, like before. When the dream began, Evie was already talking to him.

"Please," she was begging. "You have to tell me where you hid the Spellstone."

Wainwright folded up his newspaper and turned to her. "I told you, Evie – it's in the last place he'll look."

"But I don't know where that is!" Evie cried.

Wainwright patted her hand. There it was again – that strange, secret smile.

"If I told you now, Evie," he said, "then the plan wouldn't work."

Evie frowned. "What plan?"

Wainwright didn't answer. He opened up his newspaper again and started reading it. Evie was desperate.

"Please … you have to help me! I don't know what to do! I don't understand what my hidden power is or—"

She was cut off by an almighty *crash* beside her: the unmistakable sound of someone walking directly into a dustbin.

"*Argh!* Oh, my *leg*…"

Evie spun around in surprise. Someone was sprawled on the ground beside her, nursing his knee. "Rish?"

Rish looked up, and his eyes widened in alarm. Evie was confused – why was Rish here too? Why did he look so scared? What was going on?

And then she realized what was happening. This was all a dream. Rish was using his magical powers to sneak into her head while she was sleeping.

"Get out!" she cried.

Rish waved his hands frantically. "It was a mistake, I swear! I can ex—"

Evie woke up.

She was back in her four-poster bed: it was the middle of the night. It took a few brief moments to remember what had happened – the fog, Wainwright, seeing Rish – before the anger that had woken her up surged through her again.

Rish had stepped inside her dreams again. He was spying on her. Evie had thought she could finally trust the magicians – that they trusted *her* – but it turned out she was wrong. She threw off the duvet and stormed out of her bedroom, marching down the corridor until she found a door with light still spilling beneath the crack. She barged inside without knocking – sure enough, Rish was sitting at a desk in the corner and looking sheepish.

"Oh – Evie! You're up!" he said. His acting was appalling. "Er – can I help you?"

"What were you doing in my *head*?!" cried Evie.

Rish cringed with embarrassment. "I don't know what you mean…"

"Don't lie to me – I *saw* you!" She pointed at him. "You broke into my dreams! *Again!* Do you have any idea how *rude* that is?" Evie was almost shaking. She couldn't remember the last time she had felt so angry. "You can't just walk inside my head whenever you feel like it! Those are my personal, private thoughts! You can't *do* that to someone!"

There was a painful silence. Rish looked like he was ready to curl up and die.

"It was a mistake, I swear," he mumbled. "I was searching for dreams about Wainwright, like Campbell told me to. It didn't occur to me that *you'd* be dreaming about him, too. I sort of … got sucked into your head, by accident. It was so foggy in your dream that I didn't even realize where I was until I walked into that bin. If I'd known it was *your* dream, I'd have left straight away – honest."

For a moment, he looked so mortified that Evie almost felt bad for shouting at him. "What about the time you came into my theatre dream? I never gave you permission to do *that*, either."

Rish blinked. "But Wainwright asked me to do it."

"So?" said Evie. "How would you like it if people went snooping around *your* dreams?"

Rish's mouth opened and closed, trying to work out what to say. "Well… I don't know. I don't *have* dreams. I can go in and out of other people's but that's it. I haven't had my own since I was five. When I first discovered my skill."

Evie blinked. "You discovered your skill when you were five?"

Rish nodded, picking at a bag of sweets in his lap. Then

160

he looked startled and held out the bag. "Oh! Sorry – do you want one?"

Evie felt a flood of compassion. Rish looked very young all of a sudden, politely offering her a sweet. "Thanks."

She took a sweet, feeling reassured. If Rish could discover his skill at such a young age, then she might just have a chance of finding her own powers in time. It gave her some hope, at least. "Can you remember how you did it? Discovering your skill, I mean."

Rish shuffled on his chair. "Not really, no. It just … happened. I went to sleep one night, and woke up in Wainwright's dream by accident. He nearly wet himself; it was so funny." He giggled. "He said that I must have learned early because Mum was such a strong magician. That she'd passed it on to me. I guess that makes sense. I learned my skill just after she…"

He trailed off, and took another handful of sweets. He was clearly a nervous eater. Evie had forgotten about what happened to Rish's mother. She felt bad for making him talk about it. "I can't believe she made this mansion all by herself. She must have been an amazing magician."

Rish nodded, with a flush of pride. "She was. She used to make loads of places for me and her when I was a baby, before we joined the Order. Places for us to hide, that kind of thing."

"Hide?"

Rish took another sweet. "Things hadn't worked out

with my dad, and Mum's family started arguing with her all the time. So she ran away with me. We didn't have anywhere to go – but Mum had her powers. She'd find some empty cupboard or a box in an alley and build a whole house inside it for us to live." He smiled. "She could make a home out of nothing."

Talking about homes was making Evie's heart ache. She tried to move the conversation on. "How did Wainwright find you both?"

"He saw her making a new house for us one day, while he was out on his rounds," said Rish. "Said he'd never seen a magician who could do so much without any training. He told her all about the Order, and the Spellstone, and showed her the magic inside her – and the magic inside *me*, as well. He said that it was going to be dangerous – but that if we joined, we'd always have somewhere to stay. We'd have people around us, too. Mum joined right away." He gazed around. "She built this mansion the same day. She'd never tried to make anywhere so big before. I think she wanted to impress the Order. But I think it was for me, too. Our first proper home. One we wouldn't have to leave again after a few days."

Evie looked around. It was only now that she realized how neat and tidy Rish's bedroom was. His desk was beautifully organized, with cast-iron figurines lined up in perfect height order. He had even made his bed. Evie didn't know a single child in the world who made their own bed. There was a shelf beside it, with a neat row of books propped up by a little Ganesh statue and a framed photo of his mum.

"She could have been leader after Wainwright, I think," said Rish, smiling at the photo. "She was going to make more hideouts like this one all over the city. That way magicians could move around safely without being caught by Vale." His voice suddenly took on an edge. "That was how he got her. He found her while she was looking for a place to make a new hideout on the other side of the city. He tried to make her tell him where this one was, but she refused. So he stole her powers. I didn't even get to say goodbye." He picked angrily at the sweets, not meeting Evie's gaze. "He took my mother from me, and I can't even fight him. If I had a skill that let me fight, maybe Wainwright would have let me come with him the night he died. Maybe I could have protected him, too. Instead I'm just stuck in here all day, with this worthless skill. The only time I ever get to leave here is when I'm in other people's dreams."

Evie's heart went out to him. She wondered how it must feel for Rish to lose someone like that, and to know that the person who killed your mother was still out there. "I don't think that's fair. It sounds like your skill helps a lot."

"Maybe," said Rish. "But I'd give it all up to have my *own* dreams again, just once. I might see Mum again if I did." He glanced up. "And for what it's worth … I take it seriously, you know. Going into people's dreams. I know what a responsibility it is. Having the *power* to do something doesn't give you permission to do it. Mum taught me that." He was quiet for a moment. "So I'm sorry for going in your head without asking. I won't do it again. It would mean a lot to me if we could be friends."

Evie could tell he meant it. It must have been incredibly lonely for Rish, living in the mansion with no one but adults for company. "Of course. It sounds like an amazing skill to have. Maybe one day you can show me how it works."

Rish's eyes suddenly lit up. "Hang on – why not now?"

Evie frowned. "What now?"

Rish held out his hand. "If we join hands, you can see for yourself how it works. We don't have to look for dreams about Wainwright – we can look for anything! Who knows – it might even help you work out your own skill!"

Evie glanced at his hand uncertainly. Rish had a point, but she'd had quite enough adventure for one day. "Er … maybe some other time. I'm pretty tired."

Rish's face fell. "Really? There's nowhere you want to go? Nothing you want to see?"

Evie paused. There *was* something she wanted to see – something she wanted to see more than anything else in the entire world.

18
DREAMSCAPES

FIVE MINUTES LATER, EVIE WAS STANDING TO ONE side while Rish arranged his bedding on the floor to make a comfy nest.

"Do we *really* have to lie down to do this?" she asked, embarrassed.

"Absolutely!" said Rish. "Coming out of dreams can be pretty sudden, especially if you've never done it before. If you fall over, you could really hurt yourself."

Evie thought about it. "So … when you guys came into my dream the other night, you were all lying down together, holding hands?"

Rish nodded. "Yeah! We made a pillow fort in the library. It was fun."

Evie shook her head wearily. The more she learned about magicians, the weirder they became.

"First rule of going into dreams," Rish explained, "is *don't let go of my hand*. You have to stay connected to me at all times."

Evie frowned. "But the others weren't holding your

hand in my theatre dream."

"They're *proper* magicians," said Rish. "You still haven't discovered your own powers yet. If we're inside someone's head, and you let go of my hand..." He trailed off.

Evie glanced at him. "What? What would happen?"

"Er ... I'm not sure, to be honest," he said. "It's never happened before. Maybe you'll get stuck in someone's head for ever?"

"Maybe?!"

"Just don't let go," he repeated. "And ... don't open any doors, either. *Never* open any doors." He shuddered. "Doors in dreams ... they don't always lead where you'd expect. People have a way of hiding stuff from themselves – *bad* stuff, too. Trust me, it's not nice." He turned to her. "Right – are you ready?"

Evie didn't feel ready at all. For a moment, she wasn't sure that she wanted to go through with it any more – but then she remembered what she wanted to see, and it steeled her resolve. She lay down beside Rish and took his hand.

"Now – shut out *everything*," said Rish. "Forget about where you are – the room, the hideout, the city – and just focus *in*. Get lost in your thoughts."

Evie did as she was told, but she wasn't sure how you were supposed to shut everything out. It was like trying to think of *nothing*: by thinking about nothing, you made it *something*, no matter how many times you tried, until it felt like an endless set of Russian dolls getting smaller and smaller and smaller and smaller…

"There!" said Rish. "You're doing it! See?"

Evie gasped – he was right. The walls were fading around them, like stage lights being lowered. The room was drifting away: the smell, the light, the touch of moisture in the air, all dissolving into black. She felt her body leave the steady press of the floor and lift from the ground, until she and Rish were floating in mid-air…

But it wasn't air any more. It wasn't *anything*. A universe of nothing was materializing around them, stretching into fathomless black in every direction. It was like floating on the ocean at the end of the world; like ballroom dancing with the lights turned off. Evie knew – just knew – that it went on for ever.

"Argh!" she screamed.

"Great, isn't it?" said Rish.

"Make it stop!" cried Evie.

Then a patchwork of colours began to appear at the edge of her vision, blurring into view like northern lights. They came a pinprick at a time, slowly at first and then all at once, swelling like storm clouds of powdered paint until there was every single colour that Evie could think of.

She gasped. They weren't just colours: they were pictures. Whenever she looked at one of the pinpricks, a single image appeared in her head before fading away, like an ember flicked from a fire. No matter where she turned her head, Evie saw something new and incredible. There was someone riding a white headless horse; there was a person in a golden meadow, playing with their childhood dog; there was a man taking a bite out of a baguette, only for it to wriggle out of his hands and slither beneath the table like a snake.

"They're dreams," Rish explained. "Every single dream that's being had at this very moment, all over the world."

There were so many that Evie didn't even know where to look. There must have been millions of them – billions, perhaps. Every single one belonged to a different person, a different mind, a different life. It hurt her head to think about it.

"It's always like this, you know," said Rish, his eyes shining. "It's always this beautiful."

Evie looked at him. Rish seemed different, all of a sudden. He wasn't trapped inside the mansion any more: he was free, at ease with himself, doing what he did best. It was a joy to behold. Evie wondered if she would ever feel like that. "So – how do you find the right dreams? The ones you need?"

"Think about what you want to see," said Rish. "As clearly as you can. If you do it right, we'll get taken into the right dreams. You have to focus properly, though, or it won't work."

Evie swallowed. Focusing while floating in a boundless universe was easier said than done. Her head was spinning too fast, like a hundred feelings were fighting for her attention at the same time. She felt tired, and homesick, and frightened, and slightly hungry…

All of a sudden, a dreamscape of colours broke free and began spiralling towards her. She and Rish were dragged into them, slowly at first and then faster and faster. An atmosphere of light and sound was materializing from nothingness, drawing into sharper focus around them…

And suddenly, her feet were *freezing*.

Evie opened her eyes, blinking in disbelief. The dreamscape colours were gone. She was standing ankle deep in an arctic wilderness, hand in hand with Rish. Huge drifts of snow surrounded her on every side, and a fierce blizzard dashed against her face.

But the wind wasn't cold – and it wasn't snow. She licked her lips. "Powdered sugar?"

She looked down and moved her feet. The top layer of white gave way to a layer of brown, and then lurid pink.

"Ice cream?" Rish asked, confused. "*That's* what you wanted?"

Evie blushed. It was a whole landscape of ice cream: the mountains in the distance even had cherries on top. "Er … no, not really. I think I'm just quite hungry." She glanced around. "Whose dream *is* this?"

"My money's on him," said Rish, pointing to a man being chased by giant gummy bears in the distance. "Right – try again. And this time, focus properly! Think about what you *really need*, not the first thing that comes into your head."

Evie closed her eyes, a little embarrassed. She knew exactly what she *wanted*, but trying to make a single thought shine through was impossible. She'd never needed more things in her life at once: she was trying to get home, and trying to lead the Order, and trying to discover her own powers, and trying to find the Spellstone, and trying to save the world…

It happened again, faster this time. The snowstorm whipped away like a bedsheet – the dreamscape colours spiralled around them again, forming into a new world of shape and light and sound before their eyes…

Evie landed on her feet with a thump. *This* dream couldn't have been more different to the last. The vast, frozen wilderness was gone. Evie and Rish were standing in a small, dark, windowless room. The walls were made from concrete, except for a thick metal door at one end. Evie looked around. "I think we're in some kind of safe."

"You *think?*" said Rish sarcastically.

The room was stacked with shelves, and every single one was heaving with gold bars. There must have been over a million pounds' worth, gleaming under the electric lights.

"Let me guess," said Rish drily. "*Money?* That's what you wanted?"

"No!" said Evie. "Honestly! I don't know why we ended up here."

"Maybe *he* does," said Rish, pointing across the room.

There was a man, sitting on a folding chair on the other side of the vault. Evie didn't recognize him, but it had to be his dream: there was no one else there. He was wearing a security guard's uniform with a triangle logo on his sweater. He didn't seem to have noticed that Evie and Rish were there: he was too busy staring at something in his lap. What were they doing in his dream?

"Can he see us?" Evie whispered.

Rish shook his head. "Not unless we start talking to him."

"OK," said Evie. "I'll try and work out why we're here…"

She made to walk towards the security guard, but Rish yanked her back.

"No! Remember what I said earlier? People act … *differently* in dreams. He could be dangerous!"

Evie gazed at the security guard. He seemed harmless enough. She'd always been good at reading people. "Just one question – please? Otherwise, I'll *never* learn how to do this properly."

Rish sighed. "Fine – I'll be on standby to take us out if anything goes wrong."

They walked hand-in-hand to the security guard. He didn't look up as they approached. All his attention was focused on the thing in his lap: it was a single, plain household brick. Evie had absolutely no idea why he found it so interesting. She tapped him on the shoulder, and his head snapped up. It took him a few moments to register that she was there.

"Hey! What are you doing?" he cried. "You need special clearance to get in here!"

"Don't worry – I'm not really here," said Evie. "This is all a dream."

"It is?" The security guard's face fell. "Oh, *man*, I've fallen asleep at work *again*. I can't believe they haven't sacked me yet."

Evie looked around. "Where *are* we?"

"The vault!" said the security guard, nodding around him. "That's my job – I'm supposed to make sure no one breaks in. But I fell asleep at my desk the other day, and when I woke up someone had broken inside. I thought I was *definitely* going to get sacked … but when I checked the vault, no one had stolen a thing." He gazed in wonder at the gleaming shelves before him. "Can you believe it? All this gold, and they left it right where it was!"

Evie frowned. This still wasn't helping. "And er … the brick?"

She pointed at the brick in his lap. The guard frowned. "Oh, yeah. *This* was in here, too. Someone had left it behind. And now I can't stop thinking about it. Who puts a brick in a vault?" He shook his head. "That's just weird, that is."

Evie sighed. This was going nowhere.

Rish seemed to be losing patience, too. "Look – let's call it a night and try again tomorrow. Maybe after some rest you'll be better at—"

"No!" said Evie. "Please – let me have one last try. I'll really focus this time, OK?"

Evie closed her eyes, and focused again. This time, she made herself think about *exactly* what she wanted. She had to get it right. She blocked out everything – the vault, the gold, the security guard, Rish – and willed with all her heart for the one thing she wanted above everything else...

And this time, when the dreamscape colours wrapped around them, she knew that it had worked. She felt herself fly from the vault and into a new dream, a new world, a place that she recognized the moment she came to it...

19
HOME

Evie's feet came to rest on the floor. The swirling patterns undid themselves and she felt the atmosphere of a new room fall into place around her. She knew where she was before she even opened her eyes. She knew by the smell, the sound, the taste in the air. She knew it as well as she knew herself.

"Where are we?" asked Rish.

Evie opened her eyes. "I'm home. It's my bedroom."

She had never really appreciated her bedroom before: it had simply always been there. But now that it wasn't, she finally understood quite how much it meant to her. The scrapes on the wall; the patches pressed in the carpet; the Blu-tack stains on the closet doors: they were like old friends. She felt herself fill from the toes up with joy and relief and pain, all mixed together at once.

But that was nothing compared to how she felt about the person sitting on the bed.

"Mum?"

Evie's mother sat alone, staring at a heap of

photographs. All the photos were the same: Evie's last school portrait, printed over and over, piled on the bed. There must have been thousands of them. Evie's mum kept trying to pick one up, but every time she did, it turned to liquid in her hands and dripped between her fingers, puddling like oil and spreading across the floor.

"No!" Mum was crying, clawing at the photos. "Please, I need *one*, I just need one."

Evie gasped. They were inside Mum's head. And this wasn't a dream they were seeing – it was a nightmare. Evie had never seen her mother look so upset before – she had never even seen her cry, not like this. Evie made to run to her, but Rish held her back. His eyes were wide and frightened. "I – I'm not sure about this…"

"What do you mean?" said Evie. "She's crying! I have to talk to her!"

Rish looked completely torn. "But she can't know where you are, remember? It's the only thing keeping you safe! If Vale found out you'd been talking to her…"

Evie knew he was right – but she couldn't bear to leave her mother like this. "Rish – *please*."

Mum's head snapped up, as if she had only just heard Evie's voice. "*Evie!* Evie, is that you?"

She looked around the room helplessly, searching for her daughter. Rish took one look at Evie's face and understood. Evie slithered across the slick rainbow of oils that covered the carpet and threw herself into her mother's arms, dragging Rish behind her. She and Mum sat and rocked on the bed, clinging to each other like ships to the sea. Evie just breathed her in. Being held by Mum was so simple, so obvious. She had missed it more than she could explain.

"Oh, Evie," Mum whispered. "It was so awful. I dreamed you went missing."

Evie felt the guilt like a knife in her heart. "It's OK, Mum. I'm here now. It's OK."

She held Mum tight, soothing her. It was like they had switched roles – like Evie had become the parent, and Mum had become the child.

"I knew you'd come back," said Mum. "I could *feel* you were still close somehow, but no matter where we looked, your father and I couldn't find you anywhere. I've never seen him like this – he's not slept a minute since you disappeared, not one." She turned to the swelling heap of photos on the bed. "I even had to go to the police to report you missing. They said they needed a recent photograph of you in your school uniform, but I couldn't find any on my phone, so I had to go into the attic to find your last class photo, and I couldn't find it, and … and…"

Evie winced. She couldn't believe she'd made her own mother feel like this. The guilt was unbearable. "I'm so sorry, Mum. Please don't cry."

Mum clutched her hand tight. "Why did you run away, Evie? All those things you said about being unhappy at school… Oh, we should have listened! Did you think we didn't love you?"

Evie shook her head. "I didn't run away Mum, I swear. It's … it's just something I have to do. I'm doing everything I can to come back."

Mum's face lit up. "You're coming home again, Evie? You promise?"

Evie's heart filled with misery. She couldn't promise that – she had no idea if she ever *could* come home again. But how could she look her mother in the eye and say that? "I promise, Mum."

A silence fell over the room. Evie glanced at Rish, still standing behind her. He was trying to give them some privacy by looking at a poster. She wondered if this was hard for him, seeing Evie with her own mother. But she couldn't leave just yet – there was something she'd come here to ask, something important.

"Mum – I really need your help."

Mum smiled, stroking her cheek. She was completely back to her old self now, as if she'd forgotten what had happened ten seconds before. "Of course, poppet. What is it?"

Evie closed her eyes. There was no way she could say it without Rish hearing her, but this was her only chance. "There's something important I have to do. Something *really* important. Everyone's relying on me, and I don't know if I can do it. I'm *frightened*, Mum."

Saying it out loud somehow made it even more real. Mum wiped the tears from Evie's eyes and gazed at her. "Do you remember last Christmas? Your dad got stressed about dinner and your grandparents were so late that everything got burned, and all the shops were shut and there wasn't enough food for everyone."

Of course Evie remembered – it was hard to forget the sight of a grown man in a paper crown, sobbing into a pan of gravy.

"Everyone was so tired, and so fed up, and so frustrated with each other…" Mum smiled. "Except you. You were just happy that we were all together. You made everything good again. You cheered us all right up."

Evie was amazed that Mum remembered it. Maybe her parents noticed more than she gave them credit for. "But … that was just a stupid dinner. This is important."

Mum shook her head. "It's not stupid, Evie. Stuff like that matters. You have a way of finding the *good* in things. You don't get it from me, and you *certainly* don't get it from your father, but it comes easily to you. It always has." She squeezed her hand. "So, whatever this problem is – just be yourself, and you'll be fine. Look inside your heart."

Evie groaned. There it was again – the same old worthless advice. How was she ever going to see Mum and Dad again, if *being herself* was all she had? How was *looking in her heart* going to find the Spellstone and stop someone like Vale?

And all of a sudden, she was boiling over with anger. Vale was the reason Mum was crying. Why Wainwright was dead. Why Rish's mother wasn't here. Why Evie might never be able to go home again. It was all because of him. The unfairness of it all was suffocating. Suddenly Evie didn't *want* to hide from him any more. She wanted to find him. She wanted to get her hands on him. She wanted to make *him* feel frightened for a change…

"*Evie!*"

She snapped around – and gasped. The bedroom walls were fading in front of her. Rish was fading, too. He was being dragged out of the dream, holding onto her hand for all he was worth.

"I – I don't know what's happening!" he cried. "I can't stop it!"

It was true. Evie could feel the dreamscape colours pulling them both away – and this time, they were stronger than ever. It felt like they were being dragged out of the dream by force. Within seconds she was hanging in mid-air, suspended between Mum and Rish.

Mum gripped Evie tight. "Evie, no! Don't leave me again!"

Rish's hand began to slip from hers. Evie held on as best she could, but it was no use – it was like trying to fight a riptide. She felt like she was going to be pulled apart, inside and out. The thought of leaving Mum again was unbearable – but if she let go of Rish, she could be stuck inside Mum's dream for ever…

But would that be so bad? She'd be safe here – she'd be protected. She'd never have to worry about Vale, or the Order, or the Spellstone, ever again…

Evie gritted her teeth. No – it wouldn't be real. If she wanted to protect her mum, her *real* mum, she had to let her go.

"Mum – I love you," she cried. "And you were right – I'm close. I'm just around the corner, right on the canal, and I'm thinking about you and Dad every single second. I'm coming back to you, I swear it!"

"Evie!" Mum cried.

She had run out of time. The dream wrenched Evie from Mum's grip and spun her out of the room like a catapult, pinwheeling her into another dream at a thousand miles an hour. The dreamscape colours spun faster and faster – she could feel Rish gripping her hand so tightly that she thought he might crush it completely…

Their feet hit the ground at the same time and they fell sprawling. Evie lay on the floor, her vision swimming. She couldn't make out where they were. She could feel carpet beneath her, thick and luxurious – but there was something wrong with it, somehow. A scratch hidden inside the fabric.

"What's going on?" she groaned, sitting up. "Where are w—?"

A hand slapped over her mouth. It was Rish, stopping her from talking. He was staring at something on the other side of the room, and he was shaking with fear.

Evie followed his gaze. In many respects, the room that they found themselves in was a perfectly ordinary office. On one side was a giant window, gazing out across the city. The light pouring in through the glass was a rich, deep sunset red … but that was the only colour in the room. Everything else was grey. The carpet was grey; the walls were grey; the furniture was grey.

The man at the window was grey, too.

Evie froze with terror. The man was turned away from them, but she knew exactly who he was. She'd known it the moment she laid eyes on him. It was the feeling he left inside her. No goodness; no warmth; no humanity. Evie looked him up and down, and from side to side, but no matter where she looked, there was only a dead grey hole where all those feelings should be.

Rish turned to her. Evie had never seen anyone look so frightened in all her life.

"It's Vale," he whispered. "We're inside his dream."

20
THE MEMORY PALACE

Evie stared at Vale. Here he was – the man who had killed Wainwright. The man who had killed Rish's mother. The man who had spent forty years hunting down the Order and stealing their powers. She had expected him to look terrifying, but the truth was, Vale looked *ordinary*. You could pass him on the street, and never have the slightest idea who he was or what he was capable of. For some reason, that made him even more frightening.

"Look at me," said Vale.

For a heart-stopping moment, Evie thought that he was talking to her – but then she realized he was still facing out of the window. She looked outside: they were at the top of Tower 99, gazing out over the city. But the city beneath them was different. There were no buildings, no streets, no houses. Everything had been flattened to grey waste.

"That's right," said Vale. "Look at me."

Evie gasped. She understood who Vale was talking to. Far below them was a sea of people – millions and millions of people, stretching far beyond the horizon. They were all on their knees, bowing down to Vale. He leaned back, and Evie saw that the deep red light wasn't coming through the window after all. It was coming from the great ragged boulder rising from the carpet before his feet. Its surface burned like solid fire, illuminating the room in a sickening blood-red glow. Vale had both hands pressed to the boulder's surface. Wave after wave of evil power was pulsing up his arms and into his body...

"Look at me!" he cried.

Evie knew what she was seeing. Vale was dreaming about what he was going to do with the Spellstone when he finally found it. Her desire to find him had dragged her right into his dream. She spun around to Rish. "You have to get us out – quick!"

Rish shook his head, heaving for breath. "I – I'm trying, but I... I..."

He clutched at his chest – he was having a panic attack. How could Evie blame him? He was trapped in a room with the man who had killed his mother. There was no way he could focus his skill enough to get them both out of here. Evie made a hopeless attempt to do it herself, but it was no use – every time she tried, her thoughts were instantly washed away in a tide of fear. How were they going to get out of here before...?

At the window, Vale froze. He cocked his head, as if sensing something in the air.

"Who's there?" he said.

Horror filled Evie. Vale knew they were here. She and Rish were trapped – there was nowhere for them to hide, no way to escape. Vale suddenly spun around, twisting to face them – and those eyes, those *terrible* eyes…

Evie reacted before she knew what she was doing. She leaped from the floor and dragged Rish with her, flying through the office door just as Vale caught sight of them. She slammed it shut and locked it behind her, heaving for breath. They were free – but not for long. Vale knew where they were.

Rish grabbed her and shook her. "*What did you do?!* I told you *never* to go through any doors!"

Evie looked over his shoulder and was lost for words. A series of ancient stone hallways lay before them. They were broken and disordered, twisting into a hundred different directions at once: some stretched on for ever, some ended in bare brick walls, some veered left and right before flipping upside down and climbing the ceiling. Everywhere she looked were doors, doors upon doors, shifting into position for a moment before vanishing as if they'd never been there. "Where *are* we?"

"We're inside Vale's mind," Rish groaned in horror. "All his thoughts and memories, mixed up in one place… Do you realize how bad this is, Evie? I don't know how to get us out of here! We're stuck! If Vale catches up and touches us, we *die*!"

The door behind them suddenly hammered in its frame. The handle was twisting and snapping, right in front of them. Evie could hear Vale roaring like an animal on the other side. He was trying to break through; it wouldn't hold him for much longer.

"We have to run!" cried Rish.

"Run where?"

"Just run!"

They tore down the corridor as fast as they could. Rish skidded to a stop and flung himself through the nearest doorway, just as the office door burst open behind them…

They locked the door, panting in terror. Evie blinked. This room was identical to the last one. They were back inside Vale's office – there, standing behind his desk, was Vale again.

"It's … it's a trap!" she began – but then stopped. Through the window, she could see that the city was still intact. There were no people bowing down here; no devastated fields of grey waste. Vale was talking to someone on the other side of the desk. Neither of them seemed to have any idea that Rish or Evie were there.

"Bring them here – all of them," Vale was saying. "Search every station in the city, if you have to."

Evie's blood froze. The man Vale was talking to was just a black shape: a shadow. It sank to the floor and passed beneath Evie's feet, seeping under the doorway without noticing them.

"The shadow – that's Wainwright's skill," said Rish, piecing it all together. "This isn't a dream – it must be one of Vale's memories. That's why they can't see us." His breathing began to slow. "OK – maybe if we hide in here, we'll be safe for a little—"

The office door pounded on its hinges behind them. Vale had followed them again – he knew exactly where they were. Evie stumbled back from the door. "H-how did he know where we'd gone…?"

She looked down, and understood. Their shoes were still covered in smears of rainbow oil from Mum's dream. They'd been leaving a trail of footprints for Vale to follow. They tore off their paint-stained shoes and searched for another way out, but there was nothing. "We're trapped!" Evie cried.

But Rish wasn't panicking any more. A calm had settled over him. He was focused, back in his element again. "Quick – in here!"

He dragged Evie towards a stationery cupboard on the other side of the room, just as the office door exploded in splinters behind them. There was Vale again, stumbling through a burning hole in the doorway, both of his hands swarming with blue flame.

"Who are you?" he cried. *"What are you doing in my head?"*

Rish flung open the cupboard door, threw both of them inside … and Evie suddenly found herself falling backwards, tumbling onto a cold pavement. They had fallen *up* through an open manhole, onto a random city street in darkness.

"Quick!" said Rish. "This is another one of Vale's memories – we have to find another door and lose him, before he follows us!"

Evie looked around, desperately searching for another door. They were in one of the old city squares, surrounded by glass office buildings. She could make out Vale in the distance. He was standing beside the remains of a crumbling stone wall, pounding his hands against it while an audience of smoke-men watched in silence.

"*No!*" Vale was screaming. "*No, no, no, no!*"

Evie had no idea what this memory was, but she had a feeling it was important somehow. She didn't have time to wonder why – she had to find some door, *any* door, that would get them out of here fast…

And then she saw one. A giant bin on the corner of the square, its lid shut tight. "In there! Quick!"

She dragged Rish over the square and flung open the bin lid just as Vale was clambering through the manhole behind them, his face twisted with rage. They leaped inside the bin as he reached out his hands and a bolt of blue lightning burst from his palms…

Evie slammed the lid with less than a second to spare.

She felt a shuddering wave of heat as the lightning bolt passed right beside her, singeing her hair and crackling the enamel in her teeth. Another second, and it would have hit her head-on.

She staggered back. The bin lid had become a glass partition, leading to a lit stairwell. They were in a housing estate. A discreet grey car was parked at the end of a tunnel beside them. "Where are we now? Is this another one of Vale's memories…?"

She trailed off. She had just spotted him standing inside the tunnel, surrounded by a crowd of smoke-men once again. He was talking to someone – someone who hung in mid-air before him, held in place like a pinned frog.

"No," said Rish, his voice breaking.

It was Wainwright. Vale had just caught him. And Evie understood, in a flash, what this memory was going to be. She couldn't let Rish see what was about to happen. She tried to drag him away. "We – we have to find another door, right now…"

But it was too late. A dark shape shot beneath the smoke-men and streaked out of the tunnel towards them – it was Wainwright's shadow, racing to escape and heading right for them. The smoke-men tore after it, but it was no use: the shadow was going to get away. Vale turned around, and Evie saw Wainwright wrench his arm free and grab Vale by the hand…

"No!" Rish cried.

There was nothing they could do but watch as white magic pulsed from Wainwright's body and into Vale. Wainwright collapsed to the ground – the shadow stumbled and fell at their feet.

"*Wainwright!*" Rish screamed.

It happened fast. Rish ran forward – Evie tried to pull him back – and in an instant, their hands slipped apart.

Rish disappeared. He was there one moment – the next, he was gone. Evie was left alone on the concrete walkway, her heart pounding.

"Rish? *Rish!*"

But he wasn't there any more. The horror of what had just happened began to rise in Evie's chest. She had let go of Rish's hand; she was alone, trapped inside Vale's memories. There was no way out.

Her heart began to pound. She had to find another door – there had to be some other way out of here. She looked around frantically, searching for something, *anything…*

And stopped. Wainwright's shadow was lying at her feet, fading away grain by grain … but it hadn't completely gone. It was staring right at her. It had stretched out an arm, and was pointing at something behind her.

Evie turned around. The shadow was pointing at the grey car parked beside her – the open passenger door. She knew that it wasn't a coincidence.

"In there?" she asked.

The shadow nodded … just as the glass door behind her shattered. Evie screamed. Vale had caught up with her – his hand had burst through the glass, and was clawing for her. There was no time to wonder where the new doorway might lead. Evie leaped towards the car as Vale prised himself through the broken glass, bellowing in desperate rage…

21
HIDDEN SECRETS

E VIE SLAMMED THE DOOR AND LEAPED BACK, HEART thundering.

It was no longer a car door: it was an old wooden entranceway with an iron lock and key. Evie turned the key just as the handle began to rattle and shake. She could hear Vale on the other side, screaming with fury. She knew the door wouldn't hold him back for long. She had to keep moving, until she found another way out. Maybe *that* was why Wainwright's shadow had sent her here – maybe this door led to another way out of Vale's mind.

She turned around. She was standing inside an unfamiliar house. It was cold and drab and cheerless. A sterile light seeped through the lace curtains. A man and a woman were sitting on armchairs before her. The woman was watching TV; the man was reading a newspaper. A small boy was standing in front of them, his face streaked with tears. He couldn't have been more than six years old.

"Look at me," he was begging. "Mum, Dad, please, I don't know why you're doing this. Look at me. Look at me!"

But the man and the woman couldn't hear him – it was like they didn't even know he was there. The boy kept crying and begging, but it didn't make the slightest bit of difference.

"Look at me!"

Evie understood perfectly what she was seeing. The boy was Vale, and this was one of his personal, most private memories, stored away deep inside him. Was *this* what Wainwright's shadow had wanted her to see?

The door pounded in its frame behind her – Vale was catching up. Evie moved fast, skipping past the horrible scene and stepping through a door on the other side of the room.

Once again, everything changed. Evie was no longer standing in a house. She was outside, in the middle of the night in the pouring rain. The streets were awash, and the gutters were foaming. Evie yelped with surprise and ran for shelter …

… almost crashing into the man beside her. It was Vale again. He was older now, perhaps in his twenties. He had clearly been standing in the rain for some time. His clothes were completely soaked through, and his hair dripped in a constant stream. Evie followed his gaze through the window of the closest house. Inside, she could see a group of friends, laughing fondly at the end of an evening meal. They looked so happy together. The look on Vale's face as he watched them was one of open, unrelenting hate.

"Fine night for it."

Vale almost leaped a foot in the air. A woman was standing on the pavement behind him, sheltered beneath a grim black umbrella. Evie could see that she was very tall and well-dressed, in a belted black trench coat and black leather gloves. Her face was all in shadow. Vale was almost too shocked to speak.

"You – you can see me," he said. "How can you see me?"

The woman didn't reply. She held something out for Vale – a spare umbrella. Vale took it gratefully, shuddering with cold. The woman nodded at the people through the window. "Your friends?"

Vale looked between the woman and the window, still baffled, trying to find the right words. "Er – no. My flatmates. They've locked me out again. I've been knocking at the door for hours, but they can't hear me." His face began to once again cloud over with hate. "I got held behind at work, you see. The security forgot I was in the office. Again. They shut up the building before I could leave."

The woman nodded. "Happens a lot, does it?"

"All the time," said Vale quietly.

He sounded so drained, so broken. It was strange, seeing the man who was chasing her suddenly look so different. He didn't look frightening now: he looked weak and vulnerable.

"There's a reason why those people can't see you, young man," said the woman. "Why no one notices you. Why their eyes just slip over you, no matter how hard you fight against it. You've probably been wondering your whole life."

Vale glanced at her warily. Despite the umbrella, he was shivering like a child. The woman calmly pulled off a glove and raised her hand. A blue light flickered from her fingertips, warming him instantly.

Vale sighed. "Thanks, I—"

The words dried up in his throat. The flame hadn't come from a match: it was coming straight from the woman's fingers. A perfect orb of blue fire floated in the air above her palm like magic. Vale stumbled back.

"Who – who are you?" he said.

The woman brought the blue flame close to her face, and Evie realized that she recognized her. She had seen her face on the tapestry during her own initiation ceremony. She was a member of the Order.

"My name is O'Brien," said the woman. "It's a pleasure to finally meet you, Vale."

"You know my name," said Vale, stunned.

"Of course. I've been watching you for some time." O'Brien smiled. "Here – let me show you something."

She reached around her neck, and brought out the token on a length of fine golden chain. Evie's mind raced. This was no ordinary memory. O'Brien was one of the old leaders of the Order: she was about to watch the moment that Vale was recruited. And Evie suddenly knew, deep down, that the shadow had sent her this way for a reason. She was about to see something important.

O'Brien closed her eyes, whispered some unheard words, and the token lit up with a ghostly white glow. Evie saw the magic in O'Brien's chest, beating bright and strong in time with the token … but that was *nothing* compared to what was inside Vale. His whole chest had filled with light, glowing through the cotton of his shirt like a lighthouse. The puddles around him became bright white mirrors, illuminating the whole street. Vale dropped his umbrella.

"See that?" said O'Brien. "That's magic, Vale. *That* is the reason no one sees magicians like us." She smiled. "But you are special. I've never seen so much in one person before. Our society has been waiting for someone like you for a long, long time."

Vale drank in her words. You could tell, just by his face, how much praise like this meant to him. Evie got the feeling that it had been a very long time since anyone had said anything nice to him. "What society?"

"The Order of the Stone," said O'Brien. "A secret organization devoted to destroying the Spellstone. It's the most powerful magical weapon in the world – and I believe that your power, Vale, will be the one that can finally destroy it for good."

Vale stared at her in confusion. "Why do you want to destroy it?"

"To protect humanity," O'Brien answered.

Vale paused for a moment – and then gave a derisive bark of laughter. *"Why?"*

O'Brien was taken aback for a moment. She gazed at Vale, her eyes torn, as if trying to understand whether or not she was making the right decision … then her eyes fell back to the beaming glow in his chest. She returned the token to her neck, and the light faded.

"I can see you have a lot to learn," she said primly, pulling her glove back on. "We'll get started on your training straight away – the sooner the better." She held out her hand. "The Order of the Stone are going to be very excited to meet you, Vale."

Vale took her hand – and the moment he did, the street began to fade at its edges. The memory was disappearing around them. Evie had no desire to find out what would happen if she was still here when it faded completely. She threw herself through the nearest doorway…

And the scene changed again. The rain disappeared; the street was gone. Evie was standing in a vast and cavernous room, brutally tall and brutally dark. It looked like one of the old abandoned warehouses that littered the outskirts of the city. The high windowpanes were broken; the walls were piled with old, rusted machinery. The only light came from a low brazier that burned in the centre of the room. Twenty people stood in a semicircle around it, all wearing red and white robes, their heads bowed. One of them was staring right at her – it was O'Brien.

"Vale," she said. "You have been brought before your fellow magicians under the gravest of charges."

Evie turned around … and, sure enough, there was Vale beside her. He was kneeling on the dusty floor, head bowed, held in place by two other magicians. Judging by his age, it didn't look like long had passed since the last memory; but in that time, Vale had changed almost beyond recognition. He was drawn and exhausted; his back almost bent with weariness. There was no expression on his face; he looked as if he was dead inside.

"In all my years as leader," said O'Brien, her voice shaking, "I've never heard an allegation like it. Using magic to *kill* another member of the Order…"

"It's not an allegation," said a voice. "I saw him do it."

A magician stepped from the line and raised his head. Evie's heart leaped. It was Wainwright. He was younger, of course, more or less the same age as Vale, but it was unmistakably him. He was staring at Vale with absolute loathing.

"Vale and McDonald were arguing," he explained. "They always did that. McDonald used to tease him for not having discovered his powers yet. Vale said something that I won't repeat, and McDonald swung a punch at him. Vale grabbed his hand and…" He trailed off, searching for the right words. "It was like his life was drained out of him. Like Vale took it."

O'Brien turned to Vale. "Is this true?"

Vale didn't answer at first. He stayed staring at the ground, his eyes empty. Then he raised his hand. At the far end of the room, a huge piece of machinery lifted clean off the floor, as if by invisible hands. The magicians cried out in disbelief.

"That's … that's McDonald's skill!" said one. "But how could he…?"

"Don't you see?" said Wainwright. "He stole it. He *stole* McDonald's powers, and killed him in the process. And he could do it to any one of us!"

O'Brien raised her hands, trying to bring them all back to order.

"No one could have foreseen this!" she said. "It's an accident — a terrible accident. Vale had no idea that his skill would hurt McDonald, let alone kill him." She gazed at Vale, almost imploringly. "Isn't that right, Vale?"

Vale finally looked up … and Evie felt a flutter of horror. She knew, with one look, that Vale was beyond hope. Any goodness that had been inside him was gone.

He had let it die. The greyness, the coldness, had settled on him like ashes on a burnt-out forest.

"But I did," he said. "I did mean to kill him."

O'Brien's face drained of colour. Around her, the room was in uproar.

"He can't stay here!" said a magician beside her. "As long as Vale is here, we're all in danger. He must be sent away!"

"Why? So he can come back and kill us when we least expect it?" said another. "We can't risk it. A life for a life – it's the only way!"

"We are not *executioners*!" said another. "We swore an oath to protect one another…"

"And Vale broke that oath," said another. "We cannot let it go unpunished. We could use Davenport's skill to freeze him in place…"

"You can't hold a person prisoner for the rest of their lives!" said another. "What if he escapes?"

The magicians suddenly fell quiet. There was a sound that had been slowly building beneath the argument, growing louder and louder. Now, it was loud enough to silence the room.

Vale was still kneeling on the floor, howling with laughter. The magicians stared at each other in confusion.

"Listen to yourselves," said Vale. "You can't even *punish* me. It's pathetic!"

O'Brien's face hardened. "Mercy isn't *weakness*, Vale. You and I have spoken a lot about that…"

"Of course," said Vale sarcastically. "The Order knows all about mercy, don't they? That's why you've devoted our lives to protecting people who don't know we exist. Who don't even *care*!" He stared at the magicians. "The Order is a joke. *Emrys* was a joke! He had the power in his hands to rule the world, and he gave it all away. Think of the things he could have achieved, if he'd harnessed the power of the Spellstone for himself! Think of what he could have made people do!" He was getting more and more agitated. "Don't you see? We're not meant to destroy the Spellstone – we're meant to *use* it! And I'm the one to do it!"

O'Brien stared at Vale in horror. Evie could see what had happened. O'Brien had wanted so much for Vale to be good, to be the answer that the Order had been searching for, that it had clouded her judgement. She hadn't seen what was right in front of her all along, as clear as day: Vale wasn't worthy of the Order. The expression on her face was one of absolute heartbreak. "Take him away. He is beyond our hope."

Vale looked up … and his eyes flickered with hate. "Oh, I'm beyond far more than that."

He reached up and clasped the hand of one of the magicians holding him down. Only Wainwright seemed to understand what was happening.

"Banda, no!" he cried.

Too late. Banda yelled with shock as white magic pulsed from her arm and into Vale – in the space of a second, she was dead. Vale let her drop to the floor like a piece of meat and stood up. O'Brien shot out her hands, and each one instantly filled with a ball of blue flame.

"Stop him!" she screamed. "Stop him before he—"

Vale reached out a hand to the brazier. The flames roared like a furnace and smoke suddenly boiled up in torrents, swirling around the warehouse like a tornado. The room was chaos. Magicians were shouting in the darkness, struggling to breathe, trying to fight back, but no one could see a thing except Vale. The smoke formed a perfect shelter around him as he stepped across the warehouse towards O'Brien, swiping his hands left and right and sending the magicians flying. He never once took his eyes off O'Brien.

"The Spellstone," he demanded. "Take me to the Spellstone, now."

Evie understood what she was witnessing – it was the moment that everything changed. The moment that the golden age of the Order of the Stone came to an end, and the decades-long battle against Vale began. Soon, Vale would start hunting down these magicians, one by one: within forty years, every single person in this room would be dead. Vale's powers would only grow stronger and stronger, until...

"You!"

Evie spun around. There, tearing through the smoke towards her, was Vale – the *real* Vale, his eyes burning with hate and fear. He had finally found her.

"Who are you?" he screamed. "Why are you in my head?"

His eyes fell down … and he saw the token that hung around Evie's neck.

"Wainwright's replacement," he cried. "It's you… *You're* the leader!"

Evie tried to run, but it was no use – there was nowhere left to go. Vale roared with anger and flung himself at her, his fingertips clawing through the final few centimetres…

And Evie's feet were wrenched from the ground. It was as if she was being dragged from the memory by force: she swore that she could even *feel* a set of hands pulling her up. Vale missed her by millimetres as she was whipped from his grip at the very last second. The last thing Evie saw were those eyes, those *terrible* eyes, as he bellowed after her with soundless rage…

And then she was back on the floor of Rish's bedroom, gazing into his terrified face as he shook her.

"Evie, wake up! Oh, please, please, please, wake up…"

She sat bolt upright with a scream, expecting to see Vale breaking down the bedroom door and following her into the real world… But he wasn't there. All she could see were Onslow and Campbell and Lady Alinora, crying out with relief beside her.

"Evie!"

"Oh, thank goodness…"

Lady Alinora scampered into her lap. Her voice was low and urgent. "Evie – are you hurt? Tell me what happened."

Evie opened her mouth, trying to find the words to describe what she had just seen. She was back in the hideout, safe and well. She was with friends. The light, the warmth, the neatly arranged books and cast-iron figures: everything was exactly as she'd left it. "I saw… I saw…"

But it was too much. Evie slumped sideways, falling into Campbell's arms and bursting into tears.

22
AFTERMATH

THE MAGICIANS SAT IN SILENCE IN THE DRAWING room. Evie and Rish were swaddled in blankets in front of the fireplace. Onslow had made them both mugs of hot cocoa, but Evie could barely drink it – her hands were still shaking too much.

"I was trying to show Evie how to walk through dreams," Rish was explaining. "I thought it would be good practice for her. I never thought we'd—"

Campbell shushed him. "It's OK, Rishi. You're both safe. That's all that matters."

"It's *not* all that matters," said Alinora coldly. "They could have *died*, Campbell."

Onslow waved her quiet. "Maybe they should explain what happened first. Evie?"

Evie swallowed down a scalding mouthful of cocoa. The sugar helped. She did the best she could to explain about finding her mother's dream, only to be dragged out of it the moment she started thinking of Vale. She told them all about Vale's dream, and getting lost inside his memories when they tried to escape. She was about to describe the moment when she and Rish had become separated when Campbell suddenly stopped her.

"Hang on – that second memory," she asked, puzzled. "The one in the square. What was happening?"

Evie cast her mind back. "We were standing by some sort of old wall. Vale was with his smoke-men. He was really angry about something, but I don't know what..."

Campbell's eyes began to gleam. She leaned back in her chair, realization dawning on her face. "I see. So, he could have..." She shook her head. "Well I never."

Onslow frowned. "What? What are you thinking?"

Campbell began to answer – but then shook her head. "Nothing. It is just a hunch. Something I will investigate tomorrow. Keep going, Evie."

She did. She kept the details of Wainwright's death brief – Rish was clearly still shaken by it – and she decided not to tell them what had happened with Wainwright's shadow, either. It felt like all it would do was upset the magicians more – and part of her felt like it couldn't possibly have happened, either. How could Wainwright's shadow have seen her in Vale's memory? How could it have shown her where to go?

Instead, she told them all that she had seen in Vale's most private memories – everything that she had discovered about his childhood, and how he was recruited, and what had happened the night he turned on the Order. She ended at the moment that the real Vale had finally caught up with her and nearly grabbed her. The others shared a dark glance.

"You're lucky you got out alive," muttered Alinora. "You could have been stuck in his memories for ever – or worse." She glared at Rish. "From now on, *neither* of you are to mess with your skills unless one of us is around too. Understood?"

Rish and Evie nodded, crestfallen. The atmosphere in the room was strained – the mansion suddenly seemed even darker and gloomier than usual.

"There is much for us to think on," said Campbell sagely. "Now that Vale knows Evie is the leader, things are going to become more difficult for us." She heaved herself out of the chair. "For now, let's all get some proper sleep."

"I'm … going to stay up for a bit, with Evie," said Rish quickly. "If that's OK."

Evie nodded, though she had no idea what Rish wanted. The magicians wished them goodnight and filed off to bed. Soon, it was just Rish and Evie left by the fireplace.

"I – I just wanted to say sorry," said Rish. "For letting go of your hand. I didn't mean to do it. It was an accident. When I saw Wainwright, I just … freaked out." He shook his head. "I'm such a coward."

Evie felt a pang of guilt. Rish had been forced to watch the moment of Wainwright's death – she couldn't imagine how awful that must have been for him. "You weren't a coward. You were really brave – finding a way out of Vale's memories like that. Besides, if you hadn't dragged me out when you did, Vale would have got me."

Rish frowned. "Drag you out of the dream? I didn't do that. I don't even know *how* to do that."

Evie was confused. "But someone did. I felt them."

Rish gazed into his mug. "I … I don't think they did, Evie. I think it was *you*, on your own. When you took us into Vale's dream, I've never felt power like that before. The *magic* inside you…" He gazed at her in admiration. "Wainwright was right to recruit you. You *are* a sorcerer."

Rish had no idea how hollow those words sounded to Evie now. She had seen, with her own eyes, what immense power had done to Vale – how it had led him to do all the terrible things he'd done. Was the same going to happen to her? She gazed silently at her cup. Only the dregs of cocoa were left now, floating on a skin of tepid milk. She drank them down, and they tasted bitter.

"Thanks," she said quietly. "I might stay up on my own for a bit longer, if you don't mind."

Rish understood. "OK. But … Evie?"

"Yes?"

"I'm really glad you're here."

He left. Evie sat up alone, gazing at the fireplace, watching as blue flame licked the last of the logs to ash. It made her think of the fire she had seen in O'Brien's hands: another power that Vale had stolen. *All* the powers that she had seen were his now. How was she supposed to defeat that?

She glanced at the portrait above the mantelpiece. There was Emrys, standing before the Spellstone with his silver sword held high. For a moment, she hated him. If it hadn't been for Emrys, none of this would have happened. And she hated Wainwright, too. She hated him for bringing her into it; for all his secrets. She hated him for giving her nothing but smoke and shadows. She gazed miserably at the Spellstone in the portrait, radiating with a blood-red glow, and shook her head.

"Where *are* you?" she asked quietly.

23
CLOSER

"WHERE ARE YOU?"

Vale stood at his office window, gazing over the dark city. He had been doing this ever since he woke up. Ever since he lost the girl.

He had been dreaming of the Spellstone – as he always did – when he'd felt a *presence* in his head. He'd seen the two children, standing in his dream, and understood right away what was happening. They were magicians from the Order, and they had broken into his mind. The boy had looked almost familiar to him, as if he had seen his face somewhere before. But the girl – she was different. Vale didn't recognize her at all. It was only when he had chased her through his memories – through things he had never wanted to see or think about ever again – and seen the token around her neck that he had realized who she was. She was Wainwright's replacement: the new leader of the Order of the Stone. She couldn't have been more than twelve years old. And just like Wainwright, she had slipped between his fingers at the final second.

She was still somewhere out there, laughing at him.

He gazed over the city. How he hated it all – these streets, this city, this world of people. From up this high, all their achievements became so meaningless. Even the tallest towers and buildings seemed pitiful. He wanted to reach out a hand and flatten them all, driving them down to powder and sweeping it all into the river so he could watch the dirt-grey water carry it all away.

And he would. He would do it all, and more. When he finally had his hands on the Spellstone…

There was a flutter of darkness in the corner of his eye. Vale spun around. He'd thought he was alone – but his shadow was waiting for him on the other side of his desk. He had no idea how long it had been standing there.

"What?" said Vale.

The shadow reached inside itself with both hands … and heaved something out onto the desk.

Vale stared in shock. It was a mound of paper folders. There were dozens of them, perhaps over a hundred, spilling off his desk and onto the carpet. All the covers said the same thing: *MISSING PERSON*.

Vale stared at the shadow, blinking in surprise. Then he threw himself on the pile in a frenzy, opening the folders one by one. He knew what he was looking for; he knew what he needed to find. He flung each folder to one side the moment he'd read it, searching and searching for the right one…

And then he found it. He held the folder before him with trembling hands, before carefully placing it down on the desk.

It was another missing person's report. It had been filed only yesterday – a young girl, twelve years old, last seen at home, wearing her school uniform…

And there was her photograph.

Vale smiled. It was the girl he had just seen inside his head. The girl with Wainwright's token. The new leader of the Order of the Stone. The one who had just slipped through his fingers.

And her name was Evie.

"Very good," said Vale. "Very, very good."

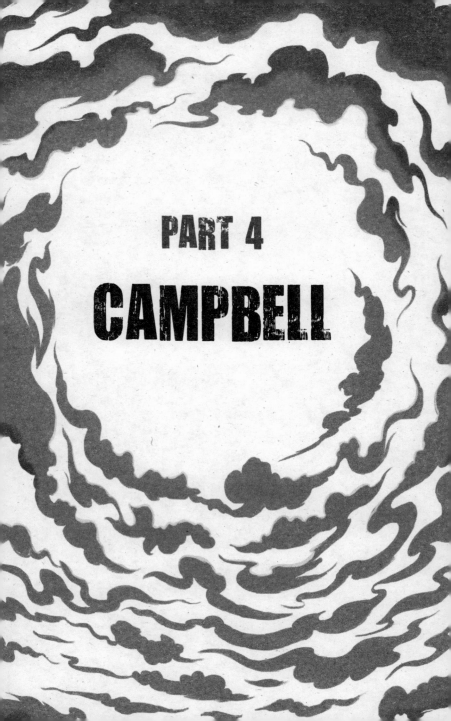

24
THE MEMORIAL

E VIE WOKE UP.

Someone had just walked into her bedroom. She peeked out from beneath the covers. Campbell was standing beside the bed, with a camel coat buttoned over her dress.

"Up up up!" she said cheerfully, jabbing her with an umbrella. "No time for this laziness. Wash the sleep from your eyes and get dressed."

Evie groaned. "What time is it?"

"Late enough," said Campbell, yanking her out of bed. "Come! We have places to go."

Evie squawked at the sudden cold. "Go where?"

Campbell didn't answer – she just bustled Evie to the bathroom and shut the door. Evie muttered with outrage, but the truth was, she quite liked being fussed over by Campbell. It made her feel loved. She felt the now-familiar surge of sadness whenever she thought of her parents: the pain in her stomach, the tugging at her chest. She wondered if it was a feeling she was ever going to get used to.

She washed and dressed herself. When she was done, she found Campbell waiting impatiently by the bedroom door.

"Finally!" Campbell patted herself down. "Map, glasses, keys, coat… All ready."

Evie gulped. "We're going outside?"

Campbell nodded. "Yes, child. And we must be even more careful now that Vale's smoke-men know what you look like. Stay close."

Staying close to Campbell was easier said than done. Evie had to race to keep up with her. The old woman was unbelievably fast for her age, and had a habit of taking shortcuts through railings and shop corners like they weren't even there. They came to an underground railway station and, sure enough, Campbell strolled straight through the ticket barriers without paying. No one tried to stop her, or even noticed her. Evie fumbled for the season ticket in her pocket and almost missed the train that Campbell was on.

"It would be a lot easier," said Evie, gasping for breath, "if you just told me where we're going."

"Nosy," said Campbell, and that was that.

They got off the train at the business district. It was still morning by the time they arrived: the sun felt like a drum roll, building to an uproar. It was already so hot that the ticket barriers had started malfunctioning: hordes of sweating commuters were pressed up tightly against each other, queuing to escape and muttering in the heat.

"*Cha!* We have no time for this," Campbell tutted. "Come."

She marched towards a locked door marked *STAFF ONLY*, dragging Evie behind her. Evie only realized what was happening at the last second. "N-no, I can't!"

Being dragged through a wall didn't feel how Evie expected it to. She thought she'd feel *nothing*, as if the locked door were simply made of air. Instead, she felt every single material as her body passed through it – the wooden warmth of the door, the chill of the metal cladding, the small queasy section of plastic on the *STAFF ONLY* sign. Each one *just* brushed the surface of her skin, drawing along the contours of her body before closing up again behind her. A second of dark pressure, and then Evie found herself standing in an empty stairwell on the other side, reeling.

"Maybe … give me a little warning, next time you're going to do that?" she gasped.

Campbell frowned. "Do what?"

"Walk through walls."

Campbell laughed, and dragged her up the stairwell. "*Walk through walls!* I don't walk through walls, dear. I ask them nicely to make room, and they do."

They came to the wall at the top of the stairwell. This time, Evie could at least prepare herself before being dragged through it. There was another moment of brief, stale darkness – the bricks felt rough and dry against her skin, like being combed with sandpaper – and then the world outside emerged into view. Campbell brushed herself down, humming a cheerful melody. No one on the street gave them so much as a second glance, despite their arrival.

"Are you going to tell me where we're going now?" asked Evie, growing impatient.

Campbell shrugged. "It's nothing. I have a hunch; something that you said last night made me think of it, but I had to wait until morning to check it out. Empty streets are no good to us now, with Vale's eyes everywhere."

Evie glanced up, despite herself. Sure enough, there was Tower 99, looming over the city like always. "Is it something to do with the Spellstone?"

"Of course!" said Campbell. "But there is something else I want to show you first."

She led Evie through the sweltering streets. The pavements were almost palpitating in the heat; Evie wondered how Campbell could stand to wear her coat. The city was different here, in the business district. The oldest buildings had been bulldozed to make way for sleek new cafes and digital billboards, but every now and then something was randomly left untouched in the exact spot it had been made centuries ago. It was like the city had so much history that it didn't know what to do with it. It felt like being in a play with all the stage scenery mixed up.

You were just as likely to walk past an ancient temple as a doughnut shop.

They came to a small park, carved out of the space left between office buildings. It was nothing special: a patch of grass with a few plane trees, hushed and cool in the shade. Campbell led Evie to a bench, cleaned it with a handkerchief, and sat down with a sigh of satisfaction. Evie gazed around. "*This* is what you wanted to show me? A park?"

Campbell nodded. "It is a *memorial* park; a very special one, too. See?" She nodded to a brick wall ahead. There, above a bed of red and white climbing roses, were a series of ceramic plaques. There were dozens of them, lined up in rows, each one hand-painted with a different person's name and a date. Some of the dates were from over two hundred years ago; some were just a few years old.

"It is not a memorial for some king or queen," Campbell explained. "It is a memorial for ordinary people: people who gave their lives to save others. They were not made to do it – this was not for a war. They did it because they thought it was right."

Evie looked closer, and, sure enough, each plaque had a brief description explaining what the person had done. There was a man who had run into a burning building to save a child, and a woman who had dived into the river to save a drowning man. There was a young boy – even younger than Evie – who had pulled his own brother from a set of train tracks. Sometimes, the person had died saving a loved one; sometimes, they had died saving a complete stranger. Evie felt a string of emotion pluck inside her. "That's so sad."

Campbell nodded. "But beautiful too, in a way. People do brave, wonderful things all the time, just for the sake of it. And they are so easily forgotten." She held out her hands. "Imagine how many *more* wonderful things are out there, that we do not even know about!"

Evie couldn't help but think of the Order of the Stone: all the magicians over the centuries who had given their lives to the cause, without reward or recognition. Through the office windows around her, she could see people sitting at their computers, sending emails and hurrying to meetings. She wondered how many of them knew about this park and the names on the plaques, right beside where they worked.

"This is where Wainwright brought me, you know," said Campbell. "When I refused to join the Order."

Evie frowned. "You *refused*?"

Campbell laughed out loud. "Of course I did! What an offer – to give up everything I had, all my freedom, the few years I had left, to spend it in hiding for people who did not even know I existed. You couldn't have *paid* me to join!"

Evie giggled. It was a relief to hear someone say how hard being a member of the Order could feel sometimes:

that in some ways, the duty was a terrible burden. She felt a tiny weight lift from her shoulders.

"I'd had my powers for almost fifty years," Campbell explained. "I discovered them myself, when I was twelve years old, just after I moved here. I wasn't born in this country, you see. My family came here to find work. I was suddenly by myself, in a new city, in a whole new country, where everything was different. *That* was when I found out what I could do. I could walk wherever I wanted, go wherever I pleased, without anyone trying to stop me. That meant a lot, back then." She sighed. "So, when Wainwright found me, and told me all about the Order, I told him to scram! Why should I give up everything I had for him? I told him where to put his stupid token."

Evie snorted. "What did he say?!"

"He wouldn't leave me alone," muttered Campbell. "That was Wainwright – when he set his mind on something, he stuck to it. I ran through so many walls to get away from him, but sooner or later I'd always find that scruffy little white man on a park bench somewhere, eating a ham sandwich in his bad shoes."

Evie giggled again.

"And then one day," Campbell went on, "he asked to meet me here. He said he wanted to talk to me one last time, and if I still said no, he gave me his word that he would leave me alone. And he showed me those plaques, and he said: *Just because no one knows about the sacrifice, Clara, it does not make it worthless."*

Campbell didn't say anything for a while.

"And that made me stop and think a little. I never wanted to leave anything behind when it was my time to go: take my clothes apart for fabric, throw my ashes to the wind, be done with it. But perhaps, I thought, I could find a way to leave the world a little better than I found it." She sighed. "It was a big decision. So, I did what I always did when I was unsure: I asked the world what I should do. And the world said that I should do what I thought was the *right* thing to do. So I joined the Order and I never looked back."

Evie didn't understand. "You talked to the world?"

"Of course! How do you think I found my skill in the first place?" She held out her hands. "I spoke to the world, and the world spoke back."

Evie shuffled on the bench. She still didn't really understand a lot of what Campbell had said. But even so, she felt like she could at least be honest with her.

"I'm really frightened, Campbell," she said. "I don't know what to do. I don't know if I have what it takes to defeat Vale."

Campbell nodded, as if she had known Evie would say this all along. She gestured to the wall.

"You see those people, Evie? They did not give their lives because they were special or different. They gave their lives because ordinary people do good things all the time. And that is what Vale will never understand. He can only see the badness – the ugliness in people. He will never see that sometimes people do wonderful things. And that is precisely what makes him so weak."

Evie swallowed. "But even if I do somehow get rid of Vale ... what about the Spellstone? Its power is still growing, right? How can we ever destroy it, if it was already strong enough to kill Emrys?"

Campbell thought about it.

"Wainwright used to tell me stories from the old days of the Order," she said. "Things that are all lost now. He said that some magicians used to tell a different version of the story of Emrys. In their story, Emrys never *really* died. When his sword shattered and he lost his powers, he hid himself in secret beneath the earth. And they said that he is still there, waiting for the moment when the world is at its point of greatest peril, and only then will he return."

Evie didn't know what to make of that. "But which story is the right one?"

"Who knows!" said Campbell, heaving herself to her feet. "But if Emrys *did* want to come back, now would be the right time. Shall we?"

And with that, she strode out of the park without looking back. Evie followed, her mind racing with questions. "But ... *why* would Emrys hide? What would he be waiting f—"

She came out of the park, and stopped dead. She realized that she knew exactly where they were.

It all looked different, of course. When she'd last seen it, it had been the middle of the night. But everything was still here. There was the manhole she and Rish had tumbled up; there was the bin they had used to escape Vale.

It was the city square that she had seen in Vale's memories. And, rising from its centre like a broken monument, were the remains of an ancient wall. Campbell was striding towards it.

"Come," she said. "There are some stones I want to talk to."

25
THE STONES

EVIE GAZED AT THE WALL IN THE CENTRE OF THE square. It was barely a wall any more. Huge chunks of stone had fallen off long ago and were lodged in the ground, and what was left stood alone like a dropped artwork, connected to nothing. "What is it?"

"*This* is all that is left of the original city walls," Campbell explained. "Back when it was a stone fortress, two thousand years ago. The rest of the city grew around it over the centuries." She patted the wall. "The fortress is gone, but these stones have stayed. They've sat in this exact spot for two thousand years. They've been here longer than anything else."

Evie gazed around. No one was paying the wall even the slightest bit of attention. People strode right by eating pastries; buses and taxis roared past on the busy nearby road. No one seemed to care that the wall had been there for twenty centuries, through wind and snow and rain. It gave Evie an ice-cream headache, just thinking about it. "And why are *we* here?"

Campbell smiled. "Where's the best place to hide a needle?"

"In a haystack," said Evie automatically.

Campbell tutted. "Nonsense! The best place to hide a needle is in a stack of needles." She ran a hand along the crumbling wall. "And the best place to hide an ancient stone … is inside a pile of ancient stones. Hidden in plain sight – just like magic itself. *The last place he'll look.*"

Evie understood what Campbell was saying. She gazed at the wall and her mouth fell open. "You mean the Spellstone's *here*? In the middle of the city? In broad daylight?"

Campbell shook her head. "No. I think it *was* hidden here, for centuries, but then Wainwright moved it. What you saw in Vale's memory made me think of it. Why else would Vale be standing here, screaming like that?"

Evie gazed around, her heart pounding. The thought that the most dangerous weapon ever created had been left out in the open was mind-blowing. But she had seen the Spellstone in the painting: it wouldn't be too hard to camouflage the boulder in among these huge fallen slabs. "How can you be sure?"

"I can't," said Campbell. "That's why I'm going to have a little chat to the stones. I want to find out what they know." She reached out her hand. "Come. Help an old woman."

It took Evie a moment to realize that Campbell wanted to climb the wall. It looked impossible. The only place to stand was a thin ledge above them, barely a few inches deep. The stones were worn smooth by centuries of rain: if Campbell slipped, she'd have a nasty fall to the ground below. But by now, Evie knew Campbell well enough to know that saying no wasn't going to stop her. She climbed onto the ledge and heaved Campbell up beside her. They stood side by side, facing the wall.

"Now take my hand," Campbell said. "And press the other to the wall. You're going to share my skill with me. We will speak to the stones together."

Evie did as she was told. The skin of Campbell's palm was warm and dry, like tissue paper.

"Now – repeat after me," said Campbell. *"I'm calling on you to show us Wainwright. Show us what you know. Tell us what you saw."*

Evie had never talked to a wall before. "Um – tell us what you saw. Show us what you know." She paused, and then added, "Please."

"Don't just *say* the words," Campbell chided. "*Mean* them. Open up to the world – listen to it. You can't hear what it's saying if you're not listening."

Evie closed her eyes, and tried again. "I'm calling on you to show us Wainwright. Show us what you know. Tell us what you saw."

She listened with every fibre of her being – not just with her ears, but with her mind, her skin, her breath. She took it all in, every scrap: the cool stone beneath her palm, the hummingbird pulse of blood in Campbell's hand, the whisper of a breeze in the hairs along her arms. Soon she was noticing *everything*: the birds in the nearby trees, the shudder of buses, the far-off call of a thousand strangers, the wind that shivered against the tips of the tallest building...

And then it began to change. The surface of the wall began to tremble against her fingertips. The stones beneath her feet hummed like an alternating current, trembling up past her stomach and settling in the space between her lungs.

"That's it," said Campbell. "Keep going, Evie."

Evie opened her eyes and gasped. The sun was running backwards above her, wheeling overhead like a lantern swung faster and faster: setting and rising, setting and rising. The city lightened and darkened with rapidly passing days and nights; cars flew past in a blur; people appeared and disappeared like flickers on the surface of a cinema screen... They were travelling back through time itself. But they were going back far further than just a few days. They were leaping backwards decades at a time, never settling in one place for more than a fraction of a second before moving on. Buildings shot up and shrank down around them as they were demolished and rebuilt in the blink of an eye. The city square was hammered by storms one moment and blanketed in snow the next; surrounded by trees and fields and water and fog and then entirely on fire...

"That's it," Campbell said to the stones. "Take us to Wainwright. Show us what happened. Show us what you know."

Evie's teeth began to rattle. The world was spinning faster and faster, until she had to press her head to the wall to stop from falling. There was no order to it, no logic – they were scanning through the years like searching for a radio frequency, ricocheting backwards and forwards. Only the stones stayed where they were, never once changing, never once altering, as the hum grew to a whine and then a roar that rang through her bones like electricity…

And then it stopped. The tumbling floodwater of years fell silent. Evie opened her eyes, gasping for breath. It was the middle of the night. The city square was still and empty around her. Everything was gone.

But there was someone running towards them in the darkness. The unmistakable sound of broken boots on pavement.

Evie's heart leaped. There was Wainwright, exactly as she remembered him on the day they met: the same clothes, the same beard. He came to a sudden stop in front of the wall, gasping for breath … and looked right at her. Evie froze – did Wainwright somehow know they were here?

"Can he see us?" she whispered to Campbell.

Campbell didn't reply. Evie turned to her, and was

shocked to see that Campbell was crying. She was gazing down at Wainwright, her eyes red with tears.

"No, dear," she said quietly. "He can't see us."

Wainwright glanced over his shoulder. He was checking to see if he was being followed. Then he reached around his neck and brought out the token.

"Show me," he said. "Quick, before it's too late. I might not have much time."

The token burst into light … but this was no pale white glow. This was nothing like the deep pink that Evie had seen in the sewers, either. The token was burning with a deep and venomous red, far brighter than Evie had ever seen it burn before. The curved question mark of its shape blazed in the dark like hot iron, lighting up every millimetre of Wainwright's face in crimson…

But that was *nothing* compared to the light that was coming from the wall.

Evie shielded her eyes as best she could. The wall directly beside her was pulsing in time with the token, so bright that it almost hurt to look at it. It was one of the bricks in the wall itself, lit from within by a swirling red light that churned like hot blood.

Evie was speechless. Campbell was right: the Spellstone really *had* been hidden here all along. But it was no vast red boulder, bursting from the earth like the one in the portrait. It was small enough to hold in your hands.

"That's *it*?" she said in disbelief. "*That's* the Spellstone?"

Campbell's eyes shone behind her glasses as she pieced it all together. "Of course – don't you see? *That's* how the Order hid it, all along. They changed it. They made everyone think it was still a huge boulder... When in truth, it looked just like a stone. They took the most powerful, magical weapon in the world ... and they made it look ordinary. *The last place he'll look!*"

Below them, Wainwright's neck suddenly snapped around – something was racing across the square towards him, swift as the wind. It was his own shadow. The edges of the square were filling with swirling black smoke, closing in on every side. Wainwright's face turned pale.

"No," he whispered. "He's coming!"

He turned back to the wall. His eyes were wide with fear – but he acted fast. He summoned all of his courage, clambered up onto the ledge beside Evie and tried to pull the Spellstone from the wall. It didn't budge. He glanced up, and addressed the wall itself.

"Please – I know it's never supposed to be moved. But Vale's coming – if it stays here, he'll find it! There's only one place left he won't think to look for it..."

The Spellstone suddenly slid free from the wall, as if slicked with oil. Wainwright held it out before him, trembling with nerves, as if holding a nuclear bomb.

"Thank you," he said, gazing up at the wall. "For all that you've done."

Then he stuffed the Spellstone into his coat ... and

threw himself off the wall. He landed in his shadow the very moment it finally reached him, disappearing inside it like he'd fallen through a hole. The shadow flew across the square, diving between the clouds of smoke that were closing in like a net on every side, and disappeared down a side street.

Evie watched, connecting it all together. In a few hours, a pigeon would spot Wainwright sneaking down a manhole on the other side of the city. He would have the Spellstone with him, concealed in his coat. But where had he taken it next?

At that moment, a grey car with blackened windows swerved around the corner with screeching tyres, almost spinning out of control before pulling up at the side of the road. Vale leaped out. Evie almost lost her footing on the ledge: she knew that he couldn't see her, but she was still terrified of him.

"Well?" demanded Vale, searching left and right. "Where is he?"

Smoke began to gather into the shapes of men. They stood before Vale, dumbstruck.

"You said his shadow came here," he said. "Did you let him get away *again*? There must be some reason it came here to these worthless old walls, or..."

Vale turned to the wall – and understanding suddenly dawned on his face. He raced over to the ruins and saw the freshly made gap in the bricks, where only moments before the Spellstone had been hidden. The muscles in his neck tightened and he pounded his fists miserably against the wall. "No. *No! No, no, no, no!*"

This was the memory that she and Rish had seen – the smoke-men watching in silence as Vale screamed at the ruins, his chance to finally claim the Spellstone stolen at the last moment.

"I think," said Campbell sagely, "we have seen enough."

The was a note of concern in her voice. Evie understood why. Now they knew where the Spellstone had been hidden all this time … but they also knew a more concerning truth. The evil inside it really had grown more powerful over the years. The Spellstone was no longer a blazing red, like in the portrait: now it glared like molten lava. It looked like it was ready to burst free at any moment. How long did they have left until the magic trapped inside it escaped? What if they ran out of time before…

Let go.

Evie started. A voice had just spoken in her head from out of nowhere.

Let go, it repeated.

Evie looked around, searching for the voice … and realized that it was coming from the wall, right in front of her. The stones themselves were speaking to her.

Don't worry – Campbell can't hear us, they said. *You need to let go of her hand.*

She glanced at Campbell – sure enough, Campbell had no idea that the walls were talking. *Why do I need to let go?* Evie thought.

If we told you now, Evie, said the stones, *then the plan wouldn't work.*

Her hair stood on end. It was exactly what Wainwright had said to her, back in her dream. Was it a coincidence? Or was it much more than that? What would happen if she let go of Campbell's hand?

She had to know the truth. She closed her eyes, drew in a deep breath – and pulled free from Campbell. She slipped – her hand left the wall – and suddenly she was plummeting backwards, falling towards the pavement. Campbell swung around. *"Ev—"*

The landing never came. Evie fell right through the ground, and the city disappeared in a finger snap. She kept falling, down and down through long turbulent darkness, as the world roared like a jet engine all around her, and Campbell's face spiralled away like she was gazing down from the top of a rabbit hole…

26
THE MEETING PLACE

A ND THEN FINALLY, EVIE *DID* HIT THE GROUND.

It wasn't the ground she expected. This wasn't the hot, hard pavement of the square: it was blissfully cool and soft. In fact, it almost felt like ... grass?

Evie sat up. It *was* grass. The roads and skyscrapers of the city were gone. Before her lay an undulating landscape, stretching out in meadows to the moon. It was the middle of the night. The old city walls were still in front of her ... but they weren't old any more. They were made of new stone, gleaming fresh beneath the stars. A fortress stood before her.

Evie filled with panic. She realized what had happened — she had somehow fallen backwards through time itself, back to when the city had first been made. And this time, it wasn't a memory. She could feel the cool breath of the night wind on her skin and the dew of the meadow soaking into her clothes. She was *really* here, hundreds of years in the past. She leaped from the ground and threw herself at the fortress walls, pressing her hands to the stone. "No — please! You have to take me back!"

She heard a voice in reply – but this time, it wasn't coming from inside her head. It was coming from somewhere far behind her.

She turned around. There was a small copse of trees in the distance. She could make out the flickering light of a bonfire inside it. She could hear the babble of far-off voices just beneath the breeze.

Evie understood. The stones had brought her here for a reason: they wanted her to see something.

She swallowed down her nerves, and made her way towards the woodland. She silently picked her way between the trees, following the light and the sound of the voices until she came to a small clearing hidden in the heart of the forest. She crouched down low and peered around the edge of a tree. After all, this was no memory: she couldn't afford to be seen now. There were a dozen people congregated in the clearing – young and old, men and women, all wearing the same red and white robes.

But they weren't standing around a bonfire. They were standing around a boulder whose surface glowed like solid fire.

Evie gasped. It was the Spellstone, just like in the painting. And the man slowly standing up to face it…

"So it begins," said Emrys. "Our final meeting."

It was really him. Emrys, the founder of the Order of the Stone, the most powerful sorcerer in history. He looked exactly like he did in the painting: his eyes were wide and watchful. His face was peaked with age and yet somehow vibrantly alive. His beard was long and flowing, gathered in knots along its length. When he spoke, his voice was deep and musical.

"It has been a long road to get here," he said. "For years, the Order has travelled this land, flushing evil from wherever it hid and trapping it inside the Spellstone."

He gestured to the boulder before him, throbbing in the darkness and lighting up the forest around it.

"And now our work is done," said Emrys. "The last of the creatures of darkness have been defeated. Our battle is over. Tonight, we finally finish what we started."

Emrys unsheathed a long silver sword from his belt: the exact same one from the painting. The magicians held hands and formed a circle around him. Evie gripped the tree trunk. This was the moment that Emrys tried to destroy the Spellstone. The moment that it fought back, shattering his sword and defeating his magic and killing him. She was about to see it with her very own eyes.

Emrys held his sword high above him. It gleamed like a streak of molten lightning: the midnight wind sang against its blade. He leaned back, to swing it at the Spellstone with all his might…

And stopped.

"But it will not work," he said, lowering his sword. "The Spellstone cannot be destroyed – not now, not by me. Our battle is far from over."

Emrys sheathed his sword and sat down on a fallen log. Evie was shocked – she hadn't been expecting that at all. Judging from the response of his magicians, neither had they. One of the magicians separated from the circle and stepped towards him. "Sir – what do you mean? Of course the Spellstone can be destroyed. You built it yourself."

"So I did," said Emrys. "But I have been mistaken about a great many things. I thought that by defeating the creatures of darkness, I would somehow end darkness itself. Instead, I have done something far worse. I have concentrated all its power into a single place. And by doing so, I have created a weapon that is far more powerful than even me."

"But … the evil magic inside it is *trapped*," said one of the other magicians. "Only your sword can open it!"

"For now," said Emrys calmly. "But its power will only keep growing. One day, it will be strong enough to break free by itself. And when it does, it will destroy the world."

The magician was baffled. "How can you be so sure?"

"Because I've seen it," said Emrys. "I've seen it all."

The magicians gazed at each other in bewilderment. Emrys turned to them, and Evie was suddenly struck by how old he looked – how tired, and defeated. It was as if all the years of fighting the creatures of darkness had worn him down in some way.

"The evil magic that I have been gathering over the years has … changed me," Emrys explained. "It has given me powers that I never expected. These have allowed me to see into the future: to see all that will happen. All that *must* happen. And I have seen what will happen when I try to destroy the Spellstone." He smiled. "It will kill me."

The magicians all leaped forward, fighting to speak at once. Emrys waved them quiet.

"There is nothing we can do to change it. I will strike the Spellstone – it will kill me, and shatter my sword into a thousand pieces. You will destroy every piece, so that the Spellstone can never be reopened. You will spend the next one and a half thousand years trying to hide it from the world – you will even change its appearance, to confuse anyone who tries to look for it. Quite ingenious, if I'm honest." He gave a deep sigh. "But all the plans will fail. One day, long in the future, a magician will rise who will open the Spellstone and release its powers. There is no way to stop it from happening."

The magicians were stunned. None of them had the faintest clue what to make of anything Emrys was saying … and neither did Evie. How did Emrys know all this?

"But there is one way," said Emrys quietly. "One way alone to destroy the Spellstone."

Emrys stood up again – and for a moment, Evie felt certain that he looked directly at her. It couldn't be – it was impossible. But she found herself crouching deeper inside the undergrowth all the same, her heart thundering.

Emrys unsheathed his sword and held it high above him. The magicians stepped back in surprise.

"Sir?" asked one of them. "What are you doing?"

Emrys giggled, like a child. "Planting seeds."

The magicians stared at each other, baffled. Had Emrys gone completely mad?

Then the ground began to tremble. A light was glowing in the centre of Emrys's chest, beating like a second heart. Slowly at first and then all at once, it began to spread until his entire body glowed, brighter and brighter. For a brief moment, Emrys was a figure of blinding, blistering white.

And then the magic burst up, soaring into the sky like fireworks. It was beautiful, lighting up the entire forest with its power. The magicians watched in amazement as the light flooded endlessly out of Emrys, spiralling to the stars and scattering in every direction...

And then it stopped, as quickly as it had started. The white light faded: the forest fell back to darkness. Emrys staggered backwards on unsteady legs. The light in his chest had disappeared completely.

"Sir – your magic!" cried a magician. "It's..."

"Gone," said Emrys. "I have given it away. Now I have nothing left to fight the Spellstone with. Because I *must* die – the Order *must* fail. It's the only way to destroy the Spellstone. It must all unfold exactly as planned."

The magicians stared at him in horror. "But ... why are you telling us all this?" asked one.

"Because in two seconds' time," said Emrys, "you will forget absolutely everything that I've said."

Silently, he drew his hands over the air … and the magicians' faces fell blank. With the final shreds of the little magic he had left, Emrys had wiped their minds clean. Then he turned around … and faced the exact spot where Evie was hiding.

"You understand now, Evie," he said. "I made a mistake, putting all that power in one place. Me dying is part of the only way to correct it. The Order has never known the full truth. But you do."

Evie's head was reeling. This wasn't happening – this *couldn't* be happening. Emrys kept talking.

"Sorry for keeping you in the dark," he said. "I needed the walls to bring you back at exactly the right moment." He smiled. "You've been busy. Bit close there in Vale's dream, wasn't it? I could see you needed a little help. Couldn't have Vale catching you. Not then. If he had, the plan wouldn't work."

Evie had no idea what to say – no idea where to begin. "You … I…" she stammered.

"I know it won't make much sense," said Emrys. "But it will, in time. There's only so much I can tell you now. You're part of a much wider plan, you see. A plan to destroy the Spellstone for good. And for that plan to work, I'm afraid you must figure a lot of it out on your own."

Evie finally found her voice. "I – I'm going to destroy the Spellstone?"

Emrys smiled. "No, Evie. You're going to open it."

Evie's eyes bugged out of her head. "Open it?!"

"You must," said Emrys. "It's the only way. But the others cannot know. Especially not Lady Alinora – she won't understand. I think the futility of it all would make her angry. You must not tell them that you are planning to open the Spellstone; only that you're going to destroy it. Do you understand?"

Evie swallowed. This was madness. After all this, after everything she and the Order had gone through … she was going to open the Spellstone herself? "But how am I supposed to open it? Don't I need your sword to do that?"

Emrys smiled. "You have everything you need. Just find the Spellstone. You'll know what to do when you have it."

Evie was losing her patience. "But I don't know where it is!"

"Yes you do," said Emrys. "Wainwright told you. It's in the last place he'll look."

"But where is that?" Evie almost shouted.

Emrys rolled his eyes.

"Talk about pushy," he said, a little huffily. "Well, if you *must* know: the last place you look is often right where you're already standing. Now, if you don't mind…"

He turned back to his followers. They had been standing in the clearing the whole time, blinking with confusion and swaying on their feet like toddlers. Emrys's smile reappeared, like a well-worn coat.

"So it begins," said Emrys. "Our final meeting."

The magicians nodded with relief, as if finally remembering what they were supposed to be doing. Emrys kept going.

"It has been a long road to get here. For years, the Order has travelled this land, flushing evil from wherever it hid…"

Evie realized what was happening. Emrys was replaying the entire scene, just as before, from the beginning. But this time, he wasn't going to stop himself. She watched in horror as he unsheathed his sword – as the magicians held hands in a circle around him – as he swung the sword at the Spellstone with all his might…

"No!" cried Evie.

The sound of steel on bedrock crashed through the trees like deafening cymbals. The Spellstone burst with a light of screaming intensity, so red and blinding that Evie had to shield her eyes. She could only just see the silhouette of Emrys burning between her fingers, his sword shattering into a thousand pieces as he collapsed to the ground…

And suddenly the forest split like a broken fruit around her. Evie was sent plummeting backwards again at the speed of light. The clearing disappeared, as did Emrys and the Spellstone and the magicians and the truth of all she had just seen, leaving only the fading image of a falling sorcerer scorched on the inside of her eyelids…

27
EPIPHANY

"—IE!"

Campbell's voice cut through the air. Evie hit the ground, hard. She choked out a breath. She was back in the square, sprawled across the blistering hot pavement. The city was just as she had left it: there were roads and skyscrapers where moments ago there had only been fields as far as her eyes could see. The stars were replaced by a dazzling summer sky.

Campbell carefully lowered herself from the wall and pulled Evie to her feet, dusting her off.

"You silly girl!" she chided. "Did you learn *nothing* from last night? *Never* let go of a magician's hand until you know your skill! Something terrible could have happened!"

Evie stood, dazed. Campbell didn't have a single clue about what Evie had just experienced. Less than a second had passed since she'd let go of her hand and fallen from the wall: in that instant, she had been sent backwards through time and brought back again. Everything Emrys had shown her was still in her mind, clear as freshly written ink. He had known the Spellstone would kill him. He had given away all of his magic and sacrificed himself. He had even spoken to her. It sounded like a hallucination – like she had made the whole thing up. It *was* real, wasn't it? It hadn't just been some dream?

Evie gazed down at her hands. Her palms were green with grass stains.

"Evie."

She looked up. Campbell was gazing at her intently, her face filled with worry.

"What's going on?" she asked. "Did something happen to you, when you fell?"

Evie opened her mouth to answer, and quickly closed it again. Emrys had told her that she was going to open the Spellstone in order to save the world … and she couldn't tell anyone, not even the Order. She had no idea why it was a secret, but she knew that it had to stay that way. "I'm fine. I just hit my head when I fell."

Campbell tutted and hugged her close. "Poor girl! Come – let's get back to the hideout and tell the others what we have learned." She sucked at her teeth. "Things are even more dire than we feared. The magic inside the Spellstone looks ready to erupt. If we don't find out where Wainwright hid it soon…"

It happened fast. A bus swerved on the road beside her; a flock of pigeons burst from the ground; Evie spun around to shield herself, looking up as the birds flew past…

And saw the skyscraper towering above them. Tower 99 – Vale's fortress. The tallest building in the city, twisting to a single point as if trying to slit open the sky. A bead of sunlight hit the highest window, where all the building's lines converged.

It's safe – the last place he'll look.

Evie let her gaze fall, following the building down to the ground. It all came to her in one go. The answer had been there all along, right in front of her, hiding in plain sight.

"The last place you look," she murmured to herself, "is often right where you're already standing."

Campbell stared at her in confusion. "Evie? What was that?"

Evie knew, immediately, what she had to do. She marched across the square, leaving Campbell behind her. For the first time that day, the old lady had to scurry to keep up with her. "Where are you going? Come back, girl!"

"We have to get back to the hideout," said Evie. "Right now."

"Why?" said Campbell. "What's the hurry?"

"Because," said Evie, "I know where the Spellstone is."

28
THE PLAN

THE MAGICIANS SAT IN THEIR ARMCHAIRS BESIDE THE fireplace, staring at Evie in stunned silence. Lady Alinora shook her head.

"Impossible," she said. "Wainwright would *never* have dared to hide the Spellstone there."

"Yes, he would," said Campbell gravely. "It's *exactly* what he would do."

"Let me get this right." Onslow could barely bring himself to say it. "You're telling me that the most powerful magical weapon in history – the very thing that we've been trying to keep away from Vale for forty years – is currently located in … *Tower 99*? Wainwright hid it in Vale's own fortress?!"

Evie nodded. "Think about it. Vale built Tower 99 so he can watch over the whole city … but that means there's one place he can't see. The place he's standing. He'd never expect Wainwright to take the most precious thing in the world and hide it right under his feet. The last place he'll look." She turned to Rish. "Do you remember that dream we ended up in – the one with the security guard?"

Rish furrowed his brow. "That guy with all the gold?"

Evie nodded. "I couldn't work out why we ended up there. But then I remembered – the triangle logo on his uniform. It wasn't a triangle: it's Tower 99. That's where he works. The vault he guards must be the one inside the skyscraper. And that's why he was holding—"

"A brick?" said Rish, still confused.

Evie shook her head. "Not a brick – the Spellstone. That's what it looks like now. The Order changed how it looked so it was easier to hide. And *that's* how we ended up in the security guard's dream. I wanted to know where the Spellstone was, so we were taken right to it. We just didn't realize what we were looking at." She smiled. "Wainwright even told me where it was, when he spoke to me about the Spellstone. I thought he said, 'it's safe – the last place he'll look' – but he didn't. He said, '*his* safe' – *Vale's* safe. The answer was right there, staring at us all along."

The Order of the Stone were flabbergasted. It was still too much to take in.

"But … *how*?" said Alinora. "How would Wainwright get inside the vault? How would he even get *inside* the skyscraper, without Vale's smoke-men seeing him?"

Evie sighed. "Well … it wouldn't have been easy. But I think I know how he started."

She strode out of the drawing room. The others quickly

followed her. Evie smiled – she was quite enjoying feeling in charge for a change. She made her way to the infinite library and stood before the towering shelves.

"I need a map of the city drains," she said. "All the manholes and tunnels, and where they lead." She paused, and then added, "Please."

There was a gentle *puff* as a rolled-up map, the size of a rug, was spat out of a shelf. Evie caught it and unrolled it across the floor.

"Wainwright used the sewers," she said. "He must have planned it for weeks beforehand, searching for a manhole that led into Tower 99. But it meant that when he needed to, he could quickly move the Spellstone, while Vale's smoke-men were still searching the streets." She glanced at Lady Alinora. "Remember that chamber – the point where the token was glowing the reddest? We *were* close – but not in the way we expected."

Lady Alinora frowned, her whiskers twitching. "What do you mean?"

"The vault of Tower 99 must be underground," said Evie. "The Spellstone was just a few metres away, on the other side of a wall. That's why the glow kept fading whenever we walked away from the chamber."

Onslow put his head in his hands. "Well, we're doomed! If it's right under Vale's feet, it's only a matter of time before he finds it…"

"He's not going to find it," said Evie. "We're going to

break into Tower 99 and get it ourselves. And we're going to do it tonight."

The magicians stared at her in shock. She knew that, at any moment, they were all going to start shouting over each other, so she spoke quickly.

"We'll do what Wainwright did. We'll use the sewers to find a way into Tower 99. With Alinora in rat form, she can sneak ahead and check the coast is clear. Once we're inside, we can use the token to track the Spellstone and find the vault. Wainwright must have used his shadow to slip beneath the vault doors – but Campbell can get us through any door in seconds." She swallowed. Now for the most important part of all. The part that Emrys had told her to say. "But we're not going to hide it again when we find it. We're going to destroy it, once and for all."

The magicians were speechless. Evie kept going, before she lost them completely.

"No matter where we move the Spellstone, Vale will always catch up with us. And that's not the worst of it. Campbell – you saw the Spellstone today. The power inside it is stronger than ever. We're running out of time before it breaks free."

Campbell nodded reluctantly. "She is right. I saw it with my own eyes."

"But *how* can we destroy the Spellstone?" cried Onslow. "It was powerful enough to defeat the might of Emrys!"

"With me," said Evie quietly. "I think that's my power.

That's why I'm here. I think I've been put here to destroy the Spellstone."

"She's right," said Rish breathlessly. "I *felt* Evie's powers when she dragged us into Vale's dream. I've never felt anything like it in my life. She's the real deal."

Evie smiled. She couldn't tell the magicians the real truth – that Emrys had told her to open the Spellstone, not destroy it. She still didn't know *how* she was going to open it, let alone why – but she was grateful for Rish at that moment. It felt good to have someone who believed in her.

"But she doesn't even have her skill…" said Alinora weakly.

"I think there's a reason for that," said Evie. "I think I have to be standing in front of the Spellstone for my power to come alive. Maybe that was Wainwright's plan all along – why he hid it in Vale's fortress. When I destroy the Spellstone, it'll somehow destroy Vale too."

That much was true, at least – Emrys himself had said that when the time was right, Evie would know what to do. If anyone but Emrys had said it, she would never have had the courage to believe it was possible. And with that confidence, she could feel the tide in the room beginning to turn – Campbell and Lady Alinora were slowly coming round to the idea.

"I mean it," said Evie. "This is what it's all been leading up to. We're the Order of the Stone, aren't we? We have to do whatever it takes to protect the world from evil – and this is it! Our chance to defeat Vale and…

"*How?!*"

They turned around. Onslow was staring at her, petrified. "Vale has hunted down every member of the Order for the last forty years," he said. "The greatest magicians of their age have tried, and failed, to defeat him. His powers are inconceivable. You want us to fight him with … *this?*" *Ping.* A glass of water appeared in his hand. "*It's suicide!* We can't possibly do it!"

The magicians looked back at her, frightened and unsure. Evie knew what they needed now – they needed a leader.

"I don't know much about magic," she said. "But I know what I see in front of me." She turned to Lady Alinora, crouched on the floor in rat form. "Alinora – you try to put on a cold front to fool people, but we all know the truth. You'd give your life to save another member of the Order. There's no one here as loyal as you."

She turned to Rish.

"Rish – you think you're a coward, but you're not. You're one of the bravest people I've ever met. It takes guts to do what you do. Your mother would be proud."

She turned to Campbell.

"Campbell – you're unstoppable. *No one* can tell you what to do, if you don't want to do it. Wainwright could see that, and so can I."

Finally, she turned to Onslow, still holding his glass of water.

"And Onslow – you care so, so much. You look after everyone. And that matters. The Order would be nothing without you."

She took their hands.

"Don't you see? You're more than your skills. The Order of the Stone was *never* about what one magician could achieve: it was about what they could do together, as a group. And that's exactly what Vale doesn't have. Together, we're more powerful than he can ever be." She smiled. "That's how we'll beat him – together. We'll break inside his fortress, together. We'll find the Spellstone, together. And together ... we'll destroy it, for ever."

It was working. Evie could feel the excitement building between them, surging between their joined hands ... and all of a sudden, it was as if there were more than five of them in the room. It felt like they were surrounded by magicians – all the members of the Order who had devoted their lives to the cause over the centuries: Wainwright and Patel and Banda and O'Brien and hundreds more besides. They were all standing with them now, willing them on, pushing them to finish the quest.

"We'll attack at dawn," said Alinora. "When Vale least expects it. For Wainwright."

"For my mother," said Rish.

"For the world," said Campbell.

Evie smiled. She was doing it for all those reasons, and more. She thought of Mum and Dad, and the life that she longed to return to. If she didn't somehow destroy the Spellstone and stop Vale, there would be nothing to go back to. There was only one way home now.

"Let's get to work," said Evie.

29
AN ADVANTAGE

A T THAT EXACT MOMENT, VALE WAS WALKING through the city streets.

He didn't come down here very often. He hated the world at ground level: the crowds, the dirt, the stink of the people. He avoided leaving his office whenever he could.

But today was a special occasion.

He walked against the flow of the crowd, watching as their eyes slipped thoughtlessly over him. No one gave him a second glance: none of them knew, or cared, that the most powerful magician in the world was in their midst. Everyone was too busy being horrible to each other. It had been another long, hot day – the hottest on record, in fact – and the city had become a cauldron. Wherever Vale turned his head, people were losing their tempers. There were couples arguing, strangers shouting at one another, people shoving each other to get on buses. A homeless woman lay slumped with heat exhaustion on a street corner, begging weakly for help, and people just walked past her.

Vale smiled. There were thousands of small acts of cruelty like this in the city. They happened so often that no one even noticed them.

But Vale did. After all, they were the secret to his power.

He closed his eyes, and drew deep. When he opened them again, the city was transformed. The streets were filled with a burning red mist – every unkind thought, every word said in anger, every selfish, thoughtless act, sent a puff of it into the atmosphere, drifting up to the clouds like smoke. It came from everywhere, all at once, all the time… And there was more of it coming every second.

It had taken Vale years to discover it. For a long time, he thought he could only steal magic from a magician. Then one day, just by chance, he discovered that there was magic in the air itself. Not good magic: *bad* magic. Every time a person did something bad, a tiny amount was released into the atmosphere. Times that by a city of ten million people and you had a constant output of magic, every single day. Once Vale had learned how to absorb it, he was unstoppable. His powers had grown and grown. And it was all thanks to the badness of people.

He turned off the main road and onto the bridge that crossed the canal. Perhaps, he thought, *that* was why he never really belonged to the Order of the Stone. Protecting *people* had always made him feel sick. He hated people: people were thoughtless, uncaring, cruel. They treated one another so badly – they treated their planet so badly. Emrys had devoted his life to them – sacrificed himself for them – and they had proved themselves to be such unworthy children.

Vale would not make the same mistake that Emrys had. When Vale finally had his hands on the Spellstone, he would not waste its power on people. He would make them bow down to him, of course.

But then...

He was getting ahead of himself. He didn't have the Spellstone yet. He didn't even know where Evie was.

For now, it was time to take an advantage.

He turned onto a residential street, shrugging on a black jacket. Perhaps, he thought, as he did up the buttons, *that* was the reason he had reached greater heights than any magician before him. He had never needed people, and that meant he had no one to hold him back. While the Order had been trying to protect each other, Vale had been focused on nothing but the Spellstone. It didn't matter if he hurt anyone along the way, because there was no one he cared about hurting.

That was the thing with people, thought Vale, as he pushed open the garden gate and strolled up to the green front door: they made you weak. That's right, he thought, as he pushed the doorbell – love made you weak.

He placed the police helmet on his head just as a woman opened the door. Vale recognized her from the missing person's report. Her eyes were red from crying: she clearly hadn't slept properly in days. It took her several moments to register that Vale was standing there, and then her face broke open with relief.

"Officer – is there any news?" asked Evie's mother. "Have you found Evie?"

Vale smiled.

"Not yet, madam," he said. "But I suspect we will, very soon. Mind if I come in for a moment?"

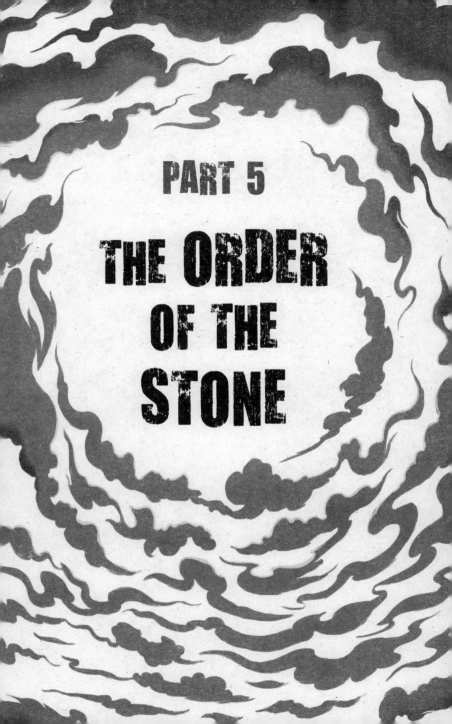

30
TOWER 99

"THIS IS IT."

The Order stood huddled in the darkness of the sewers. The chamber was exactly as Evie remembered it: the pillars, the shadowed corners, the tunnels leading to different parts of the city. It was almost dawn, and the river had been reduced to a steady trickle. The only sound was the echo of their breath against the walls and the steady *drip, drip* of water around them.

"So, what now?" asked Rish, his voice hushed in the dark.

Evie held out the glowing token. "We need to work out where Wainwright went next…"

Once again, the token had glowed steadily redder the further they went down the tunnel … and once again, it had reached a deep pink when they came to the chamber. Its gleam beat off the slick walls as Evie turned around, searching for what she and Alinora had missed the first time…

And there it was. On the furthest wall stood a set of

metal rungs, leading up to a concealed manhole in the ceiling. It was no surprise that Evie hadn't noticed it the first time around: both were so covered in grime that they were practically camouflaged. "Onslow?"

Onslow flicked on his headtorch and scrutinized the giant map of the sewers, which he'd folded into awkward sections. "It checks out. According to this, we're right beneath Tower 99. That manhole must open directly into the skyscraper's compound."

Evie's heart skipped a beat. "Then it's where Wainwright went next. If we follow his footsteps, we'll find the Spellstone." She turned to the others. "You all remember the plan?"

The magicians nodded fearfully. Despite Evie's speech earlier that evening, they still looked apprehensive about what lay ahead. And Evie could hardly blame them – after all, they were about to step into the unknown. She reached out her hands, and the five of them joined in a circle once more.

"Remember – we're not hiding any more," she said. "We're fighting back. So long as we have each other, we have everything we need to stop Vale and destroy the Spellstone."

Evie swallowed. She still wasn't certain *how* they were going to find the Spellstone, let alone achieve her final, secret mission and open it... But Emrys's words still rang in her ears.

Just find the Spellstone. You'll know what to do when you have it.

Onslow took a final breath to steady his nerves, and saluted. "Right – good luck, everyone!"

He scurried back down the sewer alone, the light of his headtorch dancing away in the darkness. Evie pocketed the token and climbed the ladder, pausing at the top so Lady Alinora could jump off her shoulder and release the catch. Together, they heaved open the manhole.

There it was – Tower 99, soaring like a sleek mountain of glass above them. It was still dark out: the stars were reflected in its windows a thousand times over, until the building seemed part of the sky itself. For a moment, Evie's courage failed her. At the very top of the skyscraper, she could see a single lit window, gleaming like the eye of a monster god. Vale was in his office – always watching, always waiting. Were they *really* about to break inside his fortress?

But she held her nerve. If she wanted to save the world – if she wanted to go back home – then there was no turning back. She carefully raised her head above the pavement and peered outside. The skyscraper's forecourt was dark and empty. There were no passers-by, no police, no smoke-men. The great glass entrance doors were clearly closed and locked up ahead. Where had Wainwright gone next?

"There!" hissed Alinora in her ear.

She pointed across the forecourt. Sure enough, at

the base of the skyscraper was a small service doorway, illuminated beneath a single spotlight. Alinora leaped from Evie's shoulder and scurried towards it. Evie and the others immediately followed, closing the manhole behind them and hiding beside a marble pillar at the skyscraper's base.

Evie glanced around the pillar's edge. There was a keypad beside the doorway, marked by a blinking red light. The sign above read WARNING: AUTHORIZED PERSONNEL ONLY.

"It must be alarmed," Evie whispered. "Wainwright probably slipped his shadow beneath the door to get inside…"

"*Cha!* Leave it to me," said Campbell, hobbling towards the door. "I'll get us through there in—"

Evie stopped her just in time. "No! You'll *still* set off the alarms if you walk through it – Vale will know we're here!" She felt a wave of panic. She had assumed that getting *inside* Tower 99 would be the easy part – now she realized how naive she had been. There was no way of getting past the doors without setting off the alarms and bringing every smoke-man in the city flying towards them. She gazed at the keypad beside the door.

"There must be some kind of code to get inside," she said. "A secret number – something that's important to Vale. We'll just have to work out what it is." She swallowed. "It's not going to be easy – it could take hours. But if we put our heads together, I'm sure we can—"

"Ahem."

They turned around. Rish had his hand up.

"I believe that I may be of service," he said grandly.

He pointed through the glass entrance. They could see a small lit booth at the end of a corridor. A man was sitting behind a desk inside it. Evie recognized him at once: it was the security guard from the dream they had entered the night before. He was back on duty.

And once again, he was fast asleep.

31

THE VAULT

THE MAGICIANS STOOD WAITING WHILE RISH LEANED against the pillar, his eyes closed and his lips faintly murmuring. Finally, his eyes snapped open. "Got it!"

He ran to the security panel and punched in a code. The red light immediately switched to a steady white and the door hissed open.

Evie gasped. "Rish, you genius! How did you do it?"

Rish grinned. "I told the security guard that I was his spirit guide, and that he should quit his job and follow his rap career. But in return, he had to tell me what the door code was."

Evie couldn't believe their luck. "Come on, let's go!"

They flew through the door and past the security booth, where the guard was still fast asleep – now with a faint smile on his lips.

The skyscraper was silent and empty around them, and their footsteps sounded impossibly loud. The walls were lined with polished black obsidian, reflecting endlessly back into itself: from every side, Evie saw dark versions of herself and the magicians racing towards each other as they made their way into the heart of Tower 99. They finally came to a central room, surrounded by lifts and stairwells that spiralled off in different directions.

"How do we know which way leads to the vault?" asked Campbell.

Evie knew exactly what to do. She walked to the centre of the room, where all the lifts and stairwells converged, and pulled out the token. "Show me magic, please."

The token glowed into life once more … but this time, the light it gave off was even more red, a scarlet glare that rippled off the darkening walls and cast shadows across the faces of the magicians. Evie turned to every side, waiting for the moment when the token's glow changed … and sure enough, just as she turned to an unmarked stairwell, the glowing light was darkened by a single drop of blood.

"The vault must be down there," said Evie. "Come on!"

They raced down the stairs. Evie led the way, her heart pounding as she followed the labyrinth of corridors beneath Tower 99, twisting deeper and deeper into the dark bowels of the building … until at last, they came to a final set of glass doors. Through them, Evie could see a thick metal entranceway at the end of a long corridor. The token in her hand blazed brighter than ever. She could even *feel* it pulling at her hand, dragging her towards the door like a magnet.

"That must be the vault," she whispered. "We're almost there! We just have to…"

She trailed off. She had just seen what lay between them and the vault doors. The long corridor wasn't empty: it was criss-crossed with a tight net of red lasers. The walls were lined with security cameras. The glass door in front of her was surrounded by a series of complicated locks and keypads.

Evie's heart sank. Wainwright's shadow could have got past all of these obstacles without setting off the alarms – but *they* couldn't. The Spellstone was right in front of them, but it might as well have been a million miles away. There was no way that the four of them could ever reach the vault.

Unless…

"Come on, Onslow," she whispered. "We're counting on you now…"

Half a mile away, an electrician was pulling his van up beside the road. He had one circuit box left to check, and then his night shift was over. It was a simple, routine job – just checking the wires for wear and tear – but it was still important. A malfunction in a circuit box like *this* could wipe out the power to half the city.

He stepped out of the van, and froze. Someone was crouched on the pavement and rummaging inside the circuit box. It was the strangest thing – the electrician almost hadn't noticed them at first. Which was weird, considering they were wearing a three-piece suit.

"Oi!" the electrician shouted. "What the hell are you doing?"

The person at the circuit box glanced over his shoulder. It was a pale, scrawny man.

"Can I help you?" he replied, in a steady voice.

The electrician marched towards him. "For a start, you can get away from that circuit box, mate. There's a fine for that!"

But the pale man didn't seem concerned at all. He slowly got to his feet and faced the electrician. "You seem a little stressed. How about … a drink?"

Ping – a glass of water appeared in his hand out of nowhere.

The electrician blinked. "How'd you do that?"

"Confused?" said the man. "Perhaps some … *hydration* would help?"

Ping – another glass of water appeared in his other hand.

"Not thirsty?" asked the man innocently. "How unfortunate! And here I am, with two full glasses. I suppose I'd better just … *throw them away!*"

The electrician's eyes widened. The glasses were

dangerously near the circuit box. "Careful now, if you get those wires wet…"

But the man wasn't listening. "You know – some people would describe these glasses as half-full. Others would describe them as half-empty. I would describe them as … *your worst nightmare!*"

He spun around and threw the glasses of water into the circuit box. The wires inside exploded in a clap of sparks. One by one, the streetlights around them shut off: first their street, then the next one, and then whole sections of the city at a time, stretching right to the base of Tower 99…

And in the skyscraper's basement, all the lights in the corridor shut off at once. The red lasers snapped away; the cameras froze in place. The glass security door hissed open. Evie yelped with delight. "He did it!"

"Quick!" Alinora cried. "We have to get to the vault before the back-up generators come on!"

The magicians tore down the corridor as fast as they could. The red glow of the token burned brighter and brighter as the entrance to the vault drew closer, leading them, step by step, to the final resting place of the Spellstone…

They threw themselves against the vault doors just in

time. The lights in the corridor slammed back on; the lasers began tracing the floor mere centimetres from their feet. Evie could have cried for joy. They had made it, against all the odds. Now, just a single door separated them from the Spellstone. It would take a master-thief *hours* to break inside … but they had no need for that. "Are you ready, Campbell?"

Campbell smiled, and reached out her hands. The last step was the easiest one of all. They simply had to join hands and step through the metal door together. The Spellstone would be waiting for them inside. Then Evie could begin her final challenge: finding a way to summon the magic inside herself and…

Her thoughts were sliced in two by a wailing security alarm. Evie jumped. The corridor was flashing black and red around them. What was happening?

"Smoke-men!" cried Rish.

Evie's insides shrivelled with terror. Black smoke was pouring through the air-conditioning grates at the other end of the corridor and twisting into the shapes of men. Within seconds, there were dozens flying towards them as fast as they could. Evie realized what must have happened. The security guard had finally woken up and seen them, or Vale had somehow worked out what they were up to. Either way, smoke-men were now flooding into the basement to stop them. They'd been caught. There was nowhere to hide from them, nowhere to run.

"We have to get inside the vault!" Evie cried. "It's our only hope!"

Campbell shook her head. "Doors won't hold back smoke, girl – hang on!"

She pressed her hands to the nearest wall, screwing her eyes shut. "Help us – please, help us now!"

The corridor rumbled … then, to Evie's amazement, the walls began to tighten in front of her very eyes. Wires burst and sparks rained down from the ceiling as the walls shrank smaller and smaller, until the corridor was barely the width of the eye of a needle. The smoke-men were brought to a shuddering stop … but not for long. Within moments, they had returned to smoke and were pouring through the hole like water.

"It's not working!" Evie cried. "If we hide inside the vault, maybe we can…"

"No."

Lady Alinora leaped from Evie's shoulder and stood in the corridor. The rat faced the cloud of black smoke that was already twisting itself back into the shapes of men before her.

"No more hiding," she said. "No more running."

Evie understood what was about to happen. "No! Alinora, you'll never be able to…"

But it was too late. Lady Alinora was already changing. Every part of her swelled and stretched: for a flash of a moment, Evie even caught a glimpse of a floating human form, her arms outstretched and her eyes closed in focus as she transformed in a blazing ball of white light…

And then a vast and hulking shape stood before them, filling the corridor and stretching from wall to wall. It was a twelve-foot-high bear, its weight cracking the floor and its shoulders bristling against the ceiling panels. The smoke-men drew to a stunned stop before it. Evie was almost speechless.

"But… I thought you'd already been a bear," she said, confused.

Lady Alinora glanced over her shoulder, her blue and yellow eyes sparkling. "That was a grizzly bear. Now I'm a Kodiak bear."

Evie blinked. "What's the difference?"

"One's bigger," growled Alinora, and flung herself at the smoke-men.

Her strength was unbelievable: with a single swipe of her paw she tore through five of them at once, then brought her whole body crashing down on twelve more, bursting them into black vapour. But even so, it wasn't enough. More and more smoke was pouring through the corridor every second: it was like trying to hold back a river.

"*Evie!*"

Campbell was calling out to her, her hands still pressed to the corridor walls. "You and Rish have to get inside the vault! Alinora and I will hold them back for as long as we can!"

Evie shook her head. "No – we won't leave you here!"

Campbell looked directly at her – then let go of the wall, snatching hold of Rish's and Evie's wrists. Evie looked up. "Campbell?"

Campbell wasn't frightened at all. Her face was incredibly calm. "Just because no one knows about the sacrifice," she said, "it does not make it worthless."

She moved fast. Before Evie could understand what was happening, Campbell swung Evie and Rish against the vault door. The last thing Evie saw before they passed through the thick sheet of metal and disappeared into the darkness was Lady Alinora as she fought and fought against the smoke filling the corridor…

Campbell let go, and Evie and Rish tumbled to the vault floor. Evie sat up.

"Campbell…!"

But it was too late. Campbell's hand was already passing back through the door, like an arm slowly lowering into a lake. The metal was sealing itself around her wrist, and then her fingers, and finally her fingertips, until Evie and Rish were left in the darkness of the vault alone.

32
THE SPELLSTONE

EVIE STARED AT THE LOCKED VAULT DOOR, HER HEART pounding. Through the metal, she could still make out the screaming alarms, the howl of Alinora as she tore through the smoke-men, the creaking of the corridor walls as Campbell returned to the fight. The realization hit her like a sudden shock of water: Campbell and Alinora were sacrificing themselves. They were staying behind, to buy Evie enough time to find the Spellstone. She scrambled to her feet and pounded her fists against the door, but it was no use – they were trapped.

"We have to help them!" Evie cried. "We have to find a way out!"

She turned to Rish … but he was shaking his head. His eyes were red with tears.

"Evie – we might only have a few seconds," he said. "We have to find the Spellstone."

"But…"

He grabbed her hand. "We need to make it count. Or they did it all for nothing."

Evie's heart was breaking, but Rish was right. This was what generations of magicians had devoted their lives to: what Rish's own mother had died for. He and Evie were all that was left of the Order of the Stone: the fate of the world now rested on what the two of them could achieve in this small pocket of time. Evie felt a shudder of recognition. Was *that* what Emrys had meant, when he'd said that the Order had to fail for the Spellstone to be destroyed?

She forced away her tears and turned to the vault. It was just as she remembered from the dream: the stacks of shelves, the strip lighting, the gold bars. Somewhere in here was the most dangerous weapon ever created. Evie pulled the token from her pocket and held it out.

"Sh-show me magic," she whispered.

The burst of blood-red light now blazed brighter than ever, lighting the walls of the vault like a demon forge. Evie felt it at once: the pull of the token, drawing her forward like a magnet, longing to be reunited with the Spellstone. She let it lead her, step by step, towards a shelf at the far end of the vault. Like all the others, this one was stacked with gold bars ... but Evie could see something hidden inside them, burning with a fierce red glow between the cracks.

She gasped. It was the Spellstone, hidden inside a stack of gold bars. It was trembling with power, rattling inside its golden prison like chimes.

"Help me get it out – quick!" said Evie.

They moved as fast as they could, heaving the heavy gold bars from the pile and stacking them on the floor. The glow of the Spellstone grew closer, until finally the last bar was unearthed and a grim radiance filled the vault. There it was: the fabled Spellstone. Its surface was like a rippling chasm of blood, bright as a burning cinder. Evie could *feel* the sick power beating from it: all of the violence and malevolence compacted in its tiny size, clamouring to escape after centuries of imprisonment.

She put away the token, and the red glow of the Spellstone faded at once. With shaking hands, she lifted it from the gold bars and held it before her. Now it looked like a simple brick, weathered and pock-marked and worn. Its only defining feature was a single crack along the top, the length and width of a matchstick. But Evie could still *feel* the evil magic inside it, bridling against the surface of her palms, hot as iron and yet freezing cold to the touch. It was like holding a coil of snakes. Was she *really* about to open it? What if the Spellstone killed her when she tried, just like it had killed Emrys? She wanted to fling it to the ground and run from it as fast as she could…

And yet another part of her – a dark and secret part – never wanted to put the Spellstone down. She wanted to keep it all to herself and not let it go, ever again. She understood, at once, why Vale craved it so much: the evil power pressed between her palms was intoxicating, mind-blowing. She felt like the voices of a thousand dark creatures were whispering to her all at once inside her head, begging *let us out, let us out...*

"Evie?" said Rish. "Do you know what to do?"

She snapped awake. She couldn't wait a moment longer. She had to do what Emrys had sent her here to do and open the Spellstone. She had no idea what was going to happen when she did – she had no idea how it was even possible. She had no sword; she had no powers.

But Emrys's words repeated in her head, over and over. *You have everything you need. Just find the Spellstone. You'll know what to do when you have it.*

It was all down to Evie now. She closed her eyes and reached deep inside herself, asking the question that she felt she had been asking her whole life...

Why am I here?

The Spellstone swarmed with evil power in her hands. Evie sought inside herself, but nothing happened. There was no answer to her call, no sudden burst of magic, no miraculous understanding of her powers. Dread bubbled up from the soles of her feet. She had the Spellstone right in her hands, but she still had no idea how to get inside.

"Evie, they're coming," Rish whimpered behind her.

He was right: the sounds of the fight were getting louder outside the vault, more urgent. They were running out of time. Evie clutched the Spellstone in her grip, digging deeper than ever before.

What is it? What can I do? Why am I here?!

And to her surprise, an answer appeared in her head, loud and clear as a bell.

If I told you that now, Evie, then the plan wouldn't work.

Evie recognized the voice. She opened her eyes – and found, to her surprise, that she wasn't standing in the vault any more.

She was back in the forest clearing. It was all exactly as she had left it, one and a half thousand years ago: the cluster of trees, the night sky, the moan of a gathering wind. Emrys stood alone before her, gazing at her with a mixture of sorrow and pride.

"You've done well, Evie," he said kindly. "You're almost there. But I'm afraid it's not over yet. Just remember, when the time comes ... the last place he'll look."

Evie stared at him with confusion. "But I found the Spellstone already. It's right here."

Emrys shook his head sadly. "I'm not talking about the Spellstone, Evie. You're looking in the wrong place."

Evie didn't understand. "What do you mean? What am I *looking* for?"

"Well, well," said a voice behind her. "This is certainly a surprise, isn't it?"

Evie snapped around. The forest was gone: she was back in the vault again. But the metal door was no longer closed. An army of smoke-men filled the open entrance, blocking any hope of escape.

And floating above them...

Evie gasped. Campbell and Lady Alinora hung frozen in mid-air, their mouths sewn shut by magic. And they weren't the only ones: there was Onslow, both his arms and legs paralysed. And floating through the air to join them…

Mum and Dad. They were frozen in place, too, staring at Evie in terror. Evie had never seen them look so frightened before, so helpless. And directly beneath them was the man who'd caught them, a loveless smile gleaming in his hateful eyes.

"You have no idea," said Vale, "how long I've been waiting for this."

33
REVELATION

Evie stood, rooted to the spot in horror. There he was – the real Vale – finally standing before her. He'd caught her; he'd caught the magicians; he'd even caught her parents. How had he managed it?

"You've got guts, I'll give you that," said Vale. "To break into the heart of my own fortress! If you hadn't left all the paperwork lying around that mansion, I never would have credited it…"

Evie gasped. Vale's eyes thinned with sadistic pleasure.

"That's right," he whispered. "I found the hideout. And it was all thanks to you, Evie." He held out a hand to her parents, floating above him. "Your mother told me all about her dream – everything you said about being close by, on the canal. And it made complete sense. *That's* where the Order had been hiding, all along! I'd never even thought to look for a narrow boat." He smiled. "It's all gone now, of course. I burned it down. There aren't even ashes left…"

"Aaaargh!"

Rish threw himself at Vale, arms flailing. He caught the magician by surprise, striking him directly in the face.

"*That* was for my mother," Rish spat. "And *this* is for Wainwright!"

He landed another punch, hitting Vale straight on the chin. It was a brave, hopeless thing to do – and it was nowhere near enough. Vale's eyes snapped open in recognition.

"The dream boy – I knew I recognized your face!" he said. "*Patel's* son! Your mother was an exceptional magician, boy; you certainly have her spirit…"

Rish bellowed with rage and swung another punch – but this one froze in mid-air. A strangled cry escaped his throat. Vale twisted his fingers, and Rish was lifted from the floor and sent to float beside the others.

"*No!*" Evie cried. "Stop it!"

Vale turned to her – and then his eyes fell to the Spellstone in her hands. His mouth dropped open in disbelief. "No – surely not. It can't be…"

Before Evie could think to react, he shot out a hand and the Spellstone flew from her grip. It sailed across the room and Vale caught it. His eyes lit up with triumph.

"I – I don't believe it," he gasped. "It's mine, it's finally mine! You brought it right to me, girl!"

Evie filled with despair. So that was it – after one and a half thousand years, after all the searching and all the fighting, it was over. The Order of the Stone had finally been defeated. The Spellstone was in Vale's hands. Evie had failed.

"Please," she begged, blinking away tears. "Please, don't do it…"

Vale didn't hear her at first. He was too busy staring at the Spellstone, his eyes gleaming with solitary pleasure. Then he glanced up, as if he had only just heard her over beautiful strains of music. "No time to lose. Come with me."

He strolled out of the vault and gave a simple flick of his fingers behind him. Evie cried out – it was as if frozen ropes had been lashed around her, turning her limbs to stone. Suddenly she was being dragged behind Vale like a dog on a leash. He gave another flick of his fingers, and the vault doors silently closed behind them. Evie took a final, desperate look over her shoulder. The magicians and her parents were slowly lowering to the vault floor, their bodies still frozen stiff as the door sealed shut. Evie was on her own now.

But her resolve burned like a furnace inside her. She was the last member of the Order of the Stone. She was its leader. Emrys had given her one instruction: to open the Spellstone herself.

You have to get it off him. You can't let him win.

Vale led her down the remnants of the shattered corridor until he came to a small glass lift. He stepped inside and drew Evie in beside him; the doors dinged shut, and the lift smoothly raised them through the body of the skyscraper. Vale hummed merrily under his breath, as if they were in a normal lift on a normal day.

Evie thought fast. She understood where Vale was taking her: to his office at the top of Tower 99. She had no idea what he had planned for her when they got there. She had no idea how to stop him. She knew that there was no way the magicians would be able to break free from his spell and escape. From now on, it was all down to her.

"Whatever you want from me, you won't get it," she said calmly. "I swore an oath to protect the people of this planet. An oath that you broke. I will never help you."

Vale seemed amused. "*Help?* Why would I need your help, Evie?"

The lift came out of the ground, and the city suddenly swung into view. A glow was beginning to appear on the horizon: sunlight was bleeding between the buildings. In just a few hours, the city would be awake.

"Do you know how many people live in this city, Evie?" Vale asked.

Evie was thrown – what a strange thing to say, at a time like this. Vale kept going.

"Ten million. And every single time one of them does something bad … a tiny bit of evil goes into the air. Isn't that amazing? It's not much, granted, but multiply that tiny piece of evil by ten *thousand* thousand…" He held out his hands to the city sinking beneath them. "It's unstoppable. And I'm going to let you in on a little secret, Evie. I've been absorbing that evil for years. It's how I've managed to become so powerful. And it's all thanks to the badness of people." He smiled. "Almost makes you wonder if they were worth all that sacrifice, doesn't it?"

Evie swallowed. She had to keep Vale talking. The more distracted he was, the greater chance she had of somehow getting the Spellstone back before they reached his office. "Just because no one knows about the sacrifice, it doesn't make it worthless."

Vale laughed. "I couldn't disagree more. What about the sacrifice Emrys made? He *could* have used his power to rule the world. Instead, he gave it all away."

The top of the skyscraper was getting closer. The relentless climb of the lift was sending everything to Evie's stomach. She was running out of time. "Having the power to do something doesn't give you permission to do it."

"And this is better?" said Vale. "Look outside. Emrys gave the world to people … and see what they did with it."

He gestured to the city, sprawled in a grey waste before them. A haze of pollution hung in the air. The river looked like a dirty shoelace trampled into mud.

"One and a half thousand years of pain and misery," said Vale. "A whole planet, brought to its knees."

The lift suddenly ground to a halt and the doors flew open. There was Vale's office, exactly as Evie remembered it: the grey carpets, the grey desk, the ceiling that rose to a spike. Vale strolled towards the window, dragging Evie helplessly along the floor after him. She held her nerve. This was it – her last chance to stop him. She had to find some way of breaking free of his spell and opening the Spellstone, before he could absorb its powers. "And what makes you think *you'll* do any better, when you rule the world?"

Vale glanced at her with interest. "*Rule the world?* What an idea. You've been listening to too many stories, Evie."

Evie was thrown. "But ... I saw your dream. All those people, bowing down to you."

Vale gazed out across the city with a distant expression. "Oh, they'll bow down to me, all right. I'll make sure that the world finally recognizes me for what I am." He smiled. "But I'm not going to use the power of the Spellstone to rule the world, Evie. Oh no."

Evie swallowed. Something dreadful was building, and she didn't know what it was. "Wh-what do you mean?"

Vale kept his gaze fixed over the city.

"Emrys thought that he could save the world by defeating the creatures of darkness," he explained. "But he had it all wrong. It's *people*, Evie. They're the ones he should have been defeating. They're the monsters." He placed the Spellstone on the desk. "So, I'm going to use the Spellstone for what it should always have been used for. I'm going to take its powers, and use them to wipe humanity from the face of the earth."

He turned to Evie and smiled.

"And *you*, Evie, are going to watch me do it."

Evie stared at him, aghast. It felt as if a hundred floors of sand were crumbling beneath her.

"You can't be serious," she said weakly. "All those people…"

"I'm being perfectly serious, Evie," said Vale. "People have been given every chance, and they've failed every single time. It's time we started over."

He faced the window in reverence. This was it: the moment that he absorbed the Spellstone's powers for himself. Evie's last chance to save humanity was disappearing, right in front of her eyes. She had to stop him: she had to keep fighting. She fought and fought against the invisible ropes binding her with all her might…

But it was hopeless. The chance was gone. Vale placed his hands on the surface of the Spellstone and focused his powers.

"Open to me," he whispered. "I command you."

Nothing happened. Vale frowned. He gritted his teeth, and doubled his efforts.

"Open to me!" he repeated.

But it was no use. Vale couldn't get inside it any more than Evie could. She felt a burst of hope – this was her chance to get Vale to release her. "Wait!" she cried.

Vale glanced at her. Evie had to get this right.

"That isn't how you open it," she said. "I know how to do it. I'll show you."

Vale thinned his eyes. "I'm not stupid, girl."

"And you're not a sorcerer, either," said Evie. "But I am. I alone have the power to open the Spellstone. Wainwright passed on the secret of how to do it when he made me leader. I'll show you, if you let me go." She paused to take a breath. "But only if you spare me and my parents. You can wipe out the rest of humanity, but I want you to let us live."

Vale smirked at her. "You'd doom humanity to save yourself?"

"Just let me go," said Evie.

Vale weighed her with a look – and then waved his hand. Evie felt the invisible ropes binding her fall apart. "Fine. But try anything funny, and I'll send you flying out of that window faster than you can think."

Evie turned to face the Spellstone. This was it – she had to figure out a way to open it. But what? She had already tried to open the Spellstone once this evening, and she had failed. Her powers were still hidden from her. How was she supposed to succeed, when not even Vale could do it?

She had to do something, fast. Vale stood waiting to see what she would do. She reached around her neck and brought out the token.

Vale rolled his eyes. "Please. I don't need that worthless piece of metal any more. The Order is finished."

Evie ignored him. "Sh-show me magic, please."

The token burst into light with a pulsing glow: once

again, the Spellstone beat in harmony with it, swarming with blood-red fury. Vale stepped back in surprise. Evie could feel the power singing between the Spellstone and the token, drawing together like magnets. She slowly stepped forward, the token held out before her. Her mind wheeled. She had mere seconds to think of something before Vale realized she was bluffing. How could she open the Spellstone?

You're looking in the wrong place.

Emrys's words rang around her head, like a fingertip tracing the rim of a glass. What did he mean? How could she look for something if she didn't even know *what* she was looking for?

That was magic all over – the truth was always hidden, always a secret. Even the truth of Emrys had been hidden inside a story. Evie thought about the first time Wainwright had handed her the token, and she had just seen a sad, twisted piece of metal. She thought about the first time she had seen the Spellstone, little more than a cracked brick hidden in a wall. The answer had always been right there, right in front of her, but in the last place anyone expected. Was *that* the answer? Was the way to open the Spellstone so simple, so obvious, that no one would ever have thought of it?

The last place he'll look.

She was just a few steps away from the Spellstone now. Her mind turned, fast and frantic, skimming across the surface of the truth like a pebble on water. Emrys hadn't been talking about the Spellstone when he said she'd been looking in the wrong place; he was talking about something else. Something else that she needed, something else that was important. Some other way of getting inside it. But what?

She had reached the desk. The Spellstone sat before her, burning like red-hot iron, cracked and broken. Evie began to sweat. Vale was waiting. She had to open the Spellstone, now. Emrys had used his sword to do it, but that was shattered and lost centuries ago. What else would get inside it? A password? A code? A key? A...

And it came to her, slowly at first and then all at once.

Her eyes flicked down to the Spellstone: to the crack across the top, barely the width of a penny. She gazed at the token, beating in time with it. It was just an ordinary piece of metal: small, unexceptional, dirty.

But why *else* would it show the way to the Spellstone?

She reached out her hand. Vale flinched. "Careful now," he warned.

Evie kept going. She held the token to the crack ... and found, without any surprise whatsoever, that they fitted together perfectly.

The moment had come. Evie closed her eyes, pushed the token inside the Spellstone, and the last piece fell into place.

The change was instantaneous. The Spellstone began to tremble – slowly at first, and then harder and harder, until it was shuddering against the desktop. Vale leaped back in surprise. The Spellstone began to crackle and groan with the sound of splitting rock: Evie only just made it out of the way before the desk collapsed in a shatter of wood beside her.

The Spellstone was transforming, swelling into the form of a giant boulder: the token, too, was growing in front of her very eyes, stretching out from the Spellstone like a stem. The rust that had covered its surface bubbled away, grain by grain, to reveal sleek gleaming silver hidden beneath it. There was the handle, there was the hilt, there was the blade…

And finally, there was the truth, right in front of them.

In the centre of the office – where once had been a broken rock and piece of withered metal – stood a gleaming silver sword in a glowing red stone. The sword had never been *completely* destroyed, as the story had said it was; the magicians had kept behind a single piece in secret, and made it their token. The key to opening the Spellstone had been right there, all along, hidden in plain sight. They had been kept apart for centuries … and now, at long last, they had been reunited.

"Well done, Evie," said Vale, breathless with delight. "Well done indeed."

34
CATACLYSM

Evie panted with shock. The Spellstone stood before her in its full glory, emanating raw power. Flecks of loose magic circled the air around it like dust motes; evil magic beat off it in waves of sickening heat. It was both beautiful and terrible to behold: it felt as if it was ready to explode at any second.

"Of course," said Vale with quiet wonder. "The final piece of Emrys's sword. The Order kept it, all along ... and only the leader would ever know the truth. *That's* why they always had to protect it – it was the only way of getting inside! Oh, how could I have been so *stupid!*" He laughed, almost affectionately. "But thanks to you, Evie, I have everything I need..."

Evie gasped. This was it – her one and only chance to stop Vale. She had opened the Spellstone – now, she had to destroy it. She threw herself at the sword...

But she never got near it. Her hands froze in mid-air.

"Nice try," said Vale behind her. "I'll take it from here."

She felt herself dragged backwards, away from the Spellstone. Vale had bound her once more with invisible ropes – she couldn't move an inch. *"No!"*

Evie screamed and fought with all her might, but there was nothing she could do except watch as Vale stepped towards the Spellstone, his face filled with wonder. He rested his hands lovingly on the surface, marvelling at the power hidden inside it.

"I was lying, of course," said Vale. "I won't spare you or your parents. I couldn't possibly take such a risk. But I promise, it will be over so, so quickly."

Evie gasped. She could *hear* Vale's hands sizzling and burning as he touched the Spellstone. Smoke was streaming between his fingers. The office filled with the smell of cooking flesh. But Vale didn't seem to have noticed. It was as if pain didn't matter to him any more. He had closed himself off from everything except what he wanted.

"Stop!" said Evie. "You're…"

She stopped herself. Suddenly she knew – not with just her brain, not with just her heart, but with her entire body – that this was all supposed to happen. Something important was about to take place: a plan that had been set in motion centuries ago. She had been sent to open the Spellstone at just the right time. Now the real fight – the *true* fight – was only just beginning.

You're going to be very important, Evie.

Vale had climbed on top of the Spellstone. He stood in silhouette against the window, the first sunrise of a strange new dawn streaming through the windows.

"It is time to finish what Emrys started," he said. "Time to rid the world of people, once and for all."

He turned to the window. The red loathing of the Spellstone lit him from beneath, making him seem suddenly much older than his years.

"But first," he said, "I'll make them look at me."

With that, Vale grabbed the hilt of the sword in both hands.

There was a beat of silence, like a sharp intake of breath: and then, the world began to shake. There was a *crack*, one so loud that it seemed to cut the entire building in two: Evie felt it in her bones, in her skull, in her chest.

It was like a key had turned inside a padlock. The power trapped in the heart of the Spellstone for one and a half thousand years was finally being unleashed. It came flooding up through the sword and flowed directly into Vale's body. Evie watched as pulses of raw red magic beat into his bloodstream, writhing under the skin of his arms and into his chest. Vale's breath came fast and flushed, his eyes dilating to pinpricks.

"My – my God," he whispered. "The power – the *power* of it…"

The walls around him blew apart like a dandelion clock.

Evie cried out. The top of Tower 99 was now completely exposed. A fierce gale had appeared from nowhere, oven-hot and blistering; the dawning sun was brighter than ever before. Something impossibly ancient was being born into the world: something that had been asleep for centuries, waiting to be released.

Vale let go of the sword, and suddenly he was floating in mid-air, arms outstretched, rising up into the sky. The evil magic kept on coming, pouring directly into him from the Spellstone. His opened his mouth and a great and terrible voice boomed out, echoing through the city like a god from a mountaintop.

"Look at me!"

Evie gazed down with horror. People were pouring into the streets from far and wide, from every building and every corner. It was as if they were no longer in control of their bodies; as if Vale was using his fathomless powers to drag every single person from their beds and make them watch him, ten million all at once.

"Look at me!" Vale bellowed. "LOOK AT ME!"

The magic kept on coming. Shapes writhed in the red waves that poured into Vale, twisting with claws and wings and wild eyes. The creatures of darkness were gushing from the Spellstone and pouring into Vale like a waterfall, more and more every second. Evil magic was beginning to spill out of him, dripping to the office floor like liquid fire...

"L-LOOK AT... LOOK AT..."

Something was wrong. Vale's voice was no longer commanding: it was frightened, out of control. Vale's body twisted in the air like a trapped fly. And still the red magic kept coming, wave after wave after wave...

The magic freezing Evie in place suddenly fell apart. Vale was losing control. Something was wrong, terribly wrong: something unthinkable was about to happen. Evie could feel the whole building pulsating beneath her. She had to get out of here, fast.

She spun around in panic. She could make out the remains of an emergency staircase behind one of the shattered office walls. She flew through it and raced down the staircase three steps at a time. The stairwell was warping and twisting around her like a metal pipe, groaning as if in terrible pain. She sprinted down a hundred storeys as fast as her legs would take her, her mind spinning faster and faster. She had to get to the basement; she had to find the magicians again, and find a way to stop whatever was happening...

But the moment she came to the ground floor, she could see that it was already too late. The whole building was twisting on its axis, wrenching itself from the ground like a muscle strained to breaking point. The great glass windows lining the reception hall were shattering, one by one ... but the glass wasn't falling. The shards hung motionless in mid-air, trembling in place like a frozen snow globe, the sound of its fracture repeating over and over and over…

The magic of the Spellstone was flooding into Tower 99 itself, filling every inch of it with evil power. Evie didn't have time to get to the vault – the magicians and her parents would be safe in there at least, trapped underground. She had to get out, before the whole building collapsed on top of her. She leaped through a shattered window, shielding herself from the hovering shards and racing across the forecourt to the city streets…

She drew to a stop with horror. Down here, at ground level, she could finally see what Vale had done. The streets were crammed with thousands of people, packed into terrified crowds. They had all been dragged out to watch what was happening at the top of Tower 99.

There was Vale, floating high above the city. But the evil power of the Spellstone was too much for him: it was like watching a raging river pour inside a teacup. The magic was overflowing, spilling out of him in droves, pouring down the edges of the skyscraper like molten lava…

"No – no, it's too much!" he begged, his voice breaking apart. "Make it stop!"

Vale fought and thrashed against it, but there was no stopping it now: a thread had been pulled, and a series of pearls on a wire were falling to the ground, one by one. Vale's body was suddenly glowing like the centre of a blowtorch as his voice built up to a horrific shriek…

And then the magic inside him exploded.

A red pulse burst down the skyscraper from top to bottom, making its glass surface ripple like the skin of a fish. All the windows shattered … but just as before, the frozen fragments stayed stuck in place. The evil magic that had poured into Vale was now billowing into the sky like red smoke and oozing down the sides of the skyscraper, gathering into the shapes of bodies and arms and legs and wings and teeth…

The creatures of darkness were finally free.

Evie watched in speechless horror. The red smoke was twisting itself into the shapes of dragons that shrieked and roared above them, darkening the sky with their wings. Thousands of ogres and monsters and demons were scuttling down the skyscraper like ants, screaming with triumph. The skyscraper kept twisting and twisting, as if trying to wrench itself straight from the ground…

And then it did. In front of the entire city, the building tore itself from the earth and showered the streets around it with dust and cement. Its framework girders twisted into legs that ended in great clawed feet; the tip of the building split and separated into a colossal beak lined with glass-shard teeth.

Tower 99 was alive. The dark magic of a thousand evil creatures had flooded directly into the fabric of the building, and turned it into a monster god. It heaved its shoulders and gazed at the world beneath it with fathomless rage and contempt, rippling with waves of sickly red magic, surrounded by its minions.

The crowds screamed. After centuries of sleep, the world of magic was no longer hidden from them: it was finally awake. And it wanted revenge.

The monster prised apart the twisted metal of its mouth, and roared.

35
THE MONSTER

THE MOMENT THE MONSTER ROARED, IT WAS AS IF A spell had been broken. The crowds turned and fled, charging down the streets like a landslide. The skyscraper flung itself down to the ground after them. The shockwaves of its landing burst through the ground at Evie's feet, splitting the tarmac and shooting lightning-bolt cracks up the walls of the shops beside her...

Evie was buffeted left and right as people tore past her, trying to save themselves. Within seconds, she was knocked off her feet and sent sprawling to the ground. No one saw her – no one noticed or cared. And she wasn't the only one: all around her, people were being knocked off their feet and sent disappearing beneath the crowds as ten million terrified people tried to escape at once.

A booted foot came down on the tarmac, centimetres from her head. She screamed: she had to get up and escape from this madness. She tore herself from the ground and fought through the crowds, searching for a way out of the mass of bodies. The freed creatures of darkness had reached the streets now. Dragons of pure red magic swooped low over the crowds, bellowing with fury...

Evie saw an entrance to a block of high-rise flats beside her – people were pouring through the shattered glass doors to find shelter inside. She leaped through the entrance and raced up the marble staircase two steps at a time, heaving for breath. She had to get up as high as she could – somewhere she could see what was happening. Her parents and the Order were safely locked in the vault beneath the ground: she had to find a way to fix this on her own. But how?

Please let there be a way onto the roof, please let there be a way to the roof...

The stairwell ended in a fire escape – Evie charged open the door, and found herself standing on a flat roof. The entire city lay before her.

Evie felt her courage dissipate. There was the skyscraper monster. It was only now that she could see how truly enormous, how vast it was. It was swinging its arms in great circles, reaping down the buildings around it like they were little more than grass, smothering the streets in grey dust. It crushed bridges beneath itself like matchsticks and tore railroads from the ground like bindweed. It was shattering the city to powder, brick by brick. The sky above it was a whirlpool of raging dragons, some of which were spilling towards the horizon. The monster and its minions weren't just going to destroy the city: they were going to spread across the world.

And its power was still growing. Evie could see the Spellstone inside the skyscraper's chest like a red heart, steadily churning out wave after wave of evil magic. Just as Emrys had predicted, the evil inside it had grown over the centuries. Now there was enough to flood the world, and there was nothing Evie could do to stop it.

She gazed at the streets below her in despair. She could see the creatures of darkness rampaging through the crowds, scurrying and slithering through the streets in packs. The air was filled with the sound of terrified screams and breaking glass. Was *this* what Emrys had wanted to happen? Was *this* supposed to be his plan, all along?

You're going to be very important, Evie.

Wainwright's words sounded so hollow now. Her chance to stop all this had come, and gone. All she could see was chaos and misery and pain. What on earth was there inside her that could stand against something so terrible, so powerful? Across the road, a man with a stick had fallen in the surging river of people; he was struggling to get up, but no one stopped to help him. No one had even noticed. They were all too busy trying to save themselves. It was just as Vale had said: at heart, people were selfish and weak. Perhaps Emrys *had* made a mistake. Perhaps people never had been worth saving.

But then Evie saw a woman race past with her two children, spotting the man on the ground as she passed. The woman hesitated for a moment – as if struggling against her own judgement – and then she turned and fought back through the crowds to reach him. It wasn't easy – she was almost knocked down several times too – but soon, she and her children had helped the man to his feet. He thanked them shakily and they joined arms together, disappearing into the crowd and seeking shelter as best they could.

It was one small act of kindness; it was gone in the blink of a moment, lost in the carnage that flooded the city. But now Evie started to notice that small things like that were happening all around her, all the time. There was a child leading another child into an empty shop for shelter; there was someone risking their own life to pull a stranger from some wreckage; there was someone holding back a horde of monsters so that others could escape down an alleyway behind them. They were hard to see among the chaos … but they were always there, if you looked for them. Single tiny acts of goodness, everywhere, hidden in plain sight.

The last place he'll look.

You're looking in the wrong place.

You're going to be very important, Evie.

And suddenly Evie realized what she was supposed to be looking for.

She gazed at the crowds beneath her … and speck by speck, like a photograph being developed, the truth began to reveal itself.

Every single person in the crowds below had a tiny, glowing light inside them. Some were no bigger than diamonds, some were smaller than grains of rice, some were so small you could barely see them at all. But they were there, if you looked for them, in every single person, wherever you turned your head. Tiny beads of magic everywhere.

"Planting seeds," Evie whispered.

It was the magic she had seen Emrys release from himself, one and a half thousand years ago: the magic that he had sent spilling across the world in every direction. He hadn't abandoned his powers: he had gifted them. He had planted a tiny seed of his magic in every single person.

And just like seeds, the magic had grown.

Evie looked around the city, and saw them all: millions upon millions of tiny lights. Emrys's magic had grown over the centuries, just like the magic in the Spellstone ... but unlike the Spellstone, his magic hadn't been gathered in a single place. It had spread and multiplied as it passed from parent to child, from generation to generation. It had been *everywhere*, hidden in plain sight, in the last place that someone like Vale would ever think to look. He had only been able to see the badness in people: he had searched for badness, and sure enough, he had found it. It was where he'd drawn his powers.

But Evie had always been able to find the good in things.

She finally understood why she was here; why she had been chosen; why Emrys had made her open the Spellstone. She finally knew how she was going to save the world.

She closed her eyes, reached down deep inside herself, and listened to everything that the Order of the Stone had taught her. She thought about what she wanted; she sharpened herself with the stress of the moment; she shut out everything except what she knew to be true; and with what was left, she opened herself up to the world. And she found, without surprise, that the world had been speaking to her all along.

And the words it said were, *I've been waiting for you.*

36
THE SORCERER

The moment had arrived: the magic inside Evie was there, alive and ready, surging through her body like a storm cloud. She opened her eyes. There was the skyscraper monster, bellowing with senseless rage as it scythed its way through the city.

Well? said the world. *What are you waiting for?*

Evie knew what to do. She reached out her hands to the river of people below her – and, carefully at first, but with more and more confidence, she drew the white lights from inside them.

They came together easily, instinctively, spiralling out of their chests and gathering above the crowd like fireflies. Within moments, the street was alive with a thousand points of white light. Evie turned to the rest of the city and, like a man conducting the crowds, drew them all towards her.

They came swirling from every street and every corner: ten million points of light, spinning and diving like birds. Evie kept going, conjuring thoughtlessly, automatically, drawing them together in a single shape. She had no idea what she was making, and no idea how to make it, but she kept going, creating something in the city centre, something great, something that deep-down she had somehow always known how to make...

The skyscraper monster stopped and turned to face the twisting white tornado of light appearing before it. It seemed to understand what was happening: the red magic of the Spellstone rippled through its body with fury. Evie kept going, until finally a shape began to emerge from the ten million points of magic she had gathered.

It was a figure of light, standing five hundred metres over the ruins of the city. Evie understood who she had made. She recognized the turn of his head; the way he stood; the sword he held in his hands.

It was Emrys. Campbell was right: the sorcerer had never truly died. He had stayed behind in secret, hidden in every single person on the planet, waiting for his moment to rise again and protect the world in its time of greatest need.

And Evie had just summoned him.

The skyscraper monster screamed with fury, slamming down its twisted claws and tearing whole districts from the ground. A circle of dust billowed from the wreckage around it. One of the dragons in the sky circling above it suddenly swooped down at Emrys, shrieking with hate...

Emrys swung his sword; the dragon was obliterated in a single flash of light. The monster reared back in surprise. All across the city, millions of people froze to the spot to watch in disbelief. Emrys and the creatures of darkness faced each other. The wind breathed. The final fight was about to begin.

Emrys raised his sword, and flew at the monster. The sound of their colliding bodies echoed like a thunderclap across the city. There was an explosion of crystal glass as the windowpane skin of the monster shattered into pieces – but in less than a second, the pieces regathered into a swirling mass of shards that circulated its body. The monster threw itself at Emrys and latched onto him, its iron claws grappling at his eyes, forcing Emrys to stumble back…

Evie gasped – she had to keep helping him. She focused everything she had on gathering more magic from across the city, sending it into Emrys's body and making him stronger. The lights were coming from miles around now: she could see them appearing along the horizon, all the magic that had spread and grown across the world. But the evil power of the Spellstone was still pouring into the monster, swelling it with greater and greater strength.

With a heave, Emrys picked up the monster and sent it slamming down to the city. The shockwave sent up a plume of dust to the sun. Emrys raised his sword in a great swing, but the monster spun out of the way at the final second and Emrys struck only earth. The monster leaped at Emrys again. Emrys fought back, slashing and slashing, sending out white strikes of light that shattered the skin of the monster over and over.

Evie's vision blurred and doubled as she struggled to follow the fight. There was no end in sight, and it was only getting worse. Clouds of white magic were still swarming into the figure of Emrys, but the monster was getting stronger too. The city was being reduced to rubble beneath them. How many people out there had already been hurt or killed? How many more would there be? Would Emrys and the monster be locked in a fight like this for ever, the red against the white, until the world was nothing but a wasteland?

If you wanted to help, said the voice of the earth, *now would be the time.*

Evie didn't understand – she was doing everything she could to draw the magic into Emrys. "Like what?!"

Look in your heart, said the voice.

Evie looked down – and there was her own magic, swelling through her chest. It hadn't joined with the others: it was all still inside her, ready and waiting for its moment.

And the moment had come.

Emrys suddenly dropped his sword. He bent down and lifted the river from the earth like a length of blue rope, and launched himself at the monster. In a single movement, he bound the monster's arms behind it with the river and held them back, opening up its metal chest to reveal the Spellstone burning inside it...

And Evie just knew what to do. She spread her arms, and opened up her own ribcage; the magic shot from her chest like a white comet and hit the Spellstone head-on.

The blast came in three stages. The Spellstone exploded; then, the metal carapace around the monster shattered, spraying glass for twenty miles in every direction; and then came the biggest explosion of all, the greatest yet, a supernova of red and white magic that burst from the skyscraper and flooded the city from end to end.

It was seismic, gargantuan. It swallowed everything in its path, engulfing Emrys and the monster and ten million people in a vast pink tidal wave of magic. Evie cried out as it swept her up from the rooftop like a blade of grass, lifting her into the sky with the shattered remains of the city…

This is it, Evie told herself. *This must be the end. There's nothing beyond this.*

You've been watching too many movies, the world replied.

Evie looked around, and gasped. Time was streaming backwards before her. The wreckage of the city was being fixed, right in front of her eyes. The dust regathered; broken bricks slotted back into place like jigsaw pieces; families who'd been torn apart were reunited, hand in hand; a million windows sang like struck notes as they unbroke themselves in a meticulous spiral, piece by piece by piece by piece by piece.

The magic was pouring inside Evie too, flooding her brain and sending her bones afloat. There was nothing she could do to stop it, no way of fighting it. Her eyes were closing, as if by invisible hands: a shadow of sleep was falling across her. She wanted more than anything to stay awake, to see what was happening, but all she could do was *sleep…*

Evie shut her eyes, and the world remade itself while no one was looking.

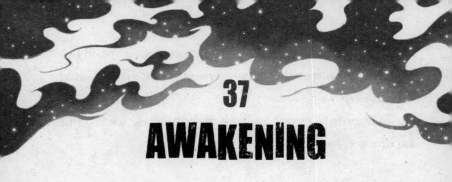

37
AWAKENING

E VIE WOKE UP.

The first thing she noticed was that she was lying on the ground. The tarmac was warm against her back; daylight shone through her eyelids like bedsheets left to dry in the sun. When she opened her eyes, the sky looked like the first day that had ever been made.

She sat up. She was back by the old walls in the city square. The heatwave had gone: the air was cool and fluid. The city stretched out before her, fixed and unbroken. The rubble had been reassembled: the buildings had been pieced back together, brick by brick. The streets were filled with people: thousands of them, on every corner, in every cafe, in every car.

And they were all fast asleep. They slumped together on park benches and leaned against shop windows, smearing their faces against the glass. They hung from the handrails of stationary buses. A whole city snored, and slept, and waited.

"Evie!"

She spun around. Someone was pushing herself to her feet on the other side of the square. Evie's heart leaped for joy as she raced towards her.

"*Campbell!*" She threw her arms around her. "I did it – I spoke to the world!"

Campbell beamed. "Well I never! How are they?"

"Quite bossy, actually." Evie glanced around. "But where are the other—"

"Oh, my *head*."

On the *other* side of the square, Onslow was sitting up and clutching his head in both hands. He looked like a man with a bad hangover. And there was Rish, on the third side of the square, scrambling to his feet for joy.

"*Evie!* Did you see that?" he cried. "I punched Vale, right in the face! *Twice!*"

Evie didn't reply. She was too busy staring at the person who was getting to their feet in the final corner of the square. It was a woman in her sixties. She was tall and poised and regal, with white hair tied on top of her head in a bun. Evie had never seen her before … but she recognized her instantly. She had one blue eye and one yellow eye.

"Lady Alinora?"

The woman turned to face her … and collapsed sideways into a bin. She appeared to have absolutely no idea how to walk on two legs.

"For heaven's sake, stop gawping like that and help me!" she snapped.

Evie beamed – it *was* Lady Alinora. She ran over and hugged her tight. "You're human again!"

Alinora chuckled in amazement. "I am! It's been so *long*… Look at me! I have hands again!" She gazed at them and grimaced. "Oh dear. I didn't think they'd look like *that*."

"I have the feeling we might have missed something," said Onslow drily, gesturing to the sleeping people around them.

Evie did her best to explain. She told the magicians the truth about the token, and the Spellstone releasing its powers into Vale until it destroyed him. She explained about the skyscraper coming to life, and the discovery of her own power, and the final resurrection of Emrys, and how they had destroyed the Spellstone together.

"It was like … an explosion of magic," said Evie. "A huge wave of red and white covering the city. And then" – she held out her arms – "it fixed everything. It's all gone back to the exact way it was."

"Not quite," said Lady Alinora.

She pointed to the skyline – and, sure enough, where Tower 99 had stood was now nothing but a bright expanse of sky. The fortress was gone. The last memory of Vale had been wiped from the earth.

"Er … hello?"

The magicians turned around. Someone else was waking up on the square beside them: a milkman, blinking in confusion.

"What's going on?" he muttered. "Where am I?"

Evie knelt down beside him. "Don't worry – it's all over now. The monster's gone."

The milkman stared at her like she was going mad. "What monster?"

Evie was shocked. How could he have forgotten something like that? But the milkman got to his feet and strode away without so much as a second glance, muttering under his breath ... and he wasn't the only one. Other people were waking up around her, taking a moment to gaze around them blankly before carrying on with their day as if absolutely nothing had happened. It was like watching a play restart itself after a fluffed line; an orchestra continue from a dropped note. In the nearest bus, Evie saw the driver sit up, look briefly confused, then roar the engine into life, driving away with a busload of snoring passengers.

The entire city had forgotten what had happened. It was brushing over the magic it had seen and was returning to the everyday, carrying on from when normal life had left off.

Campbell shook her head in admiration. "Wainwright was right about you, girl. You *are* a sorcerer! To have done all this by yourself..."

Evie gulped. It was time to tell the magicians the truth.

"But that's the thing. I *didn't* do it by myself. Emrys told me what to do. But he could only tell me so much, so that it would happen in exactly the right way. I had to work out the truth about the token at the right moment – I had to let Vale try to absorb it, so it would destroy him."

She spread her arms to the city.

"Don't you see? This was his plan all along. Emrys *knew* that he didn't have enough power to destroy the Spellstone. In order to defeat it, he had to spread and grow his own magic. It would take him hundreds of years to do it – and he had to keep it a secret from everyone, even the Order, until the time was just right. He planted seeds of his magic everywhere, all over the world, so I could bring them back together again at the right moment, stronger than ever. And now ... they've cancelled each other out. It's all gone."

"All of it?" asked Alinora wryly.

She pointed to Onslow, who was giving the waking sleepers glasses of water and wishing them a good day as they stumbled off. Campbell was popping into the toilet of a nearby cafe by strolling straight through the bank next door.

"We still have our powers," said Lady Alinora. "Which means I *should* be able to..."

Evie grabbed her arm. "Don't! You might not be able to change back!"

Alinora shook her head. "No – it feels *different* this time. Something's changed. If I just..."

There was a flash of light … and suddenly Alinora was a black cat again, just like when Evie had first found her. She leaped into Evie's arms, rubbed her head against hers, and purred. Evie giggled. "I *knew* you'd let me pick you up."

Lady Alinora leaped from Evie's arms and, in an instant, returned to her human form. She was right: things *hadn't* just returned to normal. They'd been fixed, improved, transformed for ever. It was like the plan wasn't quite over yet: like there was still some work left to do. Like…

Evie stopped. She had just seen something on the other side of the square: two people, sitting up and gazing around them. Evie was running to them before she knew she was doing it.

"Mum! Dad!"

Mum and Dad turned to the sound of her voice, just as they always did. Love lit up their faces.

"Evie!"

She threw herself into their arms, and that was it. After all the loss, after all her searching, after all the work and all the pain … she had finally found her people.

"Oh, Evie," Mum said. "I dreamed you went missing."

Evie and Mum and Dad stayed locked in place, hugging on the ground. The dream-work of the city wove back into place around them: cars began to fill the roads, people strode to work, and birds burst into the air, never settling in one place for more than a few seconds. Beneath the earth, trains rumbled in the darkness, water traced its way to the river, worms turned and bones rested. A million stories happened all at once. No one noticed three people in the middle of the city square, holding each other tight. There were too many other things to see.

Evie felt a sudden spot of rain on her shoulder: then another, and another. The heat of the last few days had finally broken, and the inevitable downpour was coming. Within seconds, rain was hammering down in sheets. Evie yelped – people were scattering for shelter on every side. It was only then that she realized the magicians were nowhere to be seen. They had disappeared.

"Quick!" said Evie. "We're going to get soaked if we don't…"

She turned to her mother and father, and saw that neither of them cared about the weather one bit. They were only looking at her. You couldn't see where the rain ended and tears began.

38
A NEW DAY

I T RAINED FOR TWO WHOLE DAYS AND NIGHTS.

There was so much water that it had nowhere to go. It burst the riverbanks and flooded the sewers. Manholes foamed and stairwells became waterfalls. Cars were lifted from their parking spots and carried ten miles down the road to other towns. No one had ever known anything like it: it was as if the city was trying to wash itself clean.

It meant that Evie couldn't leave the house. She was desperate to find the magicians and work out where they had gone, but the flooded roads made it impossible. On the plus side, it meant that Evie could spend time with her parents again. They made their favourite meals and watched their favourite shows, played games and waited for the rain to pass. Her parents seemed to have no memory that Evie had *actually* gone missing: their minds had papered over what had happened somehow. But even so, a part of them still remembered: it was like they'd suffered a terrible nightmare, and had never been happier to be awake. They hugged Evie constantly, every time they walked past her. They listened to every word she said. They didn't once look at their phones.

The rain eventually stopped. Evie put on every single waterproof item she owned – mackintosh, gloves, galoshes – and rustled her way downstairs.

"Where are you going?" asked Dad as she walked through the kitchen.

"Exploring," Evie lied. "I want to see what the city looks like now."

Dad frowned. "Hmmm – well, as long as you're careful, Squidge…"

Mum kissed Evie on the head. "For heaven's sake, Mark, she's twelve. Old enough to take a walk around the neighbourhood by herself! Aren't you, Evie?"

Evie smiled. In the last few days, she had been chased by smoke-men in the sewers, trapped inside a dream, sent backwards through time, and she had defeated a skyscraper made of evil magic … but to her parents, she was still their little girl. She guessed she always would be. "Love you, Mum. Love you, Dad."

"Love you, Squidge."

She left the house and waded down the driveway. The pavements were caked with river mud and streaked with garbage, but it was a beautiful day. The city felt different now: the suffocating heat was gone, leaving behind the peace that follows a storm. Everyone she walked past seemed to be discovering the world for the very first time.

They didn't notice Evie as she walked by: they were too busy gazing around with wonder. Evie slalomed effortlessly between them as she made her way to the towpath.

She walked past the narrow boats that had survived the storm with a sense of nervousness. Vale said himself that he had destroyed the Order's hideout – surely, the narrow boat wouldn't be there any more? But then, plenty of other miracles had happened in the last few days. A magical mansion being brought back to life didn't seem so far-fetched.

Evie almost did a double take when she finally found the narrow boat. It was in the exact place it had always been ... but it was transformed too. It had been patched up, re-varnished, gleaming with a new coat of red and white paint. The decking was polished, and the windows gleamed to a shine. She could see a warm, cosy kitchen through the glass, lit by sunshine streaming through the skylights. The boat's name, spelled out in golden letters, was *WAINWRIGHT*.

Evie ran aboard and reached for the door handle. But she paused at the final second. What if the Order of the Stone weren't there any more? What if they had disappeared?

She had to find out. She steeled herself, opened the door...

And stepped into a kitchen. There was no mansion hidden inside – no gleaming marble staircases, no Hall of

Emrys, no infinite library, no fireplace. It was just a boat. Evie stood, speechless with shock. The hideout really *was* gone: the Order of the Stone were nowhere to be seen. Had it all been a dream? Had the world of magic completely—

"*There* you are!"

Evie nearly jumped out of her skin as Onslow strolled into the kitchen, pulling on a set of oven gloves.

"You took your time," he said, good-humouredly. "*Two days!* We thought we should leave you and your parents together, after all you'd been through, but we were going to send out Alinora if you kept us waiting any longer." He pulled a cake from the oven and nodded to the boat around him. "Not bad, is it? I mean, it couldn't be smaller if it tried, but it's nice to have some sunlight in here for a change. I might grow herbs on the roof, maybe even some dahlias in the window boxes if the weather keeps up. The others are all in the back, if you want to—"

He didn't finish the sentence. Evie threw herself at him, squeezing him so tight that his back made a sound. "It's really, really nice to see you again, Onslow."

Onslow blushed, and hugged her back. "Well! Very nice to see you too, Evie."

She made her way to the back of the boat. Sure enough, Campbell, Rish and Alinora were all there, working on a jigsaw puzzle beneath a skylight. Rish was quietly, contentedly, working on a single flower; Alinora was arguing with Campbell about who was doing the edges; Campbell was ignoring her and doing what she liked. They cried out as Evie walked in and ran to hug her, and soon everyone was talking at the same time, as usual.

"What took you so long?"

"We've been so worried!"

"Do you like the boat?"

"I love it!" Evie gazed around. "But ... *how?* Where did it all come from?"

"Ahem."

Evie turned around. Once again, Rish had his hand up. Her eyes bugged out of her head. "Rish? *You* did this?"

Rish nodded. "My powers changed after we woke up. I don't know *how* it happened, or why ... but I've got Mum's skill now. I mean, I'm not as good as she was ... but I'm learning." He smiled from ear to ear. "I can't walk through dreams any more ... but that's fine. I have my own dreams now. Proper ones. I see Mum, all the time."

Onslow carried through the cake and soon they were all tucking in together. "So ... what have you all been doing for two days?" Evie asked.

"Nothing!" said Onslow. "It's wonderful!"

"It's boring," muttered Lady Alinora.

"*Cha!* Hush your noise," said Campbell, slapping her leg. "It's been a blessing, not hiding all the time. I haven't sat down this much in *years*."

"Fine for you," said Alinora haughtily. "But I didn't join the Order of the Stone to eat cake and do puzzles."

Something struck Evie, the moment she said it. "Wait —
are we still the Order of the Stone?"

The others looked at her blankly.

"Well … the Spellstone's gone," said Evie. "Emrys's
work is done. There's nothing for us to defend any more."

They all turned to the portrait of Emrys that sat on
a shelf. This was a much smaller version of the giant
painting that had once hung above the fireplace: it was
now postcard-sized, in a picture frame decorated with
teddy bears and hearts that said, *I LOVE YOU THIS
MUCH!*

"I'm being serious," said Evie. "Our quest is over.
There's nothing left for us to do. Even the token's gone."
She shuffled. There was something that had been bothering
her for a couple of days. "Do you think Wainwright knew
about all this? Did he know about Emrys's plan? Did he
know what I was going to be used for?"

Lady Alinora sighed. "I still can't work out *what*
Wainwright knew, if I'm honest."

The Order sat in silence for a moment, gazing at the
painting of Emrys. The wise, watchful eyes; the beard.
They were all trying to work out if their eyes were playing
tricks on them. If the nagging thought at the back of their
heads meant anything.

It was Evie who finally broke the silence. "Has anyone
ever noticed that Emrys and Wainwright look quite—"

"No!" said Campbell.

"Absolutely not," said Rish.

"Impossible," said Lady Alinora.

"Would anyone like some cake?" said Onslow.

Everyone suddenly started eating more cake, and with that, the topic was brushed aside and never spoken about ever again.

"Then ... the question is," said Evie, through a mouthful of cake, "what *do* we do? We still have our powers. We should use them. We need a purpose. A new quest."

Campbell chuckled. "Quests don't grow on trees, girl."

Evie swallowed down her cake. "Then let's make one. Now that Emrys is gone, we can choose what to do with the powers we have. We can find more magicians, too."

"How can we find them?" said Rish. "You said yourself, we don't have the token any more!"

"We don't *need* the token to find magic," said Evie. "We have me."

She held out her hands to the others. They glanced at each other, then took them so that they joined in a circle. Evie closed her eyes, drew deep, found her powers...

And there it was. The whole city, lit up in glorious red and white around them. White flecks of magic floated and danced across the surface of the canal; red magic hung in the air like paint in water. Every single person that walked past the narrow boat window had it inside them – a mixture of good and bad, some more than others, some almost none at all. The whole city was a swirling current of magic that never stopped moving and never once faded.

"It's my skill," said Evie. "I see magic. And the evil magic isn't trapped inside the Spellstone any more. It's *everywhere*. Spread out and scattered, but everywhere." She swallowed. "Who knows what new evil could come out of it now everything's changed – maybe something even worse than Vale. And this time, Emrys won't be around to help us at our time of need."

The magicians looked frightened – but Evie gripped their hands.

"But there's more good magic, too. *Lots* more good. That's what Vale could never see. He looked for the bad, and he found it. But if we look for the good … there's no knowing how much we might find. There could be *hundreds* more magicians out there, waiting to be recruited. And we're going to need every one of them. People who work together. People who can help us."

"For what?" asked Rish.

"A magical army," said Evie.

She gazed at the world through the window. There were billions of people out there – for a few moments, she had seen what happened when all of them came together, bringing the tiniest piece of magic with them.

"It's going to be a lot of work," she said. "*Huge*. I have no idea where to start. I don't know how to train people, or where everyone would stay…" She smiled. "But if we like a second heart, ju̶ ̶

beat, the light grew brighter, and brighter̶,̶ ̶

"Well?" said Lady Alinora. "Stop dawdling! When do we start?"

work together. I think we can do it. I think there's a chance we could make it happen."

The Order of the Stone looked at one another — and there was their magic, a white glow beating between them and ... joined in perfect rhythm. With every ... er and brighter.

of people quite like them before. There was an old woman in glasses and a bright dress, and a thin pale man in a suit, and a young boy with a neat haircut, and a regal-looking woman with white hair … but there were a dozen more beside them, too. There was a man in his eighties with a ponytail, and a teenage girl in a hoodie with a walking aid, and twin boys passing a frisbee between them, and a tattooed woman in overalls eating a box of doughnuts, and five more people behind them that he couldn't quite make out properly.

"Who are *they?*" said the boy.

Evie smiled, and got to her feet.

"My friends and I will explain everything." She offered her hand again. "Would you like to join us?"

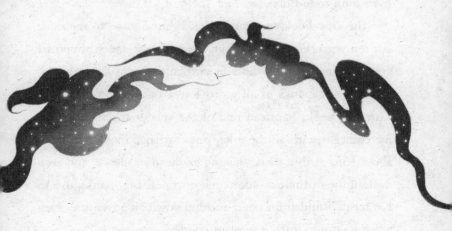

Acknowledgements

Some books go through more changes than others. The idea for *Spellstone* first came to me years ago, but it was a very different book back then. For one thing, it was set in a parallel Victorian universe, opened with a very niche joke about apostrophes, and one of the main characters was a talking head in a box. "Why on earth would you alter such a child-centric and commercially minded concept?" I hear you cry.

Barely anything has remained from that first version of the story, but at heart it's always been about magic hidden beneath the surface of a city. I owe it to the following people for their patience with me as I took this book down various exasperating paths: my agent Claire Wilson (C-Dog!), my editor Annalie Grainger (G-Dog!), and Denise Johnstone-Burt (Mrs Johnstone-Burt).

The kids' book community has been so good to me these last ten years. I'm always blown away by how much support I get from my fellow authors in particular – you lovely bunch you. Biggest thanks of all go to Katya Balen for all her help with this book. She read one of the very first drafts, helped me endlessly with all the other ones, listened to me waffle on about King Arthur while shaking her head in silence, and even came up with the title (don't tell anyone). Big thanks also to Katherine Rundell for never turning down an adventure, even when it's quite clearly a very stupid idea.

Children always ask me questions like, "How did you do the front cover? How did you make the book? How did you put all the words on the page?" They're amazed to discover that there's a whole team of people who make this happen. I'd like to thank everyone at Walker Books who's worked on this sort-of-but-not-quite-a-trilogy with me, and made it so fun and exciting. And of course – David Dean!! What a front cover – I made a noise in my throat when I first saw it. Thank you for making Evie real. I'd also like to thank A.M. Dassu, Guntaas Chugh, and everyone at Inclusive Minds for their help with the text.

I've lived in London for about twenty years now, and I've never got bored of it. You can do the same walk every single day, decide to take a slightly different route one day, and discover something totally amazing that was there the whole time. I don't think that's unique to London – I think everywhere is like that, it's just that London has an unusually large amount of surprises. Wherever you live, magic is always there, hidden in plain sight... Sometimes, you just have to look for it. Try taking yourself on a micro-adventure one day, and see what magic lies hidden around a corner – especially the kind that people walk past.

I got married while writing this book. Thank you, Helen, for making everything so much fun, and for being my wife, and for making me go outside.

When evacuee Col's childhood imaginary friends come to
life, he discovers a world where myths and legends are real.
Together with his guardians – a six-foot tiger, a badger in a
waistcoat and a miniature knight – Col must race to Blitz-
bombed London to save his sister. But soon Col is pursued
by the terrifying Midwinter King, who is determined to
bring an eternal darkness down over everything.

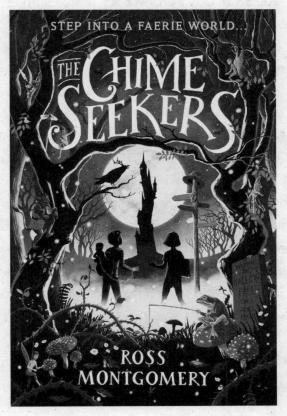

STEP INTO A FAERIE WORLD...

THE CHIME SEEKERS

ROSS MONTGOMERY

When an evil faerie steals Yanni's baby sister, Yanni and his
cousin, Amy, must travel to goblin palaces and battle-swept
oceans to get her back. But faeries delight in tricks and
Yanni will need every drop of courage, and even a few tricks
of his own, if he's to outwit the faerie and save his sister...

ROSS MONTGOMERY started writing stories as a teenager, when he should have been doing homework, and continued doing so at university. His debut novel, *Alex, the Dog and the Unopenable Door*, was nominated for the Costa Children's Book of the Year and the Branford Boase Award. It was also selected as one of the *Sunday Times'* "Top 100 Modern Children's Classics". His books have also been nominated for the CILIP Carnegie Award, while his picture book *Space Tortoise* was nominated for the Kate Greenaway Award and included in the *Guardian's* Best New Children's Books of 2018. *The Midnight Guardians*, Ross's first novel with Walker Books, was selected as a Waterstones Children's Book of the Month and shortlisted for the Costa Children's Book of the Year Award. He lives in London with his wife and their cat, Fun Bobby.

#Spellstone
@mossmontmomery
@WalkerBooksUK